Melt with Me

By

Si Elle

Publishing Company: Cinqsx Publishing
Email Address: cinqsx@earthlink.net
Author: sielle@earthlinknet

Genre: Adult, Erotic, Lesbian, Taboo

Printer and Distributor: Ingram Spark
(The Ingram Content Group)
1 Ingram Blvd. NS 395
La Vergne, TN 37086
http://www.ingramspark.com

Printed in the United States of America

Softcover ISBN: 978-0-9766321-2-2
EPUB ISBN: 978-0-9766321-3-9

First Edition

Table of Contents

Chapter 1

The Requirement

Sitting in the den with a cup of coffee saturated with sweet vanilla cream, I opened my laptop. Selecting a word document, I titled it and set the formats. Minutes had passed that seemed like hours as I struggled to organize my thoughts. Frozen in mental frustration, my fingertips impatiently wiggled about unable to strike a single key. Comparable to a math teacher describing a problem without a whiteboard, my mind had trouble gaging the point of inception.

Licking the sweetness off my lips, I pulled at my denim shorts, relieving the tautness. I unzipped them halfway down, deliberating whether I should peel them off.

"This wouldn't be the first time I've gotten things done with nothing on," I uttered, amusingly.

The uninhibited world of sensual pleasure had become my adventurous and tameless obsession. When at the beach, I love exhibiting my slim and succulent figure. Some girls would enviously gaze at my tanned bare bod. But others wanted to get close, caress, and exchange intimacies. Within the carefree impressions of the bay, ardent feminine connections were effortless, unleashing, and ceaseless. As many sought more, there was plenty to go around.

Interrupting my concentration, an itch surfaced bringing about an immediate urge to appease myself. I slipped my hand beneath my panties and caressed within the bare softness. Upon relieving the tingling sensation, the feeling became quite relaxing. So, I kept my fingers buried in the lush warmth understanding why many people unconsciously revelled in the position. Female models in fashions pose sensually with their fingers slipped under their panties. Guys sometimes place their hand under their beltline, giving them an added sense of masculinity. The position not only looks seductive and licentious but feels so instinctively natural.

Bringing my fingers to my nose, I inhaled the crisp, musky scent. The distinctive natural tang reminded me of my twin sister Alexia. Born minutes apart, she is physically like me, but our personalities and passions differ. However, our fervent devotion and sensual relationship are incessant. After we shower, my tastebuds can't stop devouring her sweet and savory succulence until she culminates upon my lips. Her taste drives me like a wild animal in heat. Thinking about our love sessions, wetness oozes under my tongue. I swallow while my eyes focus back towards the wordless page with an unsatisfied empty stare. Wanting to pull my hair out, I openly appeal like negative forces were inhibiting me from continuing onward.

"How am I going to get this paper completed."

I'm about to graduate from college with a four-year degree in psychology, but my education was far from complete. To begin the journey of becoming a sexual therapist, I needed a master's degree. With the many graduate schools around the world, there was only one program that drove my heart with burning desire. So, I confidently started filling out the online application without holding back. Yes, family has cast shadows of doubt on my ventures but I've already made up my mind. For now, anyway, I'd like to move in a direction of financial independence rather than working in the family business.

Then something led my mind to absolute hesitancy. It was an unanticipated entrance requirement.

'Write a paper describing in complete detail your experiences with human sexuality since childhood. How have these unique experiences shaped your persona and self to this point in your life?'

"What," I mumbled. "Obstacles, always obstacles. Why can't life be simple. Now, I have this daunting task to consider."

Repetitiously pondering this question in my head, I gradually stood up. Moving the chair aside, I bent over stretching my arms towards the floor. Then I raised my hands high in the air and twisted about relieving the anxiety. Walking over to the window, I looked out into the backyard. The greenery brought the feelings of the vibrant outdoors alive as I could almost smell fresh cut grass. My childhood was staring me in the face as I remembered playing like there was no tomorrow.

A bird fluttered by catching my eye. I followed the creature thoughtlessly as it lifted upward towards the bright blue sky. Gazing upward, white puffy clouds leisurely glided across as my mind remembered the days at the lycée engaged in Eros. The journey through lycée and even undergrad seemed like a flicker in time. Slowly my thoughts were gathering, organizing, and bringing back the past once more. I gently rubbed my hand on my forehead as rippling ideas surfaced through my brain.

"The first question will be quite time consuming. My childhood must come first, trailed by those playful and sensual moments. But who am I now?" I whispered with uneasiness. Peering out the window once more, I took a deep breath and calmed myself down. Realizing that there was no escape, my focus intensified as the morning caffeine stirred my nerves.

"What about my friends?" I thought. "How have they described me?"

My girlfriends have always characterized me as sensuous, easygoing, and attractive. I have a small nose, blue eyes, full lips, and olive skin. My blonde hair falls freely below my shoulders and curls at the bottom. My gifted large breasts have slightly hooked nipples and dark areoles. When I dress in a white top without a bra, my areoles display rather visibly. Some guy's stare with endless eyes as I saunter out into the public scene. To tease, I bend over to reveal my previous gems. My philosophy is that a woman should flaunt her most alluring parts but keep her inner self hidden, particularly from exploitive males.

Yes, men can be brutal. Especially when it comes to emotional support and satisfying a woman's carnal needs. In trying to get into your pants, they become very persistent and manipulative. Lying through their teeth, they play a deceitful game of unselfishness, sincerity, and empathy. Once satisfied, they're oblivious to the fact that females have erogenous parts as well. Many have tried to pick me up during my college days, but I find no interest. They serve no purpose in fulfilling my emotive, spiritual, or sensual desires.

Show and tell is a game I like to exclusively play with impassioned females. You know. The authentic and branded ones that fancy exploring an alluring and secretive acquaintance. I love the delicious taste of a woman's lips against mine. Her seductive embraces arouse my visceral thirst. Our tongues entwine in lustful craving as we drive to fulfill the aching hunger that simmers amidst compulsion. We slowly peel off our clothes, layer by layer, exposing bare soft flesh. Feeling and touching, we stimulate in the heat of passion, building into a blissful, unifying sensation. Our hearts blaze with unstoppable fever as we melt away in an ecstatic peaking moment. Encapsulated from the intensity of pleasure, we calm down into sweet and delicate kisses. Gratification often leads to a level of passivity, but the female anatomy lacks true fulfillment. In the inevitable world of sexual desire, the realm of intoxicating pleasure never ceases.

Disrupting my thoughts, a hummingbird moth captured my attention fluttering its wings in the air. Dancing and bobbing, I watched it scamper until it vanished from sight. Observing nature in the backyard has carried me back to the flora and fauna along the rue de pasture. The tranquil experiences at the creek, within the hidden woods, came alive as a rousing sensation swept through my heart. Memories began surfacing as ideas flowed without obstruction. Primed to accomplish this task, I walked over to my desk, sat down, and awakened my laptop. The blank word document stood in front of me. But this time, my fingers were ready to release my inner thoughts. Nature had unveiled its mysteries once more as memories long gone were pulling at my heart.

As I began to type, the realization that the review committee required truthfulness emerged. Slight apprehension took hold of me.

"I must reveal my deepest pleasurable experiences to gain acceptance into the school," I mumbled. "Things that I never disclosed to anyone but Alexia." But I am sure my ventures will surprise no one. Well… maybe some will need relief after engaging themselves into my past. Anyhow, the boring stuff must come first and then the salacious parts. I guess that the best place to start are the beaches in Carcene.

Chapter 2

Carcene

My name is Lizette Beaufort. Jacques, my Papa, is a well-known merchant in the Carcene community. He sells some of the finest wines and cheeses in France. Valise, my Mama, is a housewife that enjoys gardening and cooking gourmet. She lacked interest in the family business, but sometimes travels with Papa when he calls on out-of-town clients. Unlike Mama, Alexia loves working in the family business and seems to parallel Papa's passion.

I was born and raised ten miles from the ocean in the town of Carcene along the west coast of France. Carcene has a unique character when compared to vacation spots along the European shorelines. It is one of the most relaxing and spontaneous seasonal venues in the world. The beaches around Carcene are a place of leisure, naturalness, and pleasure. The sparkling brown and gray sands along its coast reflect its beauty and brilliance.

In the summer, the sun converges with the cool ocean air to craft a pleasing ether along the water's edge. The picturesque view of the ocean colors, the soothing breeze, and the sound of rolling waves make it an ideal place to sip wine, consume delights, and observe bare bodies. Locals and vacationers would plant umbrellas, roll out beach towels, and strip down without reservation. It is nothing to see gorgeous tanned bodies from around the world showing off their stuff as they strut along the bay. Girls would freely display their gorgeous tits and wax jobs as beach goers watched with wanton thirst.

The beaches are also a place that a natural family can express themselves freely, while keeping their distance from the inhibited world. Within our family legacy, the beach lifestyle has been an indispensable tradition that we religiously kept alive for decades. Generation to generation, it carried itself forward to become part of our reality that we value today. Our family blended and conformed to the beach norms, which included getting a full body tan.

During many summer weekends and holidays, my parents would take Alexia and me to the beach to soak in the sun and bask in the bay. Once our umbrella is up, Valise would strip off her bikini to reveal a pair of luscious tits, pert nipples, and a savoring female shape. Lubricating herself with tanning oil, she glistened off the sun like a golden idol. Men laying out on blankets would cunningly watch as she enticed them to arousal. Slowly spreading oil on her chest and nipples, she caressed and teased. Then, gracefully turning around like a model, her sensual magnetism captured an ecstatic craving. Her luscious feminine lips oozed as she bent over to spread oil on her calves. Papa's jealousy sometimes flared when muscular men gazed at her in great length. Staring back in defense of his property, it became quite comical. There was just no comparison. Papa had a pot belly while beach hunks had defined muscles, six packs abs, and well-hung aching cocks.

The story was quite different when hot chicks passed by. Mama's jealousy never entered the picture as Papa's eyes wandered like a kid in candy land. Girls playfully teased by bending over to display their luscious behinds and salient feminine delights. Papa would tip his sunglasses to get a full eye capturing view as their perfectly bronzed bodies enticed and aroused. Mama knew the beach life in Carcene was openly erogenous. So, she never got envious and allowed Jacque to relish within its tantalizing highlights.

Occasionally, breathtaking woman strolled by with a craving in their eye as Mama lounged in the sun. They would stop and chat while phone numbers exchanged furtively. Mama had licentious friendships, which she usually treated as mere acquaintances. Her connections would knock at the door when Papa was out of town. They would frequently wear provocative and skimpy outfits with high heels, appealing makeup, and finely polished nails. It was routine for Mama to send us off to play in the den until the guest departed.

Emphasizing good hospitality, she'd open a bottle of ninety-eight-point wine from the wine cellar. Chatting about trivial matters, they would drink until the bottle was empty.

6

Within no time at all, they cleverly disappeared into the spare bedroom, only returning later with gratifying smiles.

Carrying their shoes and buttoning up before heading out the door, they gave a passionate kiss goodbye. Their husbands never knew about the secret encounters that went on between passionate housewives. They just thought their wives merely socialized and drank with girlfriends. At restaurants, they never looked under the table to see the foot massages nor questioned the bathroom trips returning with flush faces.

Growing up with marginal freedom, our parents wanted us to enjoy life without all the social constraints. So, we basked in the natural beach scene and bared around the house. It was with this level of liberation that created full transparency within our family unit. We instinctively shared daily drama, deep personal thoughts, and intimate feelings. Mama and I could openly chat about anything and everything.

For instance, one afternoon at the beach, Mama was putting suntan oil on her breasts as we sat discussing some of life's expectations.

"I'm a little sore today," she said.

"There are so big, Mama," I said, giggling.

"Not the biggest."

"Will I get big bumps like yours?"

She raised her eyebrows slightly as to determine how to answer me. When I became too inquisitive, she would kiss me on the forehead and change the topic. Other times, she avoided my questions altogether or tell me I'd have to wait until I was older. But at my age, bumps were important enough to discuss. So, she continued.

"The natural growth cycle of females is to grow bumps sometimes into balloons. Girls have all sizes with points at the end called nipples. You will get used to them as time goes on."

"Will I get a dangler like Papa?"

"Where did you hear that?"

"Aunt Marielle told me that men have danglers that turn into banglers. Do you know what that means?"

Mama began laughing hysterically.

"Aunt Marielle told me I'd have to wait until college to learn about it. I needed to take a course in fizzy-slow-ology and a-nuts-a-me."

"That aunt Marielle, cute and inventive," she said. "I need to talk with her."

"Mama, you talk to her all the time. Sometimes you talk each other's ears off. That's what Papa says."

"Well, we talk about different adult things, Lizette. When you get older, you will also be a part of that conversation."

"You love her like us, Mama. Don't you?"

"We are a very close family. We all love each other. That's why she visits often."

Mama was sometimes too worrisome, but she persistently took care of our basic needs. Like making sure we had plenty of tanning oil when at the beach. After applying suntan oil, she'd say in a commanding tone while tapping my butt, "Go off and play, but stay close. Don't go wandering off too far. I do not want kidnappers to steal you away from me." Alexia and I would run off to play along the beach without a worry in the world.

By summer's end, Alexia and I turned golden brown like American Indian girls. Sometimes, I would sneak up behind her and place my nose against her flesh, inhaling deeply. I loved the scent of the tanning oils that lingered on our bare bodies while we sweltered in the sun. The oil blended well with our natural scent triggering a sense of innocence, excitement, and fascination.

During the winter months, I sometimes opened a bottle of sunscreen and slowly inhaled the essence with my eyes closed. The satisfying scent would bring back the sights, sounds, and smells of the summer days along the shores. Then, I put a little on my finger to appease myself as I drifted off to sleep, craving for summer to return.

Chapter 3

Auntie Marielle

Auntie Marielle is from Papa's side of the family. When we were kids, she was a nursing student studying at the local university. She usually visited when Papa was away on business to keep Mama company. Sometimes, she would even stay overnight in the spare bedroom.

When she came to visit, she usually stopped by in the late mornings, welcoming us with warm hugs and kisses. Her lips were relentlessly soft and luscious.

She'd say, "Alexia and Lizette, are you staying out of trouble?"

"We miss you, auntie. Take us to the beach," I'd request.

Then disappointment would emerge from her voice. "Not today, but we will plan another time. Look, I brought you ladies something." She'd pull out chocolate candy bars from a bag as we bellowed with boundless cheers.

Mama would comment. "You shouldn't have."

"It's nothing. Besides, I love bringing the kids' little gifts."

"Relax, make yourself at home. I will find a special bottle of wine for us to enjoy while tanning."

"You are so gracious, queen Valise."

We chuckled at Marielle's sometimes very whimsical comments. However, her humor was not only the form of words, but the way she did things, like at the beach. Marielle often had an unconscious inclination to glace at female bods as we sat on our blanket.

Alexia and I would often say, "There she goes again, making funny faces."

As an attractive girl swaggered nearby, she would first exhibit a deep, pleasant smile. Then, her long tongue extruded upwards, covering her upper lip that wiggled about. Licking her lips, she'd take off her sunglasses, giving a warm, welcoming nod with an alluring wink. Success eventually found its way by getting some phone numbers. It was an odd and amusing way to pick up chicks, but we always got a kick out of it.

Marielle loved taking us to the beach during the summer months. As she pulled up, we would run up to her car with excitement as our hands waved in the air. Wearing one of her funny sun hats, she would greet us with a warm, beautiful smile. Mama followed behind carrying our bags and lunch as we opened the car door sliding into the back seat.

Marielle would roll down her window and plant a sweet kiss on Mama's lips.

"Thanks for taking the kids today."

"No problem. We should meet up this week."

"I could use a massage," Mama would say.

"I'll call you," Marielle replied.

Their intimate kiss goodbye was more entertaining than their hello. Sometimes, we had to interrupt.

"Are we going to wait all day?"

"Patient's girls," Mama replied.

Within seconds, we waved bye to Mama as the car sped off for another day of fun in the sun.

Upon finding a location on the beach, Marielle would take off an outer layer of clothing, unfasten her bikini top, and pull down her bottoms. She revealed a beautiful and well-proportioned naked body. Purposely applying plenty of suntan oil on her breasts and nipples, she'd attract onlookers in a heartbeat. It was so funny to observe her tits bounce up and down when she walked. It made Alexia and I giggle, but men stared with deep intensity.

Marielle would often tell us, "Head for the hills if you see any saluting danglers." Then, she would put her hand to her forehead and mimic a military salute.

We giggled because it sounded funny, but we really hadn't the foggiest inclination about what it meant.

However, she took care of our every need. Like making sure we had enough suntan oil before playing on the beach. I remember her spreading oil all over us. It felt smooth, warm, and comforting.

I would say, "Your hands are so soft and pleasant. Do me again."

Marielle would caress me again with gentle motions that made me feel so good inside.

When finished, she'd say, "Now, you girls need to do me. My dorsal needs protection."

"What auntie, the dorsal," I'd say.

She'd respond, "The derriere."

Still confused, Alexia and I returned the favor by saturating her back with plenty of love. Alexia would take the right side as I took the left. Filling our palms with oil, we'd first apportion some on her shoulders. Then we massaged down to her bare butt crack.

"You're doing me nice and sweet," she exclaimed. "Massage just a little harder? Remember, ice cream treats if you girls do a good job."

Ice cream was the ultimate climax on a hot summer's day because it cooled my lips and gave love to my tummy. Thinking of a peppermint cone was motivating enough to accomplish a thorough oil job. So, when she made little sounds of pleasing relief, I added a little more pressure to soothe her tense muscles.

Upon arriving at the parlor in the late afternoon, Marielle bought Alexia and me each a double scoop. Sometimes, she'd even ask if I wanted a lick of hers. I would not argue because she was buying. Besides, it gave me more to taste.

Holding the cone in her hand, she would say, "Lick with me before it melts."

It felt so deliciously nice when my tongue brushed against hers. Then, she would lightly kiss my lips and tell me how much she enjoyed the taste of sweet ice cream on my mush. Kissing Marielle brought about my first feelings of feminine love. My stomach felt a silky sinking sensation with plenty of warm yumminess.

Craving her company was natural and innocent that augmented our ménage love. When she came over to spend the night in the spare bedroom, we would sometimes join her in bed under the warm covers. Alexia would take one side and I the

11

other. It felt so comfortable curling up in her arms. Her skin was silky warm, her touch was delicately soft, and her natural scent was like mine.

Marielle finally ignited with a female student named Lace while she was taking classes in the nursing program. Lace had no interest in boys but shared common affections with Marielle. She had a pretty face, round protruding tits, button shaped nipples, and a slim figure.

When going to the beach, Marielle would often ask Lace to join us. Lace accepted the invitation without hesitation. In picking her up, sometimes they would stop for a bottle of wine and other times for weed. After finding beach parking, they inconspicuously lit a joint behind the car. While they artfully toked looking out for cops, Alexia and I would keep busy on our cell phones. After hearing them laugh, we knew it was about time to find a beach spot.

Upon opening the trunk, Marielle would pull out an oversized beach umbrella that she literally dragged to our spot. Lace would always try to help her set it up, but they sometimes fell on their ass laughing hysterically. Without a doubt, smoking pot was the primary cause of their hilarious inefficiencies. When the umbrella was in place, Alexia and I spread our blankets and grabbed the suntan oil to lube each other. Marielle always inspected our bare bodies, ensuring that we had adequate protection. When approved, she allowed us to run off on the beach and play.

Stoned out of their minds, Marielle and Lace acted like no one else was around. They stripped to bare skin comfortably, while looking into each other's eyes. Complementing and admiring their physiques, they would speak in low seductive tones, passing intimacies. Sometimes, they would eat a piece of fruit, holding it between their mouths. They ate from each side, biting inward. As they reached their lips, enjoying the pleasures of the sweet fruit, they licked the stickiness with savoring tongues.

After undressing to bare skin, they passionately applied tanning oil, spending more time fondling breasts and nipples. It was a hot, sensuous scene, watching college girls with gorgeous bodies spread oil all over themselves. Male beach goers stared in wanton craving as two young females pleased each other with roaming hands. Aroused males tried hiding their privates under towels, blankets, and chairs. Despite some success, there were salutes that accidentally appeared.

Sometimes, Marielle laid on her towel with her butt in the air as Lace rubbed her back and buttocks. Lace had a skill of a professional masseuse and gave intermittent adoring kisses along the way. Her hand sometimes slipped in sensual places for an extended period as the sounds of enjoyment escaped from their lips. However, they didn't want us around when they engaged in passionate affections. So, they were cautious to make sure we were clear from sight. But we were not the most loyal kids, especially when Mama was not around. We sometimes eyeballed them in a secret place we called the spy hole. Seeing Marielle and Lace stoned and enjoying themselves, just transported our minds to a new understanding of love.

Chapter 4

The Spy Hole

One chilly winter night when Alexia and I were much older, we snuggled naked in bed under a soft comforter with the fireplace ablaze. I was gently caressing her back while engaging in a conversation remembering Marielle and the spyhole. As our conversation dwindled into subtle slurring, Alexia drifted off.

Closing my eyes, I reminisced. "The old spyhole. I'm surprised that no one caught us." Soon, my mind sank into a vivid dream, thinking about the lost days along the bay.

"Alexia, remember our secret hiding place."

"Yeah, it's right in front of us."

"Let's spy on Marielle and Lace," I said vibrantly. "They will never know we're watching. Well, sneak up from behind."

Alexia hesitated, feeling a bit uncomfortable with my idea. "I thought we agreed to give them privacy. We promised Mama…. remember…."

"I know, but just this once. I promise."

Grabbing Alexia's hand, we walked naked along the shoreline away from our umbrella.

When we were about one hundred feet away, Marielle yelled. "Did you put enough suntan lotion on?"

Turning around, Alexia cupped her hand over her mouth in the shape of a megaphone. "We thoroughly did each other."

As we waved, Marielle watched us disappear in the far distance. When we were out of sight, we sneakily backtracked to the spyhole with our tits bouncing all the way. We opened the door slipping in and fastened the latch to lock us in.

"Wow, it's tight in here," I said.

"That's because we were kids the last time we were in here," Alexia said.

"We have to be quiet," I said. "I don't want to give us away."

14

Amusingly peeking out of the holes, Marielle and Lace were in clear view. As we watched, they showed indecision in rearranging the beach gear. Marielle tipped the umbrella perpendicular to the ground and then accidentally flipped it upside down. Without avail, she tripped over the cooler. It was complete chaos as Lace pulled her up off the sand.

"Are you alright," Lace said.

"Yes, just lost my balance."

Alexia and I both started chuckling, enjoying their antics. It was like watching a sitcom. Marielle finally positioned the umbrella at the angle with the help of Lace. Then, she started moving some chairs back and forth several times as irresolution took control.

"What is she thinking about?" Alexia said.

"They're probably stoned," I said.

Alexia chuckled.

"Shh… I want to hear what they are saying."

Marielle arranged the beach gear under some unplanned arrangement. The angle of the umbrella partially hid them from the crowd while the chairs added to their concealment. Then, Marielle spread out the beach blanket, peeled off her bikini, and lied on her back. Lace situated herself sideways alongside Marielle, having taken hers off as well.

Lace started fondling Marielle as I watched her pink colored nails in motion.

"I'm having difficulty with chemistry class," Lace said. Lace slid her hand over her breasts and massaged her erect nipples in a circular motion.

"Don't worry. I can help you. I took comprehensive notes last semester."

Lace's nails flowed over her stomach. Then she brought them back, massaging her luscious tits.

"Thanks, I need all the help I can get." Lace moved her lips to Marielle, giving a gentle kiss as she casually gliding her fingers along Marielle's inner thigh. "The beach isn't packed today."

"That's why I enjoy getting out at the beginning of the week. So, we can have a little private party," Marielle said.

15

There was a slight pause as Marielle spoke sensually. "I like how you touch me. Let's do it.... here."

Lace spoke nervous and almost breathless. "Mm.... now that's what I was waiting to hear."

Looking into each other's eyes, Lace began uttering words of seduction as Marielle returned arousing licentious expressions. Without a broken moment, mouths opened as their tongues lusciously flickered and danced like butterflies in stationary motion. Marielle took her long tongue between her lips and began sucking as Lace's ligula slid in and out of her orifice. Her tongue plunged deeper and deeper, receiving delicious pleasure from Marielle's lips. As appetites intensified, sounds of gratification surfaced.

Without hesitation, Marielle turned her body sideways, revealing her raw, puckered hole. It glistened off the sun, sending tingling sensations across my body. Marielle's slovenly moved her mouth over Lace's nipples, lapping each drop of swelter while fondling her luscious tits. Impassioned and determined to please, Marielle devoured her flesh like succulent fruit as titillating vibrations swept through Lace's body. Her head fell backwards as she captured every ounce of pleasure from Marielle's lips.

Alexia placed her hand on my butt, stroking softly as aching desires submerged me into feminine love. Heat was building across my flesh as wetness dripped between my legs. Gradually, I moved my fingers into my puss as Alexia's stared intently at their sensual play.

Lace was kneading Marielle's breasts. Her mouth moved upon Marielle's long perky nipples, lapping, and sucking. With her luscious tongue, she licked upward toward Marielle's accepting mouth. Locking in a deep, mouthwatering kiss, their tongues savored in passion. Touching and stroking, they eased their fingers into each other's wetness. While fingers played in a torrid motion, soft moans permeated in the air. Pushing my puss closer to the wall, my fingers were secretly playing as the sensation was climbing me to a deep, pleasing level.

In a slight motion, Marielle angled her leg to allow an opening between her thighs. With gusto, Lace's finger reached for her puckered hole. Having lubricated it, she smeared some on

16

top, circling the outer rim. In relieving tension, Marielle's hole slowly flowered like a rosebud in glory. Twisting and curling, Lace eased her middle finger inward unlocking her anal gates. Then, her finger smoothy slid all the way to the knuckle. Pulling back, she started screwing and squirming her finger as Marielle squealed softly in pure delectation.

The marijuana had augmented nerve ending sensitivity, driving pleasure to the next level of satisfaction. Lace was screwing her anal cavity and licking her puss as Marielle's breathing intensified. Reaching the apex of felicity with fervor, Marielle took a deep breath inward and gripped the blanket tightly with her hands. Her head pushed against the sand as the sounds of exhilaration seeped through her lips. Her mind went totally blank as euphoria plateaued. Pulsating vibrations swept through her body as she flared in a vision of fireworks. Placing her hands on her head, she laid back in a state of fulfillment.

Lace continued rubbing her clit with vigor and drive. Marielle, having composed herself, placed her hand over Lace's. With a dual effort, Lace was on her way to an escalating release. Marielle breathed words in her ear of wanton lust as Lace started shuddering in an unstoppable state of passion. With an abrupt sound of delight seeping from her lips, Lace froze, entering the world of spatial elation.

They collapsed on the blanket, feeling satisfied, drained, and delirious.

"What a mind-blowing experience… that pot was awesome," Marielle whispered, breathlessly.

"Let's buy some more. A lot more," Lace replied.

"I was really out there," Marielle said.

"I saw stars," Lace replied.

Nervous, I opened the door, leading my sister away from the spyhole to the water's edge. We hugged, trying to comprehend what had just transpired. It was nothing like I seen before. My mind was blank, staring out into the ocean. I turned and looked my sister deeply in her eyes. My lips reached and kissed her. Then I brought my fingers to her mouth as she opened and began sucking on my juices. She was desiring my taste, not knowing that I climaxed.

17

Slowly, my eyes opened as I came into consciousness. The dream had evaporated into my mind, but I could still feel the sensations running through my pleasure zones.

Our youth had disappeared within the thousands of buried foot prints that crossed the sand along the bay. As time passed, the crowds of the beach seemed to change, but I soon realized that we were changing. We eventually lost interest in our secret hiding place, only finding out later that it was an old lifeguard storage shack. However, I remembered the fun times we had watching beach goers through the drilled holes in wall. I must look ahead toward my future, leaving childhood along the shores as a treasured memory.

Chapter 5

The Family Ritual

Realizing that pot was a psychological deterrent, Marielle went cold turkey after breaking up with Lace. While earning a master's degree in advanced nursing, she worked as a nurse's assistant at the local hospital. Her hard work and dedication paid off. Upon graduation, the hospital hired her as a nurse manager.

Marielle's indulgence in amatory pleasure with women was an obsessive game of unfulfilled desire. Wanting more, she thirsted like a hunger lioness in pursuit of her next erotic feast. Sometimes, entwining herself within female groups, she would engage in multifaceted randy play.

Valise loved when Marielle brought a female friend over to tan, drink wine, and gossip. Completely intoxicated, they disappeared into the master bedroom for hours at a time. Of course, in Mama's words, 'To shower and sleep it off.' It was just hard to imagine what three naked females were like in bed.

Sleeping naked together, Alexia and I touched, caressed, and kissed but nothing more. So, I envisioned their affections were similar. However, one day I walked past the master bedroom overhearing playful and sensual sounds. Losing self-control, I ended up taking a warm shower as fantasies unleased themselves into tantalizing contentment.

In late June, Marielle stopped by the house to visit Mama. I was in the den streaming the net. Marielle knocked and walked in as Mama greeted her in the foyer.

"How is work going?" Mama inquired, closing the door behind them.

"Patients, always complaining."

"Jacque and Alexia are away on business if you want to spend the night."

"Works out fine. I'm off tomorrow. Besides, could use a nice soapy enema and massage."

"I'll prepare it just the way you like it… just before bedtime."

"Fill me up, Valise…… You make me feel so warm inside. Then, that relieving and tingling release. The sensation drives me crazy like expelling …."

"… we'll take turns. You can do me too……. By the way, I found a ninety-seven-point cab I want you to try. I hid it in the cellar."

"Mm…. my lips and tongue are ready for a taste, if yours are."

"Is Lizette here."

"She is in the den."

In those words, distinct voices had changed into whispers. Then, silence overtook them as Valise opened a cabinet drawer and grabbed a couple of wine glasses.

As they proceeded down the steps to the wine cellar, something struck me peculiarly. Papa always kept the doors fully open when searching for a bottle. Why did they close the wine cellar door behind them? It was a little weird that they sometimes spent hours searching for a few bottles. Puzzled, my curiosity peaked. With nothing better to do, I decided to spy.

Walking through the kitchen, the sweet smell of Marielle's perfume was lingering in the air. Then, I opened the door and walked down the steps into the backyard, hiding myself by a window. Gazing into the finished basement, the adrenal began flowing throughout my body. What I saw was bringing me on edge.

Valise was sitting on the leather couch as Marielle stood in front of her. Peering deeply into Valise's eyes, Marielle peeled off her top and unzipped her shorts to reveal a hot and sexy pink bikini. Putting her arms behind her back, she untied her top, letting it fall to the floor. Her bulb like tits flopped out and bounced a bit as her perky nipples pointed upward. In fondling her tits, she brought her nipple up to her mouth and sucked. Pulling down her bottoms, she bent over, exposing her succulent glistening lips as Valise swallowed with thirst and salaciousness.

I've seen Marielle naked many times at the beach, but today was different. Now much older, my eyes looked at her with

20

a sense of desire. Her delicious nakedness revealed a slim waistline, long slender silky legs, and beautifully tanned skin. A tingling sensation swept through my body, viewing her hairless vulva. Her perky tits reminded me of bouncy water balloons. Now, I realized what men at the beach were experiencing when we laughed as kids. Unconsciously becoming aroused, I unclasped my bra and started rubbing my nipples.

Marielle stood there like a temptress of seduction. She could easily bring Valise down to her knees, begging to taste her delights.

"I'm all yours for playtime. It's your turn before we get lubed up."

Marielle's words left Valise speechless as she stared in wantonness. Looking in Marielle's eyes, Valise slowly put her hands to her back, untied her bikini top and let it drop to the floor. Then Valise slowly stripped off her bottoms. Her luscious tits, pert nipples, and savoring female figure stood out like a perfect statue as she turned around in a one-eighty. Bending forward, she placed her hands on her buttocks and opened her checks, revealing her appetizing lips and brown wrinkled hole. Standing naked together, I sensed there was something more to their relationship. Then Valise took a tube of suntan oil from a drawer without leaving the eyes of Marielle.

Marielle locked her hands above her head as Valise began spreading the oil all over her gorgeous bod. Bringing her mouth up to Marielle's lips, she passed a gentle kiss. Their tongues lightly touched and nipples brushed. Valise stood in a moment of loving affinity, waiting for Marielle to take the lead.

Passing the oil, Marielle squatted down, spreading some on her feet. She slowly massaged up to her legs, grazing her twinge, and finally reaching her chest. Moving around to her back, she massaged with pleasing intentions. Loving sounds escaped from Valise lips as Marielle teasingly reached around, feeling her breasts and nipples. Valise turned around and looked deep into Marielle's eyes as their lips stood inches apart.

"It's time for wine?" "Let's search for that delicious bottle I told you about," Valise said.

Their game had ended as they disappeared into the wine cellar, closing the doors behind them.

My head was hot and in a state of confusion. Unsure of what had just transpired, I placed my hands under my panties. Dripping wet, I smelled my freshness and put my fingers into my mouth, sucking my nectar. Then, I scurried to my bedroom, locked the door, and lied down in bed. Feeling in the mood, the woman had caught me off-guard.

"Wow, the family ritual of stripping and lubricating. Must have been going on since we were kids," I murmured. Yet, I thought nothing more about their playful act.

A few days later, Alexia had returned from the business trip. After we showered together and dried off, we lied in bed caressing. I wanted to tell her about Marielle, but there was a sense of apprehension that came over me. The words could not come out. Then, a spirit of strength pervaded as I let my words flow without inhibition.

"...not wanting to be a voyeur, it just happened..."

"... Lizette, you should not be so curious. But go on, it's sounding juicy."

"... stripping to bare skin and showing off their naked bodies seemed like an innocent game. It all happened before they walked into the wine cellar. First in was Marielle..."

With an open ear, Alexia carefully listened. As my description got more intense, she gradually turned and snuggled, placing her face on my shoulder. With her delicate hands, she was caressing my arm while gently kissing my flesh with her moist lips. After a few minutes, she glided her fingers delicately across my belly and circled my tummy with her special touch. As I proceeded, she pulled the sheets up as her wonderful scent filled within the covers. She moved her hand onto my thigh, petting softly. Feeling awakened and aroused, her hand moved downward as my breathing moderately intensified. I swallowed and tilted my head back, tensing for the moment. Giving me a nice soft gentle kiss on the neck, she placed her head onto the pillow. Unexpectedly, her eyes gradually fell shut into a sound sleep just as my story had ended.

"Well…. she's probably tired from the trip," I whispered.

My fingers touched my puss as I sat thinking about our closeness. Reaching over, I gave Alexia a soft kiss on the forehead and my mind wondered into a dream.

Awakening into the morning sun, I slowly got out of bed. I put some clothes on and made my way downstairs. Thoughts of Mama's ritual filled my mind as I made morning coffee and breakfast. Putting the breakfast on a tray, I opened the kitchen door and descended the steps to the outdoor patio. I placed the tray on a table and sat in a lawn chair. Sipping my coffee, I looked around the yard.

"This could be all mine one day to share with my sister," I muffled. "How could a middle-class family even afford such an elegant place?"

Built in the early eighteen hundred by our great-great-grandfather, our home was a gift to Papa. Constructed of stone, brick, and logs, our four-thousand square foot home sat on a five-acre plot. High cement walls with protruding iron spikes surround the spacious property.

Our newest addition comprised a contemporary kitchen, and a finished basement. In the finished basement, a set of patio doors led out into the enclosed inground hot tub, which could easily entertain twenty-five people. Enclosed by glass walls and doors, the hot tub served like a sauna in the cooler months. Natural stone pavers with cool blue interior lighting surround its edges. One could sit in the tub and stare at the stars while sipping a wine.

Walking into the wine cellar was like going back in history two-hundred years. In the older part of the home, the wine cellar contains stoned walls, brick trim, and tall ceilings. The only access to the cellar is through two large oak wooden doors in the finished basement. Further back near the rear of the wine cellar was the cheese room. We usually referred it to the cheese cave because of its cool and humid temperature. The cellar contains brick arches and metal bar cavities that can store and preserve thousands of full wine bottles. The cavities attached to the wall contains the averaged priced wines. Papa locks the most expensive wine up in antique cherry cabinetry that butts up against the cellar wall.

Our family made it a ritual to make a trip to the wine cellar and cheese cave when guests arrive. The saying 'make yourself at home' was our family's motto. Wine was not only a host gesture for our parents' acquaintances. Alexia and I would invade Papa's wine cellar to grab some cheap bottles for our girl parties.

"It is going to be one heck of a party year before heading off to college next year," I whispered.

No sooner did I finish what I was saying, when Alexia descended the stairs. She sat down next to me with a cup of coffee.

"I was just thinking about the wonderful features of our house that we will own one day," I said.

"I'd rather have Papa alive forever than think about anything else," Alexia said in a serious tone. "Sorry about last night," Alexia said. "I was tired."

"That's ok. I know you have a tight schedule this summer with Papa."

"I'll be on the road often before our last year of lycée starts."

"How's business?"

"Fine. I think it's going to be a career. It's too good not to take it over when Papa retires. I've learned so much in such a short period. Besides, Papa treats me well, and there is plenty of money. You should join us."

"Not yet, I not sure what I want to do."

My hand rested on her thigh, gently petting. We lied naked in bed together for as long as I could remember. Yet, we only continue to get closer as time goes on. Sharing many long sessions of touching and fondling has driven me to the edge of our relationship.

"Papa would love you as a partner. Well, I will always say that you are welcome. We are sisters for life."

"Sisters for life." I gave a soft kiss on her lips as we sat taking the morning sunshine in.

Chapter 6

The Secret

It was early August. The start of the school year was just a few weeks away. At age eighteen, Alexia and I would enter our final year at the lycée. Alexia seemed to find her place in the family business, but what about me? I lied back in bed, putting my hands behind my head. A cool breeze swept across my face through the open window. Taking a deep breath through my nose, I could smell the freshness of the outdoors. The thought of summer passing away left me slightly dispirited. Soon, sunbathers would gradually thin out on the beach as the weather cooled. Then, the seasonal walkers would appear bundled up and conducting their healthy routine along the bay.

In thinking about the changing seasons, a sense of relieving fullness brightened my disposition. With fall looming around the corner, a level of comfort seized my inner self. Autumn is about cuddling close and a warm lit fireplace. The woodsy scent would fill the room as the fire pops and crackles. Alexia and I would lay naked under the sheets, adding an extra layer of warmth between us. As the flames die down, we'd eventually fall asleep like snuggling playmates.

Looking at the mantlepiece, I imagined our ancestry sitting around the same fireplace. Back in those days, they had to chop the wood by hand. Mama just calls and orders it. However, we still must haul the wood up flights of stairs from the side of the house. Papa says that the delivery man puts the wood in the same spot that our family had done for decades. I guess not everything changes.

The doorbell rang, interrupting my thoughts. Mama opened the door as I carefully listened. The voice…....sounded like Marielle. She probably came over to spend a typical afternoon to sunbathe, drink wine, and gossip. Then, I remembered that Papa and Alexia were in Toulouse on business.

Retracing thoughts, I closed my eyes and slowly drifting off. Minutes had passed as the sounds of a conversation brought me back to consciousness. Rubbing my face, I got up from bed and peered outside. Valise and Marielle were sitting on the loveseat topless, wearing panties, and chatting. Their expressions were one of passion as they held hands, looking into each other's eyes. However, their conversation was faint and obscured. I pulled up a chair to the window and grabbed my laptop. I sat down and started searching for fashions on the internet. As time passed, the sounds of birds surfaced as their voices faded into the distance. I presumed they left for their usual afternoon shower and nap.

Casually gazing outside, my laptop almost dropped to the floor as my head spun in circles. Valise had her hands on Marielle's tits, caressing and sucking. Sighs of delight and appeasement seeped through Marielle's lips. They were fervently engaged in each other like a fine delicacy. I stood back from the window, trembling with my mind in a state of confusion.

"Have they been doing this for years? In the master bedroom!" I thought. "I can't believe Marielle and Mama are intimate lovers."

Then I realized Marielle had kept clothes in the guest bedroom. She would often stay overnight, but only when Papa was out of town.

"That's the reason I was hearing faint sounds of passion emanating from the master bedroom," I muttered. "All this time, I thought it was the television."

Hidden from sight, I peered out the window. My interest peaked in the heat of excitement. Erotic impulses swept through me as I observed their carnal play.

Valise was rubbing and fondling her soft tits as she looked into Marielle's glazed eyes. She sucked and licked her long, sensitive nipples like a juicy peach. Feasting like she had not eaten all day, her mouth nursed with prurience and vigor. Then, her lips compressed against Marielle's sensitive nipples, grinding as she passionately stroked. Marielle gripped the cushion on the sofa. Her nails dug in as the sensations were unsurpassable and arousing.

After lapping each droplet of sweat and slaver off her luscious tits, Valise incrementally kissed her shoulder. Then she planted moist kisses along her nape as tingling sensations ran down Marielle's spine. Valise's face brushed gently against her tender cheek. Her head turned, embracing Marielle's in a moist, luscious, full kiss. Within the thirst for oral satisfaction, tongues glided effortlessly between lips, circling, and melting.

Their unquenchable and unrelenting fervent addiction for each other lacked cessation. Plunging and playing, Valise took Marielle's tongue and sucked it like a long phallus. In and out, her tongue whisked as sounds of wantonness echoed in the air. Exchanges of intimate passion saturated their appetites. Then, their mouths opened and parted as tongues immersed in a battle of flickering stimulation.

The erotic intensity between the two females was rousing. I slid my hand under my tank top, imagining the juicy and delicious sensation of my tongue dancing in their mouths. Absorbed in their salacious play, I began teasing myself as I watched with deep intensity.

Marielle took control and guided her soft lips down Valise's neck toward her breasts. Relishing her erect nipples, she kissed and licked, enjoying the taste of her natural oils. Slowly licking towards her belly, Valise's eyes rolled upward, awakening to an unbearable tickling sensation. Marielle's hands gently caressed as her tongue brushed her tanned skin. With the tip of her tongue, she circled her belly and licked further downward. Purposely evading Valise's wet and musty minge, she vigorously teased her inner thigh like a seducing temptress.

Valise's breathing intensified as Marielle kissed and tasted her sweet, dripping juices. Inhaling her feminine scent, snares of alluring feelings surfaced. She desired to bring her into a sizzling culmination. But her tongue sailed upward, licking her smooth-shaven body like a melting ice cream cone. Then, her lips met Valises, and they embraced in a succulent kiss.

Wanting to touch and taste their flesh, I peeled off my tank top and bra. I pinched and squeezed my nipples to arousing wetness.

There was a momentary pause that emerged from their play. With mouths fully parted and eyes focused, they stared face-to-face in deep thought. But moments of nervous anxiety between deep lovers lacked containment. Compulsion overtook abstinence and mouths meshed like magnets. Tongues began darting, curling, and entwining in sizzling fusion. Cravings intensified into feral affections as moans of pleasure resonated.

Valise moved her tongue down to Marielle's breasts, licking and sucking with tenderness. Valise slurped her glistening nipples as Marielle's head leaned back in unreserved gratification. Then, Valise gently caressed her stomach, charming her like a tamed animal in heat. Softly pressing her hand inward, Valise seductively glided her fingers under Marielle's panties, feeling the soft and shaven skin. In reaching for her bare puss, Marielle accepted her advances like a sex slave in dire need of a master's love.

With moist lips bonded and tongues flaring, Valise pushed further, burying her fingers into the wetness. With penetrating fingers, Marielle's nerve endings became electrified with multiplied sensations. Pushing her pelvis against Valise's piercing fingers, their motions were moving in a rhythmic pattern. Marielle leaned back in a daze, submitting to the escalating pleasure.

Continuing with a steady pace, Valise was striking her sweet spot with precision and intensity. With breathless and broken words of want, cries escaped from Marielle's lips. Her cheeks transformed into a pink and reddish color. Her clitoral nerves sparked exhilarating vibrations. Mouths and tongues appeased as her ride to bliss heightened. Finally, entering the abyss of total fulfillment, her mind went blank and her body tensed commencing a feverish spasm.

Almost peaking, she became instantly frozen without warning. Valise stepped back like a cold shower in the dead of winter while gripping Marielle's wrist. Marielle let out a sigh of displeasure.

Marielle's breathing moderated as her mind merged back to reality. Stepping forward, Valise slowly drove her tongue into Marielle's mouth, wanting to bring her to the edge once more. Her taste was delicious as they smothered within the fervency of oral satisfaction.

Reaching for her aching hole, Marielle felt the fingers of Valise crawl under her panties. Her fingers glided easily along the wet and velvety surface as she slowly inserted two fingers into the slushiness. Filling her cavity with love, Marielle's face flaunted like a virgin, feeling her first pleasing penetration. With pervading fingers, Marielle's toes curled, attempting to grip the ground underneath her feet.

Then, Valise's fingers drove in and out, screwing with intensity as gasping sounds escaped from her lips. Marielle's heart rate increased as the heat of passion intensified. Her mouth opened wide in a silent scream as pulsating pleasures consumed her unsatisfied urges. Bounded by blazing obsession, Marielle started convulsing as she ascended into radiance.

Valise control was like a stampede of horses unstoppable and explosive. Ceasing her play, she left Marielle begging in the battlefield of pleasure. Anticipation and anxiety had descended to total withdrawal. With eyes almost tearing in desperation, Marielle was like a crazy woman in a locked cage. She wanted to be thrusted into a state of impassioned saturation.

Valise slowly moved close, slipping her fingers under her panties. She touched Marielle's erect and sensitive oyster. Marielle's flesh was nervously craving uncontrollably. Valise applied more pressure as her fingers played with eagerness. Tempos increased as Marielle's heart rate amplified achieving yet another level of gratification. Valises began driving her to the verge as nerves pleased with compelling stimulation.

Valise teased, wanting Marielle to taste a full surrender. Then, the lures of seduction took dominion. Marielle suddenly felt an easing as she opened her eyes, calming to a relaxing standstill.

Valise spoke. "You'll want me very much. Beg for my love. Beg me for it," she said, savagely.

"You know I want you Valise. I'm your…. cum slut. Give me release," Marielle whimpered.

"Tell me I'm the master of your flesh."

"I only summit to you, my mistress."

Chapter 7

Come for Me

My panties were itching wet as the desirous craving for sensual gratification intensified. Sliding my fingers into my sweet puss, I envisioned tongues all over my flesh. Then my voyeur instincts took over. I couldn't keep my eyes off their lustful play.

Within the tangs of succulence, sounds of carnal desire resonated in the air. Tongues incessantly flittered in a tenacious duel as fervent lovers pleased. They lapped and sucked, capturing every drop of oozing slaver. It was Valise's prolonged tactics in suspending Marielle culmination that led her into pure submission. Emphatically removing Marielle's panties with deviance and compulsion, Valise inhaled her scent. With determination, she propelled the journey to quench Marielle's licentious hunger.

Rubbing her vagina, Valise saturated her fingers with juicy tang. Then she slowly pushed them into Marielle's accepting mouth. Almost choking, Marielle puckered and swallowed as she felt Valise's fingers slide in and out. Before long, Marielle had sucked them completely dry.

"That's my obedient girl, savoring my delicious taste. Are you ready cum slut?"

With fiery eyes, Marielle's head nodded in pleading want. "Do me," she said, urgently.

In a mood to build Marielle to an explosive peaking sensation, Valise grabbed a small butt plug and lubed it. She turned Marielle around and commanded her to bend over. Wiggling it about, she jimmied the plug into her anal crack. Then Valise gripped her wet panties and slid them off.

"Put my panties to your nose. Inhale while I make you cum," Valise said imperiously.

Smelling her scent, Marielle was in venereous heat, yearning for a salacious surge. Using two fingers, Valise encircled Marielle's soft, erect oyster as their nipples jiggled and touched. The synergy of clitoral and anal stimulation instantaneously drove

Marielle into moans of delight. Melting away in Valise's dominating control, blood rushed through her body as nerves fired off in elation. Marielle had climbed into an ecstatic moment as her breathing intensified.

"Come my love," Valise said, casually. "Submit yourself."

Valise vigorously grinded imparting lashes of titillating pleasure. Marielle closed her eyes, feeling the rhythmic surges as she visualized a brilliance of light. Almost becoming breathless, guttural screams emerged from her lips. Then Marielle's face became flush as she began shuddering. Within an intensified moment of escalation, her mind burst into a pleasing delirium. Valise lips reached hers as tongues delicately touched, like a romantic battle between lovers had ended.

I didn't want the enjoyable pleasure to end as my breathing intensified. Marielle rested momentarily on the lounge chair, collecting her thoughts. But the amorous encounter was far from over. Within the rising heat of sweet passion, inspiration seized Marielle. Energy levels blossomed with a compulsory need to satisfy her lover. She stood up and peered into Valise's eyes with a determination to put Valise's mind into a state of absolute insensibility.

Without a word spoken, Marielle moved behind her, pressing her nipples against her bare back. She reached around, fondled, and kneaded her erect nipples. Then, she incrementally kissed along her luring neck line penetrating the tanned skin with moist lips. Valise surrendered in appeasing subtleness as soothing lips covered her bare flesh. Then Marielle moved her face, pressing lightly upon her hair while breathing softly in her ear. Words of sensuality flowed as tingling chills ran through Valise's spine. Marielle licked and teased her earlobe as she continued to knead and caress her firm tits. Valise tilted her head back, enjoying the pleasurable advances as her fingers slid between her legs.

Marielle held tight with bare skin to bare skin, touching within a bath of perspiration and natural oils. She treasured the blend of their delicious scents while they lusted in the swelter of sexual obsession. She remembered having a quicky with a fellow student after aerobics class. They stripped naked, making love in

31

a closet while sweat profusely dripped onto the floor. It felt so raw and wild as they tasted and savored each moment of pleasure. They climaxed as the steamy aroma saturated the surrounding ether.

Marielle spoke in a commanding tone. "Get my panties off the chair and relish my scent."

Valise grasped them, inhaling the wet, soiled cloth. The aroma was pure feminine tang that induced a compelling urge to fall submissively to Marielle. Holding them tightly to her face, she inhaled one last time and threw them onto the chair.

Marielle planted a French kiss on Valise's lips, sinking her tongue deep inside her mouth. Her taste was moist, soft, and pleasant. Within endless moments of pleasure, their tongues intertwined with arousing affection. Then Marielle placed her lips on Valise's tender nipples. Valise revelled the sensation as she nursed her like a newborn. With her long tingling tongue, Marielle lapped down to her lover's stomach but didn't stop. Licking and swallowing every drop of sweat, her tongue danced all her way down to her minge.

Yearning for feminine love, aching sensations swept through my erogenous zones. I wanted to taste their dripping juices as sensual cravings were ceaseless in my thoughts. Infatuated with two females in heat, my fingers were on my bare puss, masturbating with an incessant flow. Without inhibition, I daringly stepped into view as a warm breeze swept over my naked body.

Marielle got down in a sitting position, sucking and licking her lover within her musk. She spread her labia and positioned the tip of her tongue on Valise's clit, pressing, twirling, and lapping. With unceasing determination, she sucked and swallowed within the wetness. Her warm, satisfying tongue felt like a hundred feathers tenderly converging at a single point. Gasping sounds of joy resonating from Valise's lips. Her skillful play brought enrapturing sensations as the elevated stimulation led her mind into an ecstatic cloud.

Marielle softly touched her middle finger against Valise's warm anus. She looked up into her eyes with a perverse stare as she rubbed it around. Grabbing a tube of anal lube, she put a glob on her finger and placed some on her crack. Valise jumped at the tantalizing coolness, but a pleasant sensation soon emerged. Marielle circled her finger around the puckered hole until it opened wide. With a little effort, she slipped her finger in freely until it flowed like a well-lubricated machine. Screwing in a steady motion, sounds of pleasure seeped from Valise's lips. With eyes rolling upward, Valise let out cries of want and satisfaction.

Marielle then picked up a small vibrator, replacing it with her tongue. Euphoric sensation immediately intensified sending stimulating signals through her flesh. Breathing deeper, ultra-pulses of pleasure brought her to a higher level of gratification. Marielle stroked her finger with vigor as Valise was squalling in delight. Suddenly, Valise's spinster muscle gripped Marielle's middle finger with firmness. Her erect clit was becoming hypersensitive to the touch.

"Come for me. Come now," Marielle said excitedly.

Valise's body tightened as Marielle's rhythm continued. Without notice, Valise let a sound of ecstatic release as vibrating waves ran through her entire body. Marielle pulled out her finger from her gaping hole. In a mesmerizing state of sheer joy, Valise sank into a chair. The immense stimulation led to a fulfilling orgasmic rush that left her feeling dazed.

Rubbing my wet pussy, I was exuberantly ready to reach climax. The feverous heat of pleasure running through my body could not stop. Thinking of their erotic play, I began peaking in pleasure. My moans echoed throughout the backyard as Marielle looked up. She saw me in the window, naked and climaxing. I stepped back as intervals of throbs surged throughout my body like lightning. Holding onto the interior window frame with my head was down, I began reviving from the intense pleasure.

Chapter 8

St Katherines

Saint Katherine is a private girl's school on the outskirts of Carcene. Over the years, Mama developed close acquaintances with select board members and teachers at the school. Some would stop over and drink expensive wine while Papa was out of town on business. Through Mama's intimate relationships, we could attend the school with reduced tuition. Papa knew they would get a great education at a reasonable cost. So, he didn't mind footing the bill.

There was a boy's private school located a few miles up the road from the girls. The schools interacted in various activities, like dances and sports. However, Alexia and I never ventured to the boy's private school for any of the affiliated events. Mostly, we had much better things to do with our time.

The schools within the Pays de la Loire district developed an intermural girls' and boys' competitive soccer program. In initiating this program, a cheerleading program surfaced to support the athletes. Some girls at our school become cheerleaders for the boy's sport teams. However, Alexia became a cheerleader for the girls' soccer team. I was neither an athlete nor a cheer leader. However, I went to the games as a cheering fan.

One night at the beginning of the school year, Alexia got a bottle from the wine cellar. We sat in the hot tub area with our feet in the water getting a pleasant buzz discussing school.

"Some cheerleaders for the male sports team think I'm weird," she said.

"Why," I responded.

"They tell me I have a gorgeous body and can have any male on the team."

"I know you didn't want to cheer for the boys because of the way they look at you."

"Yeah… and those sexual comments."

"Alexia, you are like me. Forget about male athletes for dating, or any guy."

She kissed me on the lips as we caressed and sipped our wine.

"The Lycée aged males are chauvinistic, ego centered, and lack maturity," Alexia stressed. "They only seek personal satisfaction while caring little for female needs. Some of the cheerleaders for the boys' team tell me that once they get off, they treat their girlfriends like empty holes."

We sat back, looking into the stars.

She mockingly put her finger down her mouth and made a choking sound. "This is what I think of boys."

"That's right on point. However, your comeback when a guy tries to pick you up is so awesome."

We sat there for a minute as she collected her thoughts. "Come on, your time and not on mine, selfish boy. Donnez-moi une fille qui peut le lécher a bien et sac."

Then we laughed out of control. Boys never quite understood what pleasing a girl meant. But the words carried a lot of emotional satisfaction. We French kissed and it felt so deliciously good.

Alexia and I shared a pool of common friends within the school that included members of the cheerleading squad and athletes. The pompom girls were hot, well-manicured, and chic. The female athletes were tomboyish, avoided make-up, and kept a short hairstyle. Female athletes enjoyed wearing casual sporting attire, and mostly, baseball caps.

The diversity of social lifestyles never created a barrier or lack of cohesion. It was quite the opposite. The relationship between our friends became much closer as time passed. The sharing of spiritual and mental needs was an ongoing part of our affiliation. Physical desires such as kissing, affection, and teasing played another significant part of our cohesiveness. Some girls became deep fervent lovers, while others just shared mild affections.

When our classmates came over to the house to sunbath, they would strip down naked, displaying their gorgeous tanned physiques. The natural ritual of going nude around the house brought no embarrassment or envy, but added to our excitement and curiosity. Girls would help each other pull off tops and unfasten bras while chatting and caressing. It was nothing to see friends feeling breasts and nipples while complementing individual beauty.

However, it was not surprising to find feminine distinction among bare bodies when they were naked. The cheerleaders had delicate complexions, luscious tits, and softer bodies. The athletes were firm, slim, smaller breasted, and exhibited muscular physiques.

When our girlfriends came over to the house, some would sunbathe and others sought intimacies. Those skipping the sun headed directly to a private place in the house to share passion and pleasure. In the yard, the sunbathers would teasingly drench suntan oil all over their classmates as giggling echoed in the yard.

After tanning for a few hours, the girls would grab a glass as Alexia brought out the wine, cheese, and crackers. Filling the wineglasses to the top, the fun escalated. As everyone caught a buzz, there was laughing and toying with spontaneity.

When wine spilled on a naked body, it became a game. The girl who could lick and suck the wine up before it dripped to waste was a winner. Tongues, lips, and mouths roamed across bare skin to ensure the recapture of every drop. Some girls purposely poured wine on themselves to enjoy the luscious stimulation provided by their peers.

Some cheerleaders desired to massage athletes. So, the cheerleaders created an innovative game that focused around a total body massage, calling it the 'opulent lube job.' In this game, female athletes would lie on their stomachs. The cheerleaders' soft hands massaged in circular motions, covering all the muscles from the neck to the ankles. After massaging the back, the cheerleaders would coat their chest and stomach in oil. With tits down, they would lie flat on top of their classmates. Their bodies glided up and down like a slippery slide, giving pacifying pleasure. In swaying, the cheerleaders often uttered soft moans of delight as nipple stimulation was intensifying. Unnoticed, fingers would sometimes disappear in pleasurable places. Then, the athletes turned over and lied on their backs facing the cheerleaders. The pairs would engage in tit-to-tit stimulation with embracing lips and tongues.

The opulent lube job induced strong sensual desires, which often led into private pairing sessions after the game was over. The girls would head to the finished basement, hot tub area, or find another private location around the house for pleasuring. As early evening drew near, the pairs would converge in the hot tub for glasses of champagne and hors d'oeuvres. In the tub, new girl pairs formed to explore a fresh set of lips.

Chapter 9

Alexia's Secrets

As Alexia and I transitioned from our preteen to teen years, our Mama educated and explained the natural cycles and emotions that we would encounter. Her potent influence, mediation, and oversight led us to a philosophy of talking things out rationally and truthfully. As we progressed through lycée, Alexia and I became very transparent about conveying our innermost thoughts and feelings. We would openly express the deep personal feelings that lingered within our minds. Sometimes it was hard. But a spirit of confidence always seemed to overcome the tension within our trusted relationship.

It was a cool autumn night. The fireplace was keeping us warm, and the lights were dim. Lying in bed, I gently kissed Alexia on the lips and rested my head on her shoulder. Feeling a slight draft, I pulled another layer of blanket over me.

"Are you cold?" she said.

"Just a little."

She gently touched me on the thigh and delicately caress. Her touch was subtle and inviting. The sound of her voice was expressive, warm, and calming.

"This should provide a little warmth and comfort."

"Do you feel relaxed?"

"Yes. Your hand is so velvety. What's bothering you, my love?" I asked curiously.

My mind drifted for a moment. I started reflecting on our relationship as sisters. We were always cuddling naked under the blankets. Even during wintry nights, we wore virtually nothing. Tonight, our nakedness had an unfamiliar feeling. Something felt quite different. As Alexia touched me with a level of passion, she wanted to make me feel warm and cozy. It was like she wanted to return a favor from falling asleep when I was telling her the story about Marielle and Valise. As she continued petting, I relaxed, enjoying our closeness. I turned around and curled closer, positioning my bare bottom against her warm minge. Then, her tender breath blew lightly in my ear, giving me a tickling sensation.

"Alexia, you feel so soft. Your breath tickles," I said.

She began whispering the details about her erotic encounters with the cheerleaders in the shower as I listened intently.

"Standing naked in the shower lathering my breasts, I often glanced over at the other girls. Their gorgeousness would draw me towards them like a magnet. I imagined cleansing their bods with my soapy hands as I pleasured them with gentle touches and seductive tenderness. Teasing, I wanted to slide my hand up and down their sexy smooth legs. Before they dried off, I desired to suck every droplet of water off their wet body.

"Then, a peculiar thing happened. While rubbing their faces with closed hands under the running water, a few girls would open their fingers, peeking. As they watched, a warm, slushy feeling flowed through my abdomen. I would teasingly turn around and slide my fingers down into my puss. Pleasuring myself and hidden from view, I thought about their hands all over my flesh. I enjoyed playing with myself without shame or embarrassment as they watched my bare butt. It felt naughty, daring, and even sleazy."

Alexia took a deep breath.

"In the girl's locker room, my inner desires turned into lustful actions. I began enticing the girls in many provocative ways. For instance, I purposely stood naked, not wanting to put my clothes on until everyone else did. I leaned against a locker streaming my cell, wanting them to admire my nakedness. I sometimes took a razor and finely trimmed my pubic hair while spreading my legs wide in view.

"The girls would cunningly aim their eyes toward my juiciness while drying themselves off. It was like they wanted to lick me wet and suck me dry. Slipping their panties on with hesitancy, I could feel they wanted to join me in a session of gayety. When they put their bras on, I would help fasten it in place. In doing so, I would often touch their arms and shoulders with my gliding fingers. My nipples would sometimes lightly graze their backs, becoming hard. In those tingling moments, I wanted to unleash all inhibition and caress their tits and suck their nipples.

"To tease further, I seductively took a pair of stained panties, bringing them to my nose and inhaled with delight as they watched. Then, I would slip them on boldly, pulling them tightly to my love triangle. Some girls would volunteer to help me strap on my bra. They would return caresses with tearing lust in their eyes. I knew they were thinking about having a passionate female-to-female encounter. I sensed their inner desire to French kiss, entwine tongues, and feel bare skin. Doubting myself, I was unwilling to cross the line by making a pass."

In listening to Alexia unearth her story, I became dazed and impassioned. She never confided her flirtations or erotic inclinations. Being sincere, she continued communicating her inner thoughts.

"It was so weird. The experiences in the steamy shower with the girls were enthralling. The thought of watching the cheerleaders lather their bodies sometimes sent electric pulses through my body. Being a voyeur was unanticipated and enjoyable, but I wanted more."

Picturing what Alexia was saying, I started becoming aroused. Her voice was tantalizing and focused as she stared into the room. It was like taking a puff of marijuana and letting my mind escape into time and space. I envisioned her words creating my fantasy with characters, feelings, and emotions.

Then, her tone changed to one of ardor. "The rawness of your natural scent is also so nice when we lie together. It kindles me," she replied. "Our oils blend well, just like the beach and tanning oil. Remember!"

"I do. Coming up behind you, touching and caressing, my nose pressed against your skin, enjoying your flesh. But tell me more about your feelings with the other girls."

Changing to a more serious tone, Alexia shifted her story, focusing on the soccer team.

"When out on the field as a pompom, I felt different about the female athletes. Most are competitive sweaty jocks, unlike the cheerleaders. I watched their strength, agility, and skill as they moved the ball onto the field. Unlike the cheerleaders in the shower, there was a different type of attraction as I stood next to the players. It was better than being around boys. My mind immediately reflected on the afternoon body massages, girl pairing, and secret pleasuring sessions. I envisioned partner changes in the hot tub. You know. I wanted the same satisfaction that everyone was experiencing. But someone had to please our guests at our parties. So, I stayed sober and performed the hosting duties intentionally keeping myself out of the sensual fun."

Alexia's emotions and sexuality were coming of age as she uncovered her true self. Her thoughts and desires were like mine, but I kept an emotional distance. I wanted her to feel a genuineness about our friendship. She needed to talk out her feelings in a way that was open and honest. I wanted her to tell me every drop of detail. It was not about me but her.

"There is a soccer player that struck me with awe. She is a tall, thin blonde female with blue eyes, short blonde hair, and a round butt. Her name is Selene, a senior at the school. When I first watched her, I was just cheering her on to score more points. However, my feelings changed one day. I got excited at the games, watching her run and play against the competition. It was like being part of her at a distance. I especially liked the way she took a dominate role on the field by leading the other girls to victory. I felt a yearning desire to want to hold her in my arms. Sometimes, I purposely did not wear panties, giving her a quicky when she peered over.

I would get so horny and wet on the field, I'd rush home from school with the need to please myself silly. Then, she came close to me one day, and I looked at her. It was then that I knew she wanted me. Her blues eyes sparkled with mesmerizing strength."

Alexia swallowed and lowered her mouth. Her chin gently touched my head. Her nails gliding over my thigh in a soothing and appetizing manner. I felt very relaxed in her arms as she let out her thoughts. My mind drifted into an unconscious state, enjoying our moments of being together, touching and caressing. Then she spoke, bringing me back to reality.

"You know how girlfriends get together at our house in the afternoon loving and pleasing? Well, one night I had a dream about Selene. After cheering for her during a game, I invited her to our backyard festivities."

Alexia took a breath and continued.

"In the dream, Selene was rubbing massaging oil all over me with her firm hands. She was hinting on giving me a full body massage. At first. I felt very nervous because this was an unfamiliar experience. However, something was pushing me to get into her panties. My feelings immediately changed as I began letting go. I wanted her to slide naked on my back while coated in tanning oil. I wanted her on top of me in a tit-to-tit erotic adventure."

Alexia paused in silence for a few minutes as I continued brushing her thigh with my fingers. Her body heat was elevating as she pressed against me. I could feel the wetness against my butt. I wanted to touch her desperately and give her what I always wanted. Then, she moved her hand to my stomach, resting it.

She spoke again. "The dream led me to the bleachers. On that day, I didn't wear panties or a bra. Selene was going to meet me. I wanted to strip naked under the bleachers while the other athletes watched us indulge in lovemaking. I wanted that firm, sexy female to love every inch of my body until every nerve ending pulsated with extreme pleasure."

Feeling nervous, hot, and stirred, I became aroused by her desire to make love to a female. Turning around to face her, Alexia began caressing me on my inner thigh. Never has my sister touched me so close to my sweet spot. She placed her arms around my neck and gave me a warm kiss. Her tongue penetrated my mouth. I was feeling drunkenly awakened by her advances. The fantasy of Alexia having pleasure with a female athlete was electrifying. Our lips parted, and I calmed myself down. I needed to change the tone or lose self-control. I wanted to deeply share sister sex.

Nervously shaking with wantonness, I said. "A female-to-female erotic relationship is great. You should not let social norms stop you, sis."

Our sister's intimacy had unleashed to a new level. The innocence we experienced as children has turned into romantic vibrance. Up to this point in our lives, we would lie in bed together all night long without the slightest inclination of engaging in sexual intimacy. On colder nights, we would hold each other close to keep warm and even caress each other's hair before falling asleep. It was never anything like this. I could not get any closer to her. Not now, anyway.

"Alexia, I need to take a quick shower," I said.

With escaping words, I went into the bathroom and locked the door behind me. I took out a dildo hidden in the bottom drawer.

"This is what I need right now," I thought.

Alexia had turned me on like a bright lightbulb telling me about her deep intimate feelings. The thought of a female soccer player making hot, sweet love set my pussy ablaze. I imaged her licking my toes, moving her tongue up my legs, and sucking and licking on my triangular lips. I pushed the dildo in and out of my orifice in a smooth, pulsing pattern. Breathing deeper and deeper, I was reaching a penetrating moment. Then, a gushing sensation came over me. Clenching onto the dildo, a euphoria thrill swept through my mind. I mushroomed in a cloud as my body vibrated with satisfying pleasure. Leaning back against the shower, I held my head down, having enjoyed the pleasing session.

I hid the dildo back into the drawer. I turned on the water and doused myself in complete relaxation. After drying off, I walked out into the bedroom. My sister had fallen fast asleep; her hand was between her legs. I could smell her musky scent as I slipped under the covers besides her nakedness.

Chapter 10

The Soccer Team

St. Katherines had stringent policies when it came to girl-to-girl love on school grounds, especially in the shower. So, most girlfriends just avoided passionate kissing and erotic behavior while in the locker-rooms. However, without adequate enforcement, rule breaking was inevitable and the soccer team took full advantage. Female soccer players hid in places around the school connecting in amorous encounters. Whether in bathroom stalls, closets, under the bleachers, or in the wooded areas behind the school, they always found a place for some playful privacy. Rumors spread throughout the boy's school, suspecting the female soccer team as being an underground sapphic organization. To the female soccer team, it was merely fun and games. They took a lighter view in that a little feminine play can make their day.

The girls' soccer team also had a knack for adding extensions to school rules. For instance, one lycée rule was that sports players and cheerleaders must maintain proper feminine hygiene. The soccer team's addendum to this rule included that all players must always shave pubic hair to bare skin. After practice, teammates would help shave or wax their fellow players to a smooth-shaven surface. It was nothing to see the players in the locker-room feeling each other's soft skin after waxing. This activity sometimes led some of the girls to find their favorite hiding spot around school to take care of their needs.

The school had another rule mandating that athletes must maintain good sportsmanship while in a match or practice. The female soccer team wholeheartedly agreed and added a procedure to penalize poor sportsmanship. If the team lost a match, the player with the most penalties would be subject to the dreaded 'penalty shower.' Even though there are unscrupulous players from competitive school, dirty play would not bring their team down.

The penalty shower had special procedures, but only if the team lost a home game. The girl with the most penalties had to lie naked face up in the middle of the shower after the game. As the soccer team players took their showers, the girls would take turns pissing on the penalty player.

It sounds cruel at first but, the penalty shower ended up being a fun game the girls loved playing amongst themselves. What really transpired was that the players let it flow on each another like a battle of competitive piss. There was a lot of laughing and giggling leading to good clean shower fun. It let out a lot of frustration that helped the team overcome an emotional loss.

In my last year at lycée, I regularly attended the girls' soccer matches. Alexia supported the team as a cheerleader. Selene, a forward on the team, became my sister's girlfriend. One day, Alexia and Selene approached me.

"Lizette, how about a little excitement? Selene can get you in as a substitute for the penalty shower," Alexia said.

"What!"

"You know the penalty piss," she said. "If the team suffers a loss."

Standing slightly oblivious at first, the teams sportsmanship rule slowly came into my mind.

"Shouldn't that be for team members? I would feel a little uncomfortable," I said, apprehensively.

Selene stepped in. "I don't mind at all. Besides, the team may never experience a loss."

"You need a little excitement, sis. You lead a boring life," Alexia said jokingly.

"It will be fun engaging with the sports players," Selene said.

"It's you last year. Come on," Alexia interjected. "You always go to the games anyway… supporting the teams' efforts."

Becoming more optimistic, I accepted their offer. Through Selene's persuasive efforts, the team captain granted me permission to substitute for one loss.

Attending one of our last soccer games at home, we were playing a match against a team from Cholet. Falling behind by a goal, the score was two to one. I was cheering for our team as the clock was running down.

"Let's go. Come on. Let's get one," I yelled.

The crowd clapped and shouted chants of encouragement. The girls ran up and down the field with great determination to tie. When time ran out, the sound of disappointed echoed throughout the bleachers.

Then I realized. "Wow! This is my chance to become involved in the penalty shower," I whispered.

I waited for the team to get off the field. Then I made my way to the athlete's locker room while calling Selene in my cell.

"Selene, sorry about the loss. I'm on my way to the showers. Is Alexia with you?"

"Alexia is coming. How long will you be?"

"I'll be there in a few."

"Hold on to your pee for dear life," Selene said jokingly.

"Don't worry, I drank plenty of fluids during the game. I'm ready for action."

As I turned the corner, Selene appeared. Her arms embraced me with a hug. The smell of rough perspiration emanated from her body as her sweaty jersey dampened my blouse.

"It was close," I said.

"There will be other games. Besides, we have a winning season," she said.

I brought my lips to hers and gave a moist kiss. Her long tongue penetrated my mouth, swooshing vibrantly. It filled me with a deep, warm feeling. Now, I realized why my sister was dating her. Unnoticed, Alexia came up behind me.

"It's my turn," she said.

I backed away, and she planted a deep kiss on Selene's lips.

"Where are you off to?" I asked.

"We are going to our house to shower and relax," Alexia replied.

Selene went into the locker room and reminded the team captain of the substitution. As she came out, there was a big smile on her face.

"It's all clear. Find a locker and follow the other players," Selene said. "We'll catch up with you later. By the way, have some fun."

"You might get lucky," Alexia said. "Catch you at home."

Giving my sister a look of doubt, I twisted my smile in defiance of her thought. Then, they sped off for an afternoon of girl fun.

I nervously strolled into the locker room wearing a blouse, a short skirt, and sneakers. Silence filled the room with disappointment. The girls were tired and beaten from the game. I found an empty locker and sat down on the bench. I bent over and started taking off my sneakers. The locker room smelt of old cleats, perspiration, grass, and dirt, which reminded me of sweaty sex. The girls slowly stripped off their damp and dirty uniforms. They displayed firm stomachs, muscular legs, and shapely breasts. Some wore their hair short and others had a ponytail. Seeing raw, naked, athletic bods sent chills up and down my spine. I began getting aroused, wanting to let myself go.

Anais was a senior on the team that had accumulated the most penalty minutes during the match. The team captain approached her as she was getting undressed.

"Anais, you're up. Most penalties."

Appearing tired and slightly beaten, she spoke. "I know… be there in a minute."

Anais was a tall girl with an athletic shape, firm arms, and long fingers. Absorbed by her traits, I felt submissive as I stared at her beautiful figure. Her legs were well-developed from running countless miles on the field. She reminded me of an aerobics instructor on a fitness channel. My knees felt feeble as she unfastened her sports bra and let it drop to the floor. She had large tits, round big nipples, and medium-colored areolas.

"Her tits were a little bigger than mine. How could she run so fast?" I thought.

After taking off her slider, her wet panties were sticking to her legs as she awkwardly pulled them off. She placed them to her nose, inhaled, and tossed them to the floor. Shaven and steamy, her pussy glistened. She turned around and bent down to get a towel from her locker. My mind went blank, staring in total amazement. Anais was hot, luscious, and overwhelming. Her puckered hole was like sweet candy waiting for a licking. Her beautifully shaped pussy lips sent chills up and down my spine.

Slightly blushing, the realization occurred that I was desiring a female athlete. Feeling horny and aroused, I casually placed my hand over my panties and stroked. At that moment, Anais turned, looking straight into the eyes with a carnal gaze. I began melting away in her stare as she noticed my fingers tenderly touching. Her wet tongue appeared from those succulent lips and curled upward. At that moment, I wanted her hands all over my body.

The shower's mist engulfed my entire body, awakening me from a gaping stare. Anais headed to the shower with a towel and a face cloth in her hand. Many girls were in the shower already and others followed.

A little embarrassed and aching to pee, I wanted to be the last one in. So, I looked in the locker, pretending to be searching for something. Then I heard sounds of relief coming from the shower as the girls let their bladders flow. Unstrapping my bra and pulling down my panties, I placed them in the locker. I walked over to the shower and glanced in. It was amazing. The players were giggling, laughing, and screaming. Anais was on the floor, lying on her back. A few targeted her, but most were playing peeing wars with each other. Pee was going all over the place and the girls were loving it. The mood in the shower was one of jubilation, as the athletes had forgotten about the game. Then the athletes started coming out of the shower one by one as they dried themselves off. Extremely nervous, I peered in and felt a bit hesitant.

Chapter 11

My Turn

As the last girl left the shower, I anxiously walked in, ready to explode. The lingering scent of shampoo, soap, and perfume permeated the air. To my surprise, Anais got up and peaked her head into the locker room.

"Hope everyone has a great weekend. See you Monday... in practice."

In good spirits, the athletes finished dressing and left to catch their rides home. Anais took her position on the wet floor, waiting for my advances. Feeling anxious, daring, and desirous, my mind lost apprehension watching her in a state of submission. Savoring the moments ahead, I was ready to play the naughty and amusing game.

Then I noticed the mood in the locker room had instantly changed. As Anais peered into my eyes, the shower finale was not about laughter, fun, or releasing tension, but something quite different. The game was about fulfilling carnal desire. It was about two people engaging in kinky and sensual behavior. A game where girls play with girls in a playground of passion without shame. The winning goal is to achieve ultimate satisfaction.

Shyness quickly left me like a dark cloud had moved onward as arousal and wantonness appeared. Feeling free of all inhibition, I spread my legs anxiously over her body, desperately wanting to drown her face with my fluids. My aching puss was craving for a satisfying tongue as I impulsively moved my fingers over my clit. I was rubbing frantically and gasping with pleasure while the need to pee was imminent.

I was about ready to let go while Anais stuck two fingers in her hole. Screwing herself briefly, she brought them to her mouth and tasted the deliciousness with a gratifying smile. Staring with thirst, I wanted to suck her fingers dry one by one. Then she moved her fingers over her pussy pleasuring furiously.

"Squirt it while I cum for you," she whispered, sleazily. "I'm your penalty girl."

The penalty had turned into an erotic fantasy. Submerged with a feverish thought of peaking while peeing was driving me crazy. Vigorously frigging, she looked at me, wanting my hot steamy flow. Nervous delight passed through me as she opened her mouth wide. The threshold of pain was upon me. I could not hold it in any longer.

"Let it go now," I thought. "Soak her."

She continued rubbing her pussy in circles. I squatted down, relaxed my muscle, and blasted my pee all over her mouth, face, and tits. Absorbing the impact with pleasure, my fluids doused her like a hose putting out a fire. As I delivered the last drops to her face, she grinned like she wanted more.

I continued to play with my clit, standing over her. She was watching me like a pervert in a peep show. Her own fingers plucked a rhythmic beat, leading her to a heightened feeling of pink pearl delight. With knees bent and eyes closed, my mind imagined the female athletes. Beautiful naked firm bodies with legs spread wide open, massaging their smooth pussies. Then the girls aroused each another with passionate kisses and gentle caresses. I pictured myself standing in the middle of the all those luscious melting hands, lapping tongues, and moist satisfying lips. My blood flow increased. I was breathing at a more intense level while letting go. All the sudden, I stiffened in an escalating climax as sounds of joy escaped from my lips.

"Oh, that was so good," I said in relief.

Opening my eyes, I awakened from the trance. Catching my breath, I gradually came back to the reality. Anais was reclining on the floor, having spasmed in an elated state. Her hands covered her pink cheeks. She slowly stood up, recouping from the intensity of our female play. I grabbed some soap and turned on the shower. I washed, rinsed, and placed a towel around my body. Feeling a little embarrassed, I walked out into the locker room and opened my locker slightly peering back.

Suddenly, with eyes glued on me, Anais came out of the shower and approached. I turned facing her. Completely energized from her kinky pleasure trip, she stood naked in front of me.

"You want more of me, don't you? I saw how you looked at me at while undressing. Your hands were on your puss, wanting my passion," she said, almost breathless.

I could not say no. My tongue pressed against my lips as the moment intensified. She reached over, untied my towel, and it fell to the floor. My mind was not clear, as her eyes were gleaming in a deep, wanton stare.

Releasing my inner self to her, I spoke in an expressive tone. "Touch me all over with your long fingers. I want you to play with my succulent body like it's yours. Make me climax once more, slut."

She immediately slid two fingers into her soaking hole of wetness. Bringing them to my mouth, my lips parted, accepting her juices. Her fingers went in and out like a lubricated dildo as I sucked like a baby. Drops of saliva dripped from the corner of my mouth. Removing her fingers, she grabbed my chin and brought her mouth to mine, giving me a deep, warm kiss. Her firm fingers gently gripped my mound of pleasure. She felt so good feeling me up that submission took hold of my flesh.

Her lingua slowly sank into my mouth. The sensation of her lips and tongue were slippery, tingly, and teasing. We tongued and tasted, enjoying deep oral satisfaction. Saliva dripped to the back of my throat and I swallowed. She wrapped her long arms around me, hugging tightly. Her soft, feathery fingertips started working on my butt as I melted in her arms like ice on a hot day.

"Soccer girl, play ball with me," I said seductively.

Grabbing my hand, she said, "It's your turn."

Leading me to the shower, I got ready for another adventure. Ordering me to lie down on the floor, my thoughts were obedient, passive, and burning for her love. I looked in her eyes as she stood over me with her pee hole pointing toward my face. Without a second's notice, her warm fluids penetrated my mouth and tits like a faucet. I felt slutty, dirty, and refreshed. She immediately got on top of me. She placed her mouth on mine and began playing with my pleasure zones. Her thick tongue filled my mouth with a full delicious kiss as she moved her fingers up

51

and down my sweet box with pleasing force. She opened my lips, found my erect oyster, and was playing around. Her motion was bringing me off. My face was getting hotter while waves of vibration shook me. When I was about to reach a state of elation, she stopped.

Anais repositioned her body, easing her legs between mine. Forming a scissors position, our slits were touching like missiles ready to fire. Gradually, we began humping our bodies back and forth into a relentless, steady motion. Our pussies grinded as Anais's strength augmented the mounting pressure. Pleasuring within the heat of passion, I was driving myself into an electrifying orgasm. Almost breathless, I could feel my body escalating into a twinge. I stiffened as tremors penetrated through me like explosive energy. Letting out a shrilling sound of enjoyment, I climaxed ecstatically as we slowed down to a restful state.

Coming to reality, Anais finished getting herself off. Exhausted, we lied motionless, naked, and satisfied. I put my fingers to my nose and inhaled not realizing that after school events could get so wild. Not wanting to shower again, I walked into the locker room with a vibrant smile upon my face. I dried off and finished putting my clothes on. Anais walked over to me and put two thick leather bracelets on my wrists. I sniffed the leather, ravishing our kinky game. Giving her one last sensuous, I headed out the door.

While driving home, my thoughts just kept thinking about the unforeseen encounter in the shower. Wanton hunger emerged within the depths of an unusual ritual. A ritual that I would have initially rejected on my own, but persuasion led to acceptance. Walking off the bleachers, I ended up in a kinky affair with an offender of the game. It could have been anyone, but it was Anais. Her domination and strength pushed the golden ceremony into a gushing desire for an afternoon of lustful gratification. Our impulsive rapture erupted into a multitude of pleasant creaming 'oohs and ah's.' No one in their right mind would have believed what happened, nor was I going to tell anyone. I guess it's better to archive the erotic shower encounter under the title of 'The Secret and Forgotten World of Scholastic Functions.'

Pulling up to the house, I was feeling exhausted. I turned off the car and held onto the steering wheel. I closed my eyes for a second and brought the lather bracelets to my nose. Inhaling the raw hide made me feel sensual, libidinous, and feral. This journey of self-satisfaction was unquestionably a random exploration. It was a new founded liberation that opened its doors providing a path into boundless avenues of passion. The deeper I venture into the exploration of female-to-female love, the more I could lose my soul. This compelling female craving could destroy my chances for that eternal reward, but I didn't care now. I only wanted more.

Getting out of my car, the need to pee suddenly emerged. I did not head for the bathroom inside the house. I walked into the backyard, grabbed a couple of towels from the hot tub cabinet, and hid behind some bushes. Sensing freedom without inhibitions, I took off my sneakers and socks. My bare feet settled on the rough ground. My toes curled, gripping the dirt. I purposely left my panties on and pulled up my skirt. I crouched and let it go. A stream of warm pee flowed, drenching my panties, and scooting down my leg, getting me dripping wet. The warm, vibrant stream sent anxieties through my flesh.

"This feels so deliciously good," I whispered. "Defying social convention is the greatest feeling in the world. I just hope it is not addicting."

Placing my hand on my wet panties, I felt my sore puss.

"I'm not ready for any more action today," I muttered.

I stripped naked and dried off. I tied a dry towel around my body and walked into the house dropping the dirty clothes in the hamper. I took the bracelets off and placed them in a hallway drawer.

As I walked into the bedroom, the scent in the air was pure feminine fauna. Selene and Alexia were lying naked in bed on their stomachs. I briefly envisioned what must have transpired within the tumbled wrinkled sheets.

"You girls probably spent the afternoon exploring nature," I said, presuming.

"Did you have a nice day at the pee festivities?" Alexia said.

"You didn't warn me. It was more than I expected, but turned out to be worth my pleasing time."

I gracefully walked over and put my hand on Alexia's back, caressing her tanned skin. Selene got out of bed and picked up her clothes from the floor.

Lifting her head up, she said, "Have to run."

After putting on her clothes, Alexia gave Selene a warm kiss.

"Call me tonight. My love." Alexia responded tenderly. "Luv you."

Selene dashed off, leaving Alexia and me alone in the room. I sat onto the bed pulling the sheets to my nose inhaling the savoring scent. They were a little damp and smelled of naughty sex.

"It looks like you girls had a party today."

"Just some goo-girl fun," Alexia replied with a deep, penetrating smile on her face.

"Well, I'm going to take a well-deserved shower."

I untied my towel letting it fall to the floor. I was naked, standing in front of Alexia.

With eyes and mouth wide opened, she spoke. "You look so hot as usual, sis."

"Can't have a piece," I said, jokingly. "A little sore. Anyway, why don't you take a shower with me?"

Alexia looked at my bare body with an appetite in her eyes. Her words slightly trembled with nervousness.

"I'm headed down to the hot tub. Need to relax. Let's meet up there?"

"First, let me dose myself fresh."

"I hid an expensive bottle from Papa's collection," she said enticingly. "We can open it after you finish. I'll prepare some snacks."

"I think we could both use a little winding down," I said. "Give me about a half hour."

Heading into the bathroom, I adjusted the valves of the shower until the water reached a perfect temperature. I walked in

54

and closed the doors. The thought about a domineering woman taking full advantage of every part of my flesh filled my inner self with a warming sensation. Lathering my body, the utter desire to engage in further deviant sensual behavior entered my mind. The force of lechery had taken over. Moderation was no longer an obstacle in my life desiring to further explore luscious passion.

"Golden showers," I thought. I just entered the world of exotic female passion. What next?" Then thoughts of Alexia and Selene enjoying each other in passion set my spirits to a new dimension. "A threesome!"

Chapter 12

Le Chic Club

During her lycée years, Alexia worked in the family business, helping Papa with sales, marketing, and the books. In the summer, Papa and Alexia traveled to different European cities on business, which I sometimes tagged along. Papa usually gave us a credit card with a Euro limit to shop for clothes. According to Mama, his underlying generosity was for Alexia to look highly fashionable for his clientele. Knowing Papa's shrewdness, he probably wrote it off as a business expense.

But it didn't matter what his intentions were because we loved him. To Alexia and me, he was a warm-hearted man, buying plenty of gifts for his daughters while we grew up under his loving household. He even paid for tuition at St Katherine, so we could have the best education in town. Mama insisted Jacque was a tightwad, but we never saw that side. Valise was probably not getting enough…. to spend. Maybe that's why our parents complained about money all the time.

With many shopping sprees behind us, Alexia and I always looked voguish at school wearing the latest Paris, London, and Italian styles. Classmates complemented our trendy look, but it wasn't our fashions that made us popular. It was our spiritedness, commitment to school events, and, of course, our wine parties that really got us well accepted among our peers. As a school leader, I wanted to do something special for the senior class but hadn't quite figured it out.

It was Saturday morning. Alexia and I were chatting while enjoying our morning coffee on the outside patio. Thoughts of forming a special organization entered my mind.

"Alexia, let's create something unique to our senior class that would make a lasting impression. Something exciting that we can get everyone involved," I said sincerely.

Raising her eyebrows. "Like what?" Alexia responded, questionably.

"Maybe we can create a new type of club."

"A club for what purpose? Anything in mind?"

"Well, I was thinking of something to do with fashions."

She looked at me square in the face. "Don't be silly, a fashion club! Lizette, most students attending this school can't afford to buy high end fashion wear. We got lucky because of Papa. How about the athletes? Aren't they part of the class... and you know what they wear?"

"They like things loose and shabby because it comes off easy. You know, those moments under the bleachers and in the woods."

She tittered. "Lizette, you're a naughty girl."

Alexia took a sip of coffee and rubbed her eyes as I pondered with perplexity.

"We need to think about something that will serve a benefit to all the senior students. Remember, whatever we do is for them... not for us," Alexia remarked pragmatically.

"Okay, but should we keep the idea about a club?"

She swallowed and shook her head with a slight level of affirmation. "I definitely like the idea, but what type of club?"

"Why don't we invite some friends over and brainstorm," I said. "We can figure it out as a group. Mama and Papa will be out of town next weekend. Let's get them over on Saturday when they're gone."

"That will work. I'll send out text messages and emails out on Monday to get some interest," Alexia said.

"Also, set aside a case of Papa's low-end Riesling.... and ask Selene if she can bring some joints," I added.

"Yes, your queen," Alexia said sarcastically. "Do want me to do anything else?"

"Just bring a working laptop," I said. "It's another party. When Mama's away, the mice will play...."

"But this one has a good purpose," Alexia said in a serious tone. "I feel good about this."

We invited our girlfriends over on the following Saturday afternoon to brainstorm ideas. When they arrived, we gathered around the hot tub. The turnout ended up to be more than expected. Alexia was pouring the wine generously as the joints circled around the large room. When everything settled down, I opened my computer and pulled up a word document. Getting the group's attention, I started ringing a small bell.

"Attention! We brought you here today because of a special request as indicted in your emails. Alexia and I need your thoughts about creating a special senior class group like a club. The discussion is now open for ideas."

The room fell silent as the girls stared into space, sipping, and enjoying their spacy marijuana high. With a total lack of participation, the need to rephrase my question was essential.

"Well, let me express it a bit differently," I said. "What type of club would be cool and exclusive for the senior class?"

Lightbulbs went off as they began catching my drift.

"Let's create something with tradition to be passed on to the upcoming senior class. Like passing the torch," Anna said.

"Yeah, I like that idea," Camille commented. "The club can conduct various events throughout the year."

Then, a brief silence filled the room once again as everyone was gathering their thoughts.

"We could make up strict rules and policies like no boys allowed," Selene added.

Everyone started laughing and loving the idea as the room lit up like a flare.

"We should limit the club size with selective membership," Collette said.

"We could have a board electing the student membership," I interjected.

"I nominate Lizette and Alexia and to be the board president and vice president," said Desiree.

"I second it. Also, we would need a name," Yvette said.

"Ok, let's start with a name," I said.

We poured more wine as the group became highly involved, intoxicated, and stoned as the afternoon progressed. Taking a day off from all vices, my fingers worked diligently. Keeping up with the pace, my ears focused on the many ideas expressed. Finally, the hot tub quieted down like something immediately sucked the energy out of the group.

"Any more ideas?" I said, waiting. "Okay, give me some time to compile the data. We need to put these ideas to a vote."

As the girls were lounging and chatting away, I assembled the list of suggestions by organizing, summarizing, and deleting repetition. Then, I read each idea one by one as the group deliberated and voted. After about an hour, we finally narrowed the suggestions down to a final comprehensive list.

I stood up in front of the group. "Thank you for your participation. I'll organize the list into a final document. We will need the signatures of all the elected board members as voted today by the group. Ladies, finish enjoying the afternoon party. Do not forget to give complements to Alexia and Selene for the wine and pot."

As the week passed, I composed the draft into a final document comprising the club's name, rules, policies, and bylaws. The 'Chic Club' was the voted name of the group. This organization would be an exclusive club for only the lycée senior girls. As founders, Alexia and I were on the board, along with three of our close girlfriends. The club required a board majority vote to gain membership, which had a limitation of ten students outside of the board leaders.

A few of the rules, among many, were as follows. Students selected for club membership must always maintain good standing by following the policies and procedures. Any member not adhering to the rules and policies would be subject to dismissal. Chic members must always preserve secrecy concerning club matters. Boys could not attend the private member parties but could attend the main events. Members must also dress appropriately and be well-manicured for all activities. At year end, the club would formally hand down the club to the subordinate class.

The board members met to complete the official formation of the club and planned an advertising campaign to get the word out. As information circulated around the senior class, the club became the new happening thing everyone talked about. Every senior girl wanted to be a member, which created a fierce competition among the applicants. However, our friends that were involved in our brainstorming session got special consideration. After the application deadline date, the board reviewed submittals and voted on the new club members.

When the club met for the first time, we established a meeting schedule to plan future events. As Alexia put it, the club's purpose was to serve the entire senior class. So, the overall aim in planning any event was to get every senior student to take part.

Throughout the year, the club conducted many events, such as beach bonfires and outings, hiking, dancing, and park cookouts, which always included food and drinks. Many seniors, teachers, and school administrators attended the events. However, the only event that was exclusive to members was our occasional private club party.

It was the middle of May. The club scheduled a final meeting to create a theme for our last event, the members' private party. Alexia opened the wine bottles as the meeting came to order. Each member received a notepad to write their ideas.

"The year flew by so quickly," Yvette said, in a disappointed tone

"I do not know about you all, but I'm going to miss the good times we had," Anna commented.

"We accomplished a lot for the senior class," Camille interjected.

"But the best part is about to come. We are going to finish the year with a party of a lifetime," Alexia said. "That's why we are here today."

I rang the bell. "Okay, let's get started. I am going to give everyone ten minutes to write suggestions for our private party theme."

Few pens were writing as members looked like they had lost basic creative writing skills. Not being able to come up with any ideas, I looked at my leather band that Anais gave me. My mind drifted towards the delicious encounter that ensued in the school shower. Smelling the leather, thoughts of sensual satisfaction, liberation, and exploration drifted into my mind. Thinking of Anais, I wanted some more of that penalty piss all over again. Then it struck me. A girl-to-girl fun loving party. With that, I began scribbling erotic ideas on the pad.

"What an experience," I said loudly while lifting my head and taking another sip of wine.

"What experience," Anna said.

"Being our last event, how about a theme based on something erotically kinky?" I interjected. "Carnal interaction with plenty of wine and pot."

Eyes widened as a high-level of interest spread among the group members.

"Something hot, steamy, and highly stimulating," Camille said, shyly.

Lifting her eyebrows, Alexia spoke. "A sensual game of many pleasurable activities."

Smiles emerged on faces as ideas developed within their brains.

"An event based on sensuality, escalating arousal, and bondage," Collette said. "I'm feeling it."

"With a climatic ending," Desiree remarked.

The girls immediately went into hysterical laughter as agreement embraced the room.

"We even invite a couple of nonmembers from the senior class for a treat," Anna said. "I'm getting aroused just thinking about the newbies."

Yvette intervened, "Why don't we call this event a night to celebrate Eros?"

As electrifying emotions cascaded through the room, the members were anticipating a thrilling event leading to an explosive ending. Hence, the erotic side of the chic club was born out of the penalty shower.

Quieting the group down, I rang my bell. "Now, I want all of you to write about all of your sexual passions and carnal vices. No names required. Write them down on paper, fold it in half, and place them in the box at the end of the table."

One by one, the members dropped their deepest secrets into the box. When they all finished, I vigorously shook the box. Coming back to the head of the table, I began pulling and reading their erotic desires. The list comprised dildos, leather plugs, S &

M, retention, grinding, strapping, harnesses, whips, and anal satisfaction among other ideas.

As the group collaborated, we narrowed the theme interests into kissing, bondage, dominance, anal pleasure, clitoral stimulations and changing pair partners. It was by our third glass of cabernet that we finally came to vote on the toys, procedures, and activities.

Unanimously voted, Eros was the name given to the event. The club voted that Alexia and Selene will be hosts for the party within our finished basement, which was renamed the playroom. A few members volunteered to decorate the playroom into a Greek mythical scene. The game had a two-hour limitation with a break towards the final round. Members would give and receive within certain restrictions and time limits. The critical rule during the event was that members could not reach orgasm until the fourth round.

Upon entering the mythical playroom, the girls would strip down bare. Then, each member selected one piece of paper out of a bowl. The written words on the paper would be a leather chastisement belt, strapon dildo, or butt plug and whip. They would proceed to a designated area to pick up their toys.

Leather chastisement belts would suppress members from playing with their clit throughout the event. However, there would be a large opening in the back for anal love. The slaves will wear the chastisement belts. Masters would wear a strapon dildo with an allowed name called a dick. On the interior base of the strap-on shaft would be a clitoral stimulator. The selected edible lube for the event was cherry. All masters must use the sanitizing station at the end of each round.

Only two girls would have the assignment of dominatrices. Their job would be to keep the action going while ensuring everything was slippery wet. There would be four rounds to the night of Eros. After each round, the girls must find a new partner. Chic members agreed with a sworn oath they will role play seriously. With all details in order, the meeting adjourned.

Chapter 13

Eros

It was the night to celebrate Eros. To prepare for the event, I got a manicure and pedicure using a vibrant white nail polish. Having shaven to bare skin, I took a long bath and gave myself a warm, soapy enema. Stark naked, I walked down the steps into the mythical play room. Alexia and Selene had dressed in Greek Goddess costumes, showing bare breasts. Alexia took the wine decanter, poured me a half glass of red, and handed it to me.

"One of Papa's best... ninety-seven points," she said.

Nervously, I gulped it down, spilling some on my tits. Alexia bent over, licking it up and teasingly tongued my nipple. As her head raised to my rosy lips, she gave me an impeccably luscious kiss. Tasting the wine on her lips, I wanted more, but she stepped back.

"Sorry sis, can't be a partner today because of my duties. Besides, Selene is watching," she said, tittering. "Don't forget to pick out your assignment from the fishbowl."

The chic members arrived through the patio door, shedding clothes to bare skin. The feeling of feminine fauna intoxicated the air as hot, tanned bodies circulated with anxious desire. One by one, each member pulled a piece of paper from the bowl. Impatiently, I pulled a folded piece and opened it.

'A leather chastisement belt,' "My part for this evening was now a slave in anal captivity," I thought. I reached behind and felt my crack, starting to feel randy.

Looking over at the coach, there was one leather belt left. Walking over, I picked it up and sniffed the leather, savoring the raw sensual scent. Ever since Anais bound my wrists, leather had become one of my kinky obsessions. After putting it on, Alexia came over and locked it, placing the key in her pouch.

"Good lust tonight.... I meant luck," she said, grinning.

Giving her a wink, I replied, feverishly. "Sweet sex. Anyway, I can get it."

Alexia raised her tongue to her nose and wiggled it about. "Naughty dirty girl," she said, teasingly. "You can lick my backdoor when your done with tonight's festivities. I need some lovin there."

"Not tonight sis," I said. "My tongue is going elsewhere." With that, I began looking in the crowd.

Sustaining from sex for an entire week, I ached for female love to satisfy my carnal urges. With many bare bods around, I needed to find one to begin tonight's journey. Some girls were wearing well hung strapons and others wore leather belts. Selene had rolled plenty of joints that circulated around the room. Soon, the air filled with the sweet scent of marijuana. Grabbing a joint that passed near me, I took a long drag. Trying to hold it in, surges of coughs erupted. Then I noticed Yvette standing nearby wearing a seven-inch black dick. She looked so appetizing that it sent tickling sensations across my pleasure zones. Getting her attention, I reached over and touched her arm.

"Wanna do this round," I said.

"I love to," she replied promptly.

In taking another hit off the toasty reefer, I brought my mouth to hers. I exhaled the smoke into her mouth as her warm, sensuous tits rubbed against mine. After she exhaled, we slowly kissed as I evaporated into her pleasing comfort. Her lips were deliciously moist and magnetizing. Her long sensuous tongue glided between my lips, swirling lusciously. The succulence was driving me crazy as we entangled passionately with darting tongues and roaming hands. Savoring her alluring sweetness and delicate tang, my mind drifted into a suspended state of satiation. I desperately wanted to remain within this pleasurable sensation for hours.

Then, we gradually parted lips to catch a breath. We began giggling in pacifying delight as a mist of her sweet perfume lingered between us. Stepping back, she placed her hand on her rubbery dick, stoking it with a devilish look in her eye.

In a soft delicate tone, she spoke. "My dick is getting ready for you, my love. Want it now!"

My mouth moved onto her erect nipples, sucking, and licking while I caressed her breasts. Her body felt so earthy as I was turning her on for more.

"Mm… I like how you taste me. It feels so good," she said, softly.

My skillful lips plied her fleshy tits, getting her wet. My tongue licked upward reaching her neckline. As we were ready to French kiss, the bell rang like an alarm clock, shaking my nerves in a frenzy.

Alexia spoke as the sound of the bell reverberated in my head. "Remember the agreed-upon rules. All members must role play as a master, slave, or dominatrix. No orgasms until the fourth round. Each session has a time limit. Immediately stop what you are doing when you hear the bell, no exceptions. Dicks must use the sanitizing stations after every round. Members find a partner. Sweet pussies, get ready for an evening of toying, gaming, and loving."

After a moment of silence, the host read the last instructions. "Slaves suck off your masters. Drop to the position. Masters, turn on your vibrators."

The pot intensified the sensitivity around my lips as I embraced her dick desiring the oral pleasure. Upon puckering, every inch of her sedative cock filled my womb with loving joy. Saliva drizzled down my chin as the shaft flowed in and out at a steady pace. Captivated in the sensation, the vibrator pressed against Yvette's clit as hums of delight trickled from her lips. Feeling every ounce of pleasure with want in her eyes, my butt was stuck with a cracking whip.

"Come on, suck that dick harder. Get more lip action."

The dominatrix snapped my butt again.

"Ow, that stung," I whimpered.

Playing the part of a sex slave was making me feel submissive, slutty, and extremely horny. Then, the bell rang.

Alexia spoke in a commanding tone. "Change positions. Masters tongue the love hole. When you hear the bell, start with one finger penetration. Dominatrix lube fingers and crevices."

Yvette got behind me and licked my buttery hole. Her tongue was like a piece of soft leather that sent gratifying sensation throughout my love bits. Probing with her darting tongue, my hole was opening. Reaching around, she began fondling my jiggling tits. She rubbed and pinched my nipples as her tongue was lapping me into dreamland. Stoned out of my mind, the pleasure was astounding sending my mind into sweet satisfaction.

The bell rang. "Begin the insertions. The last step in round one," Selene said.

A dominatrix placed a glob of lube in Yvette's hand. Smiling, she spread it all over her index finger and took a whiff. Then, the dominatrix filled the rim of my puckered hole. The aroma of the cherries smelled deliciously appetizing as I reached behind, spreading it out like jam to bread.

Taking her index finger, Yvette circled my hole until it opened. Her finger incrementally pressed inward centimeter by centimeter as she stimulated with depth and determination. Driving her finger in and out, I could feel the outside air fill my love tunnel. Then I pressed my anal muscle around her finger, receiving a breathtaking jolt of appetizing pleasure.

As her finger began squirming like a worm, a stream of instantaneous satisfaction flowed endlessly through my love tunnel. The incredible sensation filled me with a feeling of pleasing warmth and fullness. Grunting, moaning, and oooing, I let my body become totally encapsulated by the nerve ending pleasure.

The bell rang, Selene spoke. "Change partners and get to know them."

Yvette gradually pulled her finger out of my hole as I squeezed my sphincter tight once more.

"Wow, that felt so great," I said.

Appreciating our love session, Yvette kissed me with sincere affection. She left my hole in activation mode, ready for another round of titillating indulgence.

With one round complete, the chic girls entered a world of role playing with greater gravity. The division between master, slave, and dominatrix had become distinctly clear. As the pot took control of our minds, the new reality filled the room with a feeling of control, subservience, and carnal craving.

Looking for a partner, I scoped the room. Camille had just finished with her partner. Without hesitation, I got up from the floor and strolled over. She had blonde hair, a slim figure, firm tits, and a hot shaved puss. During our club meetings, I itched to lick her wet and suck her dry. Without effort, our eyes locked in wanton thirst.

"New partner pairing. Want to connect?" I said enthusiastically.

"Let's give it a whirl," she responded.

She brought her finger near my nose. "Take a whiff."

I inhaled the pleasant smell of cherries.

Without hesitancy, she stuck her finger in my mouth. "Suck my juices, slave."

I sucked for a few minutes as she twisted and turned. Her finger screwed me as I puckered my lips.

"I'll be doing this to your squeamish hole," she said, perversely. "I can't wait to pluck your cherry."

Wanting to toy with her gorgeous body, I teased her firm breasts and hardened nipples. After a few minutes, my lips reached her savory chest. Her beautiful teats melted in my mouth like sweet chocolate as I sucked and lapped. Enjoying her taste, I felt her dick press against my twinge.

Lifting my head, our mouths instinctively embraced like there was a new founded attachment. She tasted fruity and scrumptious, like she had been chewing juicy fruit gum. We explored French kissing like lovers with brazen obsession. Enmeshed in oral passion, someone tapped me on my shoulder. I lifted my lips from hers. A joint had come my way, and I took it with pleasing desire.

After taking a long hit, I gave the joint to Camille. She inhaled and passed it back. The warm smoke filled my lungs as my mind drifted further from reality. Within an escalating high, Camille started pinching and sucking my nipples playfully. The pleasure dissipated through my body as the pot augmented the sensation. Her long penetrating tongue journeyed up my shoulder onto my neck. The moistness of her wet lips was pleasantly soothing. She kissed and bit delicately, making my body tense in delight.

67

Then, our lips met again as we slipped into deep oral indulgence stoned out of our minds. The texture of her wiggling tongue sent stellar vibes through the lining of my gums. The satisfying sensation absorbed my inner self as my mind escaped into a fog. Her play was so fervent that I wanted to have an all-night private party of our own. The bell rang...... awakening my thoughts.

Alexia emphasized the rules for round two. "Remember, the Eros motto is for everyone is to perform impulsively and effectively but with sincerity," "Now, slaves, drop into a doggy position and begin sucking. Masters, make sure the clit stimulator is on."

I got down on all fours, feeling her warm, rubbery dick. I took control by placing the shaft firmly in my left hand. As she surrendered to my play, I pressed it against her clit. Moving my mouth around the tip of the soft shaft, the vibrating pressure was driving her in pleasing delight.

"Suck me off, slut. Suck me until I cum," Camille said, with a savage tone.

Camille's face was flushing. She was on the verge of multiple pulsations. Drips of wetness ran slowly down her inner thigh. Then, the bell rang, interrupting our play. Camille sat for a moment, sighing with dissatisfaction.

"Change positions. Masters, get ready for round two of licking anus and double finger penetration," Alexia said.

Camille was looking hot as she got behind me with her shaking tits.

Smiling maliciously, she said, teasingly. "I going to push my big dick up your ass."

Out of nowhere, my legs felt weak as Camille knelt behind me. She was lapping my puckered hole while pressing the vibrator against her clit. Loving my crack like a kid enjoying an ice cream cone, she was licking every drop. My hole slowly opened as I felt her tongue in vivacious execution. It felt smooth, tantalizing, and electrifying. Repeating her drilling motions, it was like she was eating up the cherry lube like sweet candy.

Moaning in contentment, her hot, wet tongue was driving me crazy. Yearning to cum, I gripped onto the rug shaking my ass around. Pushing my chest toward the floor, my nipples rubbed against the carpet adding to the rapturing pleasure. Within no time at all, the bell sounded. Camille stopped licking me. Before I could cool down, the dominatrix appeared.

"It's time to loosen you up," she said.

I brought my head to the floor as my butt stuck high in the air. A dominatrix filled the rim of my hole with lube and cracked the whip on my butt. Not whimpering, the pain was flaming through my body. Camille brushed her fingers delicately up and down my crack. She repeated this motion in a playful manner getting me aroused and wet. Then, her fingers slowly pierced through the gaping entrance and my hole felt like it split in two.

"We have to make it nice and wide," she said. "Your cherry is popping like an anal virgin in need."

In one motion, Camille slid her two fingers all the way in. Holding them in place for a few seconds, she twisted and turned. Then, she pulled them out in a single motion alleviating the pressure. Dabbing more lube on my hole, I wiggled my butt around wanting more. Then, her long fingers glided easily inward as she started screwed me with her loving skill. Within the momentum of her rhythmic insertions, my sphincter muscles relaxed like a baby humming on Mama's lap.

"Keep going, I'm sizzling for an anal orgasm," I said.

Her fingers were driving me in crazy delight as trickles of wetness dripped down my thigh through the belt. Then, I squeezed my sphincter muscle, and the pleasure escalated to a new level.

The bell rang ending round two. "Change partners and get to know them," Selene said.

With one last thrust, Camille pushed inward as far as she could go. Giving one last ride, she pulled her fingers out. We kissed quickly as she departed for the next partner.

Colette was standing against the wall like a seductive hustler on a street corner. I looked in her direction as she peered back at me. I got up and walked over. Our bodies pressed together in a hug. Her tits felt very lush and warm.

We sat next to each other during the chic meetings, whispering dirty words. She could get me wet on the spot with her lustful thoughts. We sometimes played a petting game under the table. She would reach under my skirt to toy with my puss. It was often hard to keep a straight face as others never knew what was going on.

Collette had a gentleness about her as we touched lips meshing in delicate kisses.

"Now we can do it in the open," she said teasingly.

"I always loved the way you played with me," I said.

The bell rang. "Member's kiss and fondle your new partner," Alexia said.

Colette was an exciting, sensitive, and passionate person in every aspect of her life. Her lips were round, thick, and rich. Her slender body comprised petite breasts with button nipples. Within our friendship, we often had deep conversations about erogenous pleasure. However, there was nothing emotional or deeply physical about our relationship, except at meetings. I fantasized twice about making love to her while achieving a vibrant orgasm. Her style of sexuality encompassed strapon sex with females. She loved a females delicate and sensuous touch that can bring on a scrumptious orgasm.

Collette was wearing a pink eight-inch dildo that hung down. She walked over to a center table, grabbed a sanitizing cloth, and wiped it shining clean. Her mouthwatering dick jiggled as she walked over to me in a swanky manner.

She placed her arms around my neck and whispered, "You are going to suck my tasty dick until it squirts. Then, my cock is going to jizz your tunnel. Just remember open wide for Mama because I'm going to love you deep."

My flesh melted with desire as she whispered words of sensualness in my ear.

Eagerly, I responded, "Suck my ass until your tongue gets pulled right in. Pop my cherry hole b…"

The bell rang.

"Slaves suck on all fours. Masters turns on vibrators."

I got down on all fours, grabbing her dick with my left hand as my butt was sensitive entering round three.

I hummed, swallowed, and nurtured her dick like there was no tomorrow. My tongue moved up and down the shaft like I wanted it deep inside me. My grip on her dick was pressing against her clit as I primed Colette's sensitive clit to want. Loving every minute of the pulsating pleasure, she was getting off with my skillful efforts.

"You like my dick, don't you slave? Suck me good, then."

Taking my tongue, I slurped it up as I relished the oral satisfaction once more. Violating a rule, my mouth quickly moved up to hers and I unloaded my savory juices. The bell rang.

"Change positions. Dicks lick ass and prepare for butt plug insertions. Plugs must be kept inserted during the break right until the fourth round," Selene said.

The dominatrix passed out the butt plugs and cherry lube. The plugs looked a little larger than expected. I got down on all fours as Colette came up behind me. She started licking the crack of my ass with long, penetrating strokes. My sensitive hole was loving her tongue with delightful fulfillment. It felt like her tongue was finding every ounce of cherry juice left in me. With rectal nerve endings linking to my brain, the ultimate fervor was driving me crazy. Then Colette pressed her thick lips tightly over my puckered hole and drilled her tongue down as far down as she could. Her slippery lingua was squiggling and screwing my cherry tunnel as I entered anal bliss. Then I heard female moans reverberated throughout the room as the last licking ride was for the splendor of Eros.

The bell rang again. "Masters insert butt plugs," Alexia said.

Collette took the plug and rubbed some lube on it. The dominatrix came by and smeared a glob on my open rosebud. Collette inserted one finger, working my hole with smooth strokes. Creating space, she put two fingers inside and wiggled around. She began screwing me until I was ready. Pulling her fingers out, she took the butt plug and rubbed it against my puckering hole. She rotated it around and was pushing inward. The pointed round end was going in fine, but the bulky part was giving her trouble. My head fell to the floor, trying to spread my cheeks further apart. Upon jimmying, she was trying to gain full access, but was unsuccessful.

The dominatrix, noticing the slight struggle, began snapping my butt continuously, turning it pinkish red. The stinging sensation took my mind off the plug, releasing tension in my body. Without resistance, the plug oozed inward, filling my hole with a pleasing delight.

As it fully entered, the feeling was filling, warm, and relieving. Colette began playing with the plug by pulling at it slowly, making my hole larger. The awesome sensation sent my muscles into a pleasing mode. Colette left the plug in my hole as her hand grabbed the shaft of the pink dick. Wanting to cum so desperately, she pulled it against her clit, making sensual sounds.

Then, against the rules, Colette moved her body in front of me and spread her legs. She unstrapped one side of the dick, revealing her pink lips. I crawled up, desperately placing my mouth between her open legs as my ass stood in the air. Putting my tongue on her clit, I began working away licking her into bliss.

"Lizette, finish it now," she said breathlessly.

She tensed as I feverishly increased my efforts to get her near orgasm. When her facial checks started blooming in pink as I immediately backed away.

"No climax till the last round," I said. "Remember." Then I giggled a bit in a toying manner.

Discontented, her eyes rolled onto the back of her head.

"We have some unfinished business, but somewhere else," I said. "My beautiful babe has to wait until it's time."

Within moments, the bell rang, ending round three.

Alexia announced, "There will be a fifteen-minute break. Grab drinks at the wine bar before we start the final round. Find a new partner when you get a chance. Do not forget to get your belt unlocked during break. But you must keep it on until the end."

I walked over to Alexia. She unlocked my belt, and I headed to the bar.

Chapter 14

Finishing Eros

Wet and wanting, the anticipation was building for some pleasing anal penetrating love. I desperately wanted to rip off my belt, grab a chic member, and have her drill me to oblivion with her big cock. I walked over to the bar tenderly rubbing the plug as it filled my insides making me feel sexy. Thoughts entered my mind in getting on all fours and playing the role of a submissive anal slut for one last time.

"Looks like I graduated from a voyeur to a player," I muttered, impishly.

Upon reaching the bar, I grabbed a glass of wine and took a sip. Then I accidentally bumped into Colette and started a conversation about the pleasures of the event. Before long, the discussion casually shifted towards us as we began revealing our secret affections.

"I always wanted you as we collaborated with the various club events," I said. "I guess my inner apprehension took the best of me. Sort of held me back from asking you for some playtime."

"Before graduation, maybe we could even role play in private."

My eyebrows lifted as I gazed into her wanton eyes. "We could even wear lingerie without restraints. I dislike the idea of stopping the play."

As chatter surrounded us, Colette glanced around the room and faced me again. "I wouldn't mind a few toys, if that's alright with you."

"I'd like that," I said, amusingly. Then I kissed her passionately on the lips.

Looking across the room, I noticed Anna. "Let's talk later about our little rendezvous. I'll call you. Just need to talk with Anna."

Walking over to Anna, the delicious cherry scent caught my attention as a joint crossed my path. Taking a slow long hit, my lungs filled with the warm harsh smoke. As I let the smoke flow through my nose and mouth, my high escalated making me feel relaxed and on top of the world.

I reached Anna and we immediately embraced in a welcoming hug. Putting the wineglass on a table, I became captivated by her gorgeous body.

As we both tittered, enjoying the fun, she said. "Lizzette, look at my plug."

"Could I touch yours?" I replied.

"Give it a little push, if you like."

Within a second, the spontaneity of female-to-female bonding struck like a polarized magnet. We faced each other, brought our lips together, and started French kissing.

Taking a breath, I spoke. "Your tits are so soft."

Then I brought my mouth over her nipples and suckled. She was enjoying my lips and tongue as I squeezed her tits playfully. I brought my lips upon hers once again as the oral stimulation connected like a running current of electricity. Savoring our interlaced tongues, my mind wondered in space entering a trance of passion. Then Yvette interrupted by tapping my shoulder.

"Let me have a taste," she said.

Instantly, we started a three-way session trading off lips, tongues, and mouths. Their alluring oral skills consumed my inner thirst, and the savor was endless. Without notice, the bell rang, breaking our intimate session.

"This is the final round. All members must keep their toys on until you hear the command. Find a new partner and get sensually acquainted," Alexia said.

Preoccupied with Anna, I did not find a new partner. There was a nudge on my shoulder as a thick joint passed. I took another hit as I peered around the room.

Desiree did not have a partner and acknowledged herself by waving. I walked over, handing her the joint. She took a hit and passed it on. Our bodies pressed together in a warm hug. There was an attractive frivolity surrounding her aura. As our succulent lips pressed together, my flesh immediately eased into her arms. Her skin was the softest of the chic girls.

74

Our tongues passionately flickered in tangling and slithering pleasure. Then I nibbled on her neck, reaching for her earlobes as she caressed my body with her supple fingers. Massaging her tits, she continued to explore my body. Sensing the mounting anticipation, the smell of leather, cherry, and mustiness surfaced in the air. Now I was ready to climax.

The bell rang. "Start sucking. Anal play all the way to the big O," Selene said.

The retentiveness of the leather belt intensified my want. My tenderly aching pleasure zone was desperately in need of a gratifying orgasm. I could not hold back any longer as the heat of passion was ripping through my flesh. Getting down on all fours, I sucked with urgency wanting her dick to fill my orifice. With deviance intent, I pushed the vibrator against her minge as I sucked her to glory. My tits swayed as she slid her dick in and out of my mouth. Driblets of saliva oozed from my mouth as my tongue recaptured the cherry taste, only wanting more. Then, the dominatrix smacked my butt, awakening me with an unpleasant sting.

"Get sucking slut. Make your girl cum," she said.

The bell rang once more, saving me from further unpleasantness.

"Take out butt plugs, lube dicks, and get ready for insertions. There will be no anal licking for this final round," Alexia said.

The dominatrix made sure there was globes of lube to go around. Desiree was staring at me with amatory, seductive eyes. She was stroking her dick, looking at me like she wanted to screw me to insensibility. Taking her thumb and index finger, she gently pried out the plug. The pleasure overcame the discomfort, leading to pleasant relief. My anal cavity, now unfulfilled, wanted an exhilarating ride of pleasure to eternity.

The dominatrix smiled and looked at Desiree's dick. "Lizette, you will squeal by the time Desiree gets done with you," she said.

The heat of passion was striking my insides as I placed my head on the floor with my arms extended. Wanting my master to fill me with her deep affections, my hole opened effortlessly.

75

She looked at my orifice while generously smearing her dick with plenty of lube. Without notice, the head of her dick touched my anal rim. I jerked slightly as I took a deep breath to relax. Desiree was ready to take my anal virginity. Inch by inch, she inserted and dislodged. Her dick was going deeper and deeper with every attempt. Finally, seven inches filled my crack, displacing my mind with pure divine gratification.

The world of prurience had opened its doors as she was driving me into ecstasy. The feeling of her hot dick was flowing, pacifying, and stimulating. Every ounce of tension throughout my body had left as thousands of nerve-endings vibrated in pure jubilation.

I remember Mama putting suppositories up my anus as a young child. As they melted within me, it felt so good. I would sneak some out of the bathroom. Then, I would go out in the yard behind the bushes, wanting to feel the releasing sensation endlessly. As Desiree rode me, she broke my anal virginity. Her dick felt like hundreds of suppositories melting all at once, giving me ultimate anal gratification that I longed for.

The dominatrix approached and snapped her whip repeatedly on Desiree's ass. "Work that butt." Then she started cracking. "Work faster, master. Push, push, push!"

The wavelike contractions were unceasing as Desiree's pace continued. I could feel the exhilarating oscillations as she moved with a constant rhythm. The pressure on my vaginal wall was building with pleasure as my breathing intensified. It felt like a million vibrators all over my body as her coitus play led me to deeper want. How much more could I endure without going into blissful insanity? I rode her dick like a bronco in heat, bumping, grinding, and propelling.

I could hear the other girls getting their fill as the sounds of pleasure echoed throughout the room. They were squalling and screaming, which intensified my desire to peak. Feeling on the verge, Desiree started screwing with intensity. In achieving rapture, a continuous stream of delight flooded within me as intense shuddering overtook me. Ripping off my belt, I cried out in absolute relief and bucked back hard.

"Oh, my gosh." Stars were bursting in my head as my body vibrated in ultra-appeasement. Completely lost in time, my mind went blank into absolute sanctifying goodness.

"That's my girl," Desiree said. "I popped your anal virginity tonight."

Never have I experienced such a breathtaking erotic adventure that led me to such fulfillment. My virginity was no more as I have achieved my first full anal orgasm. Desiree dismounted me like a cowgirl and rubbed my behind. I turned around gently kissing her. My puss was sore from the restraint and my clit hypersensitive to the touch.

"Lick my clit to orgasm," I commanded Desiree.

She came around quickly, unstrapping the dildo. We immediately fell into a sixty-nine. I was licking her with an endless lashing tongue. As I licked away, her tongue dove into my puss. Her tongue was driving me wild and crazy as electrical vibes filled my brain. Her licks were creaming me into glory. Within minutes, pulsations swept through me like a lightning bolt. I tensed and slowly closing my legs. Desiree finished herself off as I sat with my head against the carpet.

The club that I initially envisioned had come to fruition. With my creation, came the many followers that fell into an erotic illusion of mischievous role playing. The result was that there was a stronger sense of cohesion that blossomed among us. We could meet anytime and help each other take care of our needs. However, playing the role of a submissive female brought me to a new level in discovering my sexuality. Greater than the one experienced with Anais.

Chapter 15

After Lycée

A couple of weeks after receiving my lycée diploma, the family finally went out to celebrate at our favorite Italian restaurant. My mind had finally settled down from the excitement of graduation and all the parties that followed. After ordering dinner, I sat staring at the lit candle on the table in a daydream. Thoughts of leaving friendships behind left a void in my heart.

"Lizette, why are you looking so down?" Papa said.

He awoke me from a deep trance as I looked at him with desolation. "Well, you know," I said. "Our friends will go off to college or finding jobs elsewhere. We became like an extended family, especially forming the Chic club."

"I know how you feel," Alexia said. "Things just won't be the same."

Mama put a hand on top of ours. "Life is not over," Mama said. "Cheer up, you will meet new friends through your new ventures in life."

Papa took a sip of wine, holding it high in the air looking at the color. "Wine puts food on the table, but family really matters."

There was a brief silence as Papa took another sip.

"That's what I thought when I graduated. Life seemed to stop. But I met your mom and had you two. Look at my business today. We have plenty of friends and a wonderful family."

Putting a careful ear to Papa, I felt more optimistic. Then he looked around the table, expressing himself further.

"Girls listen, life moves in constant progression without ceasing. Those who do not follow the momentum of time will not fully benefit from what life offers. Change can be for the better, but one must be prepared to face the challenges of change. But most important.... remember, there is always a level of risk with any path you take."

78

In Papa, I always found a level of support and understanding. Then, a sense of relief struck my inner-self freeing me from the hollowness as future opportunity became clearer.

"It's great to have a family for sustenance," I said. "I'm lucky to be have loving parents and, of course, Alexia."

We all raised a glass of wine and toasted as mama spoke. "Cheers to a bright future. May our family live on to greener pastures."

My experiences at lycée would always remain a part of me. But as Papa put it, our lives must go on. I didn't want to make the family business my career. Not yet anyway. My decision was to stay in Carcene and attend college full-time. I loved to help people and often thought about a career in psychotherapy. So, I declared a major in psychology at the local university. If it didn't work out, I could always fall back on the family business.

Upon entering college, Alexia was a beautiful young lady of fashion that typified the features of a perfect model. Her voguish flare was captivating to bystanders as she liberally strode in confidence. Alexia had dirty blonde hair that she wore straight and well below the shoulders. Her finely manicured nails displayed various shades of pink. She wore French and Italian knee-high skirts to show off her sexy legs and nice ass. Alexia completed her stylish desires by having a diverse European shoe collection in her closet. Sometimes, she didn't wear panties on warm summer days to add a little excitement to her life. When shopping or at the movies, she would flash a bare bottom without hesitation or embarrassment.

Just like we did when we were kids, I wished Alexia would have taken some time off in the summer to enjoy the beach. However, she had a strong interest in making a career in the wine and cheese industry. So, Papa was training her to become a high-class business professional within the company. While attending college, she worked full time with Papa, helping with sales, marketing, and operations. Papa would spoil her with bonuses when sales were strong because of her hard work. She would take the extra cash to buy expensive jewelry, clothing, and shoes that added to her elegance and outgoing personality. Besides, Papa wanted her appearance to look exceptional well when meeting high revenue accounts.

In the summer months, Alexia would tag along with Papa on work related trips to some of the most fashionable places in Europe. They would venture to cities such as London, Paris, Milan, Barcelona, Vienna, and Rome. Valise and I sometimes went on some of these work-related vacation ventures. While Papa and Alexia were in business meetings, Valise and I would head out to the shops, catch lunch at a bistro, and meet up with the other half of the family for dinner. Alexia and I would have a separate hotel room that usually comprised a king-size bed, jacuzzi, and a private bar. It was nice to travel around Europe as a close-knit family, but it was usually on a conservative budget.

Alexia had broken off with Selene since leaving the Lycée. I knew she needed some loving hearing her in the shower playing around. It was during the summer before college that I started having fantasies about making love to her. We always kissed, hugged, and caressed, but nothing more. I imaged us in bed savoring our fraternal bodies while our parents were away. I wanted to explore and experiment, strip her naked in public, and play with her wet, hot pussy.

Chapter 16

Parents Night Out

It was Friday night with the weather being cool and rainy. Our parents just left to go out to dinner with some friends. As they left, I walked into the kitchen. Alexia was leaning against the island, biting into a ripe strawberry. Her lips looked moist and delicious. Droplets of juice dribbled from the corner of her mouth. Licking her lips, she took a napkin and wiped her chin.

"Have they left?" she uttered.

"Yes," I responded enthusiastically. "They probably won't be back till later cause the restaurant is out of town. Looks like we have the entire house to ourselves."

Without pause, Alexia unhooked her bra and pulled it from under her tank top. Her thirty-six-Bs slightly jiggled as they pressed outward against her top. Her nipples penetrated through the fine cloth outlining her dark areoles. Then she lifted her breasts and settled them in place.

Straightening her top, she spoke quite blatantly. "That's a relief. I'm going to enjoy a little freedom tonight. I remember when Papa allowed us to walk naked around the house. That was until Mama put an end to it during lycée. I know he misses looking at our natural bods."

"He still thinks we are the hottest things on earth. It sort of turns me on when he calls me 'my hot bun'," I said.

"He never says that to me," Alexia replied, surprised.

"Sometimes, I tease him in the morning when we run into each other in the bathroom. I would allow my towel to drop to the floor so he can get a full view. It gets him nervous and aroused, especially when I'm not wearing panties."

"Lizette, you are a naughty little girl. Mama better not find out."

"I'm sure Papa will never tell."

Alexia selected another strawberry from the container holding it between her thumb and forefinger. Turning it around, she looked for imperfections. As her teeth bit down, minuscules of juice squirted into the air. It looked so hot that I wanted to taste the fruit right from her lips.

She swallowed and wiped her lips. "At work, Papa is different, strictly business. He treats me like an actual business professional, but still makes me feel warm and loved. That is why we work well together. Remember, the business is always open if you want to join us."

"Not now. I want to focus on my degree first. Besides, we can work the rest of our lives."

"Just remember, you're always welcome," Alexia said candidly.

"I appreciate that."

Delicately finishing the berry, Alexia turned her head and looked at me with a focused smile. Peering at her five-foot five slim physique, she could easily be a fashion model. Her naturally dirty blond hair was classy that shined like the sun. The tight pair of gym shorts displayed her tanned legs and trimmed buttocks. Her pair of brown leather boots flashed style and appetizing appeal. The thought of her wearing leather drew me into a trace. Since Anais, rawhide just melts me away like butter on a steamy hot potato.

Approaching Alexia from behind, I placed my hand on her back, massaging in a circular motion. Her body felt warm and vibrant as my fingers nestled into a relieving motion.

"Mm… that's so nice." She whispered. "Press a little harder. My lower back also needs a little love."

Teasing playfully, I worked my way down to her waist.

"Hey sis, since Mama and Papa are out to dinner, we can have a little party of our own," I said.

"We can do this all night instead? I love how you touch me. Your hands are so seductively masterful.…. Remember Marielle."

"If we do this all night, my fingers will wear themselves out."

Taking a deep breath, I continued working my hand up and down her spine as she tilted her head back. The smell of her fruity perfume drifted in the air. I moved closer, savoring the alluring scent as my fingers touched her with sensuality. As my sensual craving climbed, I put one hand on my shorts. I rubbed my zipper gently while stoking her with my fingers.

My thoughts wandered thinking about a female-to-female erotic encounter. As I fantasized, darting pulses spread through my body. Layer by layer, we peeled each other's clothes off. Her soft hands unbuttoned my blouse while I stared deep into her eyes, feeling wanton affection. With exposed bare breasts, our nipples gingerly touched with a salacious desire. I caressed her breasts while she fervently stoked my nipples. Then, my mouth opened to hers, joining in an appetizing kiss. Her tongue slid between my lips feeling soft and slippery as a tingly sensation flowed throughout my inner cavity. We passionately French kissed with thirst right into sensual intoxication. With tenderness, my hand reached downward, invading her with delicacy. It felt so deliciously soft, natural, and arousing.

As my fingers caressed, Alexia flinched, lifting me out of my trance. Removing my hand from my shorts, I stood next to my sister, feeling somewhat embarrassed. The submersion into my fantasy left me in a longing for sweet passion. Then, the trace of Alexia's leathery scent drew me closer. Wanting to taste her flesh, I nuzzled her hair to one side. My mouth moved to the base of her neck and my lips pressed lightly against her warm skin. I kissed her gently as we continued to converse.

"About tonight... your idea... about getting buzzed sounds succulently randy," Alexia said abruptly.

"Alexia, you are a naughty girl. I'd like to have a special night with you while enjoying a bottle of Papa's finest wine. Maybe ninety-nine points."

Alexia teasingly turned and faced me, displaying those red luscious lips. We stood close enough to pass a passionate kiss.

"Yes, I'll get a couple of bottles of Papa's highest rated wines from the cellar. He'll never miss them," she said, breathing her words delicately.

My thoughts left me in a lingering state of sheer arousal. The desire for incestuous love germinated within my innermost feelings. I sensed the need for titillation and indulgence. With impulsiveness, my lips met hers in a spellbinding kiss as I gazed into her angelic eyes. We interlocked tongues in a craving for affection. Nervous and aroused, the passion for a deep, sensuous encounter was igniting. I wanted to rip her clothes off and make love on top of the kitchen island. However, I needed to control myself by showing slight indifference. It was not the right moment or place to fully engage in sexual intimacy.

Our bodies slowly drifted apart as we held each other's hands, not wanting to let go. Heading to the wine cellar, Alexia glanced at me with a gaze of longing. Her feminine attributes absorbed my fascination. She had blue eyes and luscious lips. Her nipples were erect and flawless. I stood watching her jiggling breasts and tanned legs strut across the kitchen. The sounds of her boots striking the floor were mistress demanding. Her swag and scent filled the room with desirous temptations.

Calming down, I walked over to the living room and sat on the recliner. As I relaxed my anxious urges, my sister descended into the finished basement. The sweet smell of her leather boots remained in my mind.

"Leather," I thought. "Passionate intimacies with an assertive woman clad in tight leather garments, high heels, and a crop will excite me into capitulation." Planning to take a quick nap, I pushed the recliner back and closed my eyes.

As my eyes slowly opened, my body felt weightless and suspended on a drifting cloud. The dreamlike ambience was calming and pacifying. In a matter of minutes, the glaring haze had dissipated and my vision became clear.

"Where am I," I thought. "This is so surreal."

Coming to full consciousness, I lay naked on a leather divan with its influence freeing my inhibitions. Turning my head, I saw a tag and flipped it over. It read, 'Fresh animal rawhide. Real full grain leather.' A sensual feeling drew my consciousness inward. I hugged the cushion with both hands while pressing it against my face. I inhaled the deep, invigorating scent. The vibe of the thick, rustic material made my body quiver. I sank into the richness of the hide, feeling warm, relaxed, and tamed. Then, a strong seducing force had taken control of my senses. The temptations of the pelt against my bare flesh brought me into a tameless world of savage submission. It was like riding a wild buffalo naked while feeling its hairy flesh between my legs.

Impelled in lust, I turned onto my stomach, pushing against the leather while spreading my legs. Moving in a rhythmic pattern, my eyes rolled behind my head. I was imagining myself lying on top of a voluptuous woman humping into a frenzy. Our penetrating bodies caressed and rubbed as we relished our feminine scents. Tongues pressed into passion as we spiraled into climatic nourishment. I desperately wanted to explode into the bright lights of oblivion and never descend.

Then, out of nowhere, a voice caught me by surprise.

"Hello, my name is Amour. I am here to serve you," she said.

A young virgin girl with a pretty face, thin waist and a gorgeous tanned appeared from nowhere. She wore a braless pink top, a cowgirl hat, a leather skirt, and leather gloves that came to her elbows. As she approached me, her leather boots struck the floor with a confident, controlling stride. Then she snapped a crop to the floor as her hardened nipples protruded from the silky material.

In a commanding, seductive voice, she spoke. "I want to give you something special,"

I looked at her with depth and admiration. My mouth salivated as my tongue brushed against my upper lip. I swallowed with a burning impulse as my eyes teared in desire. Without notice, the ether had cast another spell over my mind. Leather straps held my hands to the divan, leaving me practically immobile.

"You want me, don't you?" she said.

I sat speechless and motionless as she turned around, displaying her gorgeous anatomy. Twirling around, her skirt lifted, exhibiting white panties. As I sat powerless, she melted me with magnetism and decisiveness.

"Do you like what I bring?" she said.

With a wave of her hand, the rustic leather scent diffused intensely in the air, arousing my senses.

"It's hot party time, but I forbid you to taste, feel, or finger," she said with a devilishly tempting stare.

Removing the cowgirl hat, her long blonde hair fell elegantly across her shoulders. Her curls were soft, wavey, and shiny. Extruding from her alluring lips, her tongue curled upward playfully. Then she sat down next to me and pulled off a boot. Bringing it to her nose, she inhaled, smelling it like a fresh bouquet.

"I like the smell of a dirty worn leather boot. It gets me so horny." Then, taking off her other boot, she placed it under her nose and inhaled with animation. "Mm delightful. You might like my scent? I am sure you would like a whiff."

Bringing her boot to my nose, I smelled the sensuous, leathery fragrance. Her raw scent carried me into escalating submission as I eagerly tried to escape. In one fluid motion, she got off the coach and unzipped her leather skirt, letting it fall to the floor. Peering deeply into my eyes, she turned around, displaying her firm sweet ass.

"Do you like my attractive butt? I'm sure you want to lick my sweet hole."

Mesmerizing me with her gaping stare, she mounted me by putting her knees across my lap. Warmth emanated from her body while the smell of her sweet candied perfume drifted between us. Then she slowly peeled off her white top, revealing her luscious tits. Her nipples were tender and appetizing as she looked at me with a devouring smile. She jiggled friskily while stimulating them against my bare skin. Getting wet and aroused, I desperately wanted her to drive me into sheer bliss.

She stood up and peeled off her panties, revealing her finely shaven muff. She brought her panties to my nose, exposing me to her natural scent. As I took a breath inward, the naturalness of the musty tang drove me into a confined state of frustration. Putting her fingers on her juicy minge, she caressed herself with selfishness as she teased me with her provocative lures.

"Cum with me. Touch my nipples, feel my lips, lick me all the way down."

Wiggling frantically to break free, I wanted her long, thick tongue all over my flesh. Without expectation, her hands fell upon my nipples, pinching, and rubbing, and making me squirm in pain.

"Come, kiss me," she said.

As I moved my lips to hers, she backed away, wanting me to beg for a taste. Subdued at her mercy, her lips began sucking my nipples as her fingers vigorously stimulated my puss. I twisted and turned, craving culmination as she drove her hand with piercing pleasure. Without haste, she got off my lap and spread my legs wide. Putting her mouth between my legs, she vigorously started licking my inner thigh. Satisfying sensations swept throughout my body as her flaming tongue was driving me to a state of insanity. Then, her wet lapping lingua found my erect clit. She sucked and licked me, giving intensifying pleasure. With every thrash, I squirmed, climbing steadily into ecstatic fulfillment. Sliding her fingers into my love hole, I immediately lit up in jubilation. A yearning compulsion overtook my flesh as she screwed with unrelenting fervor. Quickening her pace, I was on the edge of climatic relief. Vibrations swept through me.... Suddenly, a glaring haze blocked my view.

Chapter 17

Heating Up

Alexia descended to the wine cellar and reached the last step. Falling into a trance, she looked around the large room as memories surfaced, bringing her to childhood. The spacious finished basement served as a playroom that gave her a private place to plunge bare into its imaginations. Calling it her stage of performance, she would pretend to be the ballerina in a play. The play was in a kingdom with many hidden treasures. She turned and twirled around a large support pole until her head spun. Tumbling to the floor with teasing aspirations, she would close her eyes and envision herself in the enchanted world of make believe.

Years later, spontaneous moments of sensuality emerged in the mists of her playroom. Making sure no one was at home; she would descend into its lusciousness wearing sexy lingerie. Holding the pole like an exotic dancer on stage, she would strip to full exposure while practicing the art of seduction. She would spread her legs, pressing her inner thighs against the pole's firmness, feeling sexy and uninhibited. Playing with her beautiful body, she climbed too many peaking moments of delectation. The grandfather clock struck, bringing her back to reality.

"The wine. I need to get the wine," she muttered.

Getting the key, she unlocked the large oak doors and pulled them wide open. Upon walking in, the smell of dampness, antique furniture, and aging cheese emerged from the darkness. Turning on the lights, she gazed upon the old stone walls that connected to the high brick arches. Supporting the floors above, my eyes glanced up at the tall ceilings that contained original logs dating back centuries.

Positioned horizontally and affixed to the walls were hundreds of metal cavities that stored median priced bottles of aging wine. Also attached to the walls were a long row of antique cherry cabinets that stored the most expensive bottles under

Papa's lock and key. The prices of these bottles surmounted to well over a thousand euros.

Our family usually drank the lower quality wines that sat in boxes on pallets in the room's corner. Most of these wines were samples given to us by the vineyards. Papa allowed Alexia and me to take wines from these boxes when family and friends came over to party. Mama had special privileged to take the good stuff in the cavities whenever her heart desired.

Alexia began searching within the metal cavities to uncover a few expensive bottles that Papa accidentally misplaced. She discovered them one day while searching for a wine from a specific vineyard. The bottles were supposed to be in the cherry cabinets under lock and key. Through a bit of luck, these wines would be for a special sister party.

Finding the bottles, she pulled them from the cavities. "Here they are. Chardonnay-Burgundy, that's perfect," she whispered. "There are so many bottles, he probably wouldn't miss a few. Especially the ones he misplaced."

Then she noticed the one-hundred-year-old mirror standing in the corner. She slowly walked over and stood facing it. It was a well-priced antique that had been in the family for years. Staring at her beautiful piercing nipples, she put the bottles down. She folded her hands under her breasts, lifting upward.

Teasing her nipples with her thumbs, she turned around to admire her figure. She loved having her sensitive nipples touched and sucked as she slid her fingers across the firmness. Then she moved her hands under her tank top and massaged her breasts. Her head tilted slightly back as she let out a soft sigh of relief. She imagined a client of hers completely naked, standing behind her, kissing her neck. Catherine always dressed in high fashions, wearing provocative clothing and expensive shoes. Sometimes, she would bend over and flash her gorgeous tits. One day, sparks went off as they touched while Alexia passed her a glass of wine.

Impulsively, she pulled down her gym shorts to her thigh and rubbed her puss gently under her panties. Watching her reflection like a horny voyeur, her fingers caressed within the moistness. Aroused in pleasure, she gave fine attention to her precious erect gem. The sensation was breathless as nerve pleasing pulsations drove through her body. She always wanted Catherine to make the first move and take dominion over her flesh. Taking her fingers from the wetness to her nose, she inhaled her feminine scent. Bringing her fingers to her mouth, she licked and sucked like a delicacy.

She remembered how she would sneak a pair of her sister's dirty panties from the clothes hamper. Then she'd lock herself in the bathroom, holding the soiled panties tightly to her nose. She inhaled intensely, enjoying the scent while achieving a vibrant orgasm.

Awakening from my vivid dream, I rubbed my eyes. Getting off the recliner, dazed, I went into the kitchen. I opened the door and yelled down. "Alexia, how are you making out?"

"Coming, be there is a second."

Alexia pulled up her shorts, picked up the bottles, and locked the heavy doors. She put the key back to its hidden place and proceeded up the steps.

As she strolled back into the kitchen, lingering urges stuck in her mind.

"What took you so long, girl?"

While sniffing her fingers, she said. "I forgot where the expensive bottles were hiding. Probably cost over one hundred euros retail…. Remember how Mama used to spend hours searching with auntie."

"Mama and Marielle were doing other things. All over… even in the cheese room……. Anyway, thanks to Papa it's going to be a hot time."

"He definitely knows how to take care of his daughter's needs," Alexia said spontaneously.

I giggled, realizing what my sister intended.

"How can you say that, Alexia? I know he loves us…. completely bare, of course. Anyway, he is the best, as long as he doesn't find out about his petty thieves stealing his high-end wine."

Digging into the cabinet door, I began pulling out the unique style glasses and placed them on the counter.

"What are you doing?" Alexia inquired.

"Looking for the lightweight ones with the wide rims. Where are those glasses?"

"Why those?"

"I enjoy sipping and swirling from the better wine glasses. It makes me feel like a connoisseur, giving that certain level of sophistication while I get smashed."

"Sis, that sounds funny."

"Ah, here we are. By the way, what type of wine did you get?"

"Your favorite chardonnay fermented in oak."

Alexia brought the bottle under the island light.

"The label shows it has flavors of nuts, toast, spice, and caramel. I wonder how they get the nutty flavor?"

"It is probably the smelly and sweaty nuts of the grape crushers. You know, they stomp grapes naked as their balls bounce up and down?" I said, humorously.

"Don't tell me we have to pick out the hairs in our teeth," Alexia replied.

"Supposedly, they shave their balls clean before plodding. Just think, hairless, naked men bouncing around, breaking their balls on grapes. Hence, the nutty grapey flavor."

Unable to contain ourselves, we broke out in a hysterical, continuous laugh that took minutes for us to settle down. Taking a deep breath, I realized that our youth had slipped away. Staring at my sister, we were now adults entering the world with our uniqueness. Our closeness had changed, but not with distance. Yet, something was missing.

"Hey, this wine needs some chilling," I said. "Could you pull the chiller from the pantry?"

"Sure."

Alexia went over to the pantry and pulled out the chiller. She plugged it in, placed the bottles inside, and turned it on.

In placing the wineglasses on the island, I noticed the dead silence in the room.

"It's too quiet in here."

"Turn on the soft rock station that we like," Alexia said.

Going into the living room, I powered up the smart TV and selected our favorite music station. As I bent over, my jean shorts tightened, irritating my crotch. Immediately pulling them down, I peered over into the kitchen. Alexia was looking at my butt with an interesting stare.

"Wow, you look hot, Lizette," she said in a provocative tone.

As the music played softly in the background, the mood in the room changed from silence to passion. Teasingly, I turned to Alexia and slowly unzipped my shorts a quarter of the way down. With my hand held on the zipper, Alexia licked her lips, staring at my crotch.

"Should I go further? What do you think?"

Alexia slightly blushed. "Go down as far as you want." Then Alexia looked at me with a bright grin, raising her eyebrows. "You look sexy to me with your shorts on or off," she said in a sexy tone.

"Are you getting frisky with me?"

"If you take them off, I could get a better picture of those nice silky legs of yours."

The timer went off as the wine reached the desired temperature.

"We definitely need some wine," I said.

I walked over to where Alexia was standing. She uncorked the bottle, filled two glasses, and handed me one.

"Cheers, to girls' night…. at home," I said, smiling.

We stood standing at arm's length, clinging glasses, and sipping as our eyes gradually met. Alexia had the most beautiful blue eye color that kept me staring. Not wanting to get too expressive, I dropped my eyes. I briefly gazed at her nipples and peered into my glass, looking at the color. Then, I held the glass towards the light to view its clarity.

"This wine taste delicious. Let's chug this one down," I said casually.

Within no time at all, we guzzled our first glass of wine. Alexia immediately poured another.

"Alexia, I got to get out of these tight shorts. Do you mind?"

"Be my guest."

I watched her eyes intently, slowly peeling off my shorts, revealing my panties. As I was pulling them down, Alexia's eyes never left mine.

"I like your pink panties."

"My favorite on the weekends."

"By the way, what have you been up to?" Alexia remarked.

I blushed.

"I just took a quick nap on the recliner while you were downstairs. You know how amour goes."

"Come on, tell me more. Anyone I know."

"Maybe later, while we get snuggling…"

"Your words tantalize me. Watch me like a… voyeur," Alexia said nervously.

She widened the elastic band of her gym shorts and slipped them off. Raising her shorts above her head, she twirled them like a stripper and tossed them aside.

"I see you were enjoying the wine cellar. A little damp down there," I smiled.

"You know… it always gets damp in the basement," Alexia replied.

"That must have been a special moment."

"I was just thinking about someone I encountered. Nothing came of it."

"I'm sure it's a delectable female," I said, assumingly. "Alexia, fantasying about erotic desires at work. What would Papa think?"

"I hope he wouldn't. You know Papa when two women are getting into it. Remember French kissing naked with nipples touching. Papa accidentally caught us for literally minutes before we noticed him."

"As Marielle would say, it was an instantaneous salute."

Alexia took another sip of her wine, leaning up against the countertop. She stood in black leather boots, white stained panties, and a braless top. With her eyes focused towards the floor, she held onto her wine glass like something was bothering her. She looked up and turned her head towards me. Her glass was almost empty.

"Looks like you need another," I said.

Taking the bottle gently in my hand, I filled her glass while looking into her eyes. "Thinking about Selene. Those were some good times," I said, sincerely.

Her stare showed she did not want to talk about it. To preserve the mood, I put my lips on hers and gave her a soft passionate kiss as pleasant feelings swept through me.

"Hey, do you want to take a shower? I'm feeling a little sticky."

"I definitely could use one."

Her words filled my head with fervid meaning as intuition told me that a shower was going to be a start of an interesting evening.

"Well, I'm headed upstairs."

"I'll follow you. But don't forget the wine."

Turning off the wine chiller and the TV, I started heading toward the stairwell.

"Wait a minute, sis," Alexia said in a mumbled tone. "I need to take off my boots."

Alexia was sitting on the recliner, struggling. Giggling, I realized it was probably the wine.

"Wait, let me help."

Buzzed, I set the bottle and my glass on a table. I walked over to where she was sitting.

"Which one first."

"Try the left."

I gradually tugged at the left boot and it gave in. It slid off, revealing her naked foot. She was wearing pink nail polish that matched her panties. My nipples had gotten hard as I looked into Alexia's eyes. Then, I put my nose into the shaft and took a deep whiff, getting a sensual high.

"I love the way leather smells, sis, especially when you're wearing it."

"Are you getting kinky on me?"

Alexia lifted her leg, pointing it up and outward. She caressed them with both hands, moving her hands toward her thighs. In swallowing, I observed her with my eyes almost tearing in desire.

Speaking in a relieving tone, "Wow, a full body massage is what I really need. Are you up for it?"

The wine was taking effect. Her tongue danced around her lips as I felt tingling sensations running throughout my body. Like a stripper on stage, I was helping a beautiful woman undress to a waiting audience. I steadily pulled off the other boot, exposing her bare foot. Putting my nose over the shaft, I inhaled. Her scent cast a stimulating signal to my brain, arousing me even more. Thoughts of rubbing my pussy against her naked foot came into mind. I wanted to play with myself while enjoying the luscious scent of her leather.

Delicately putting my hand over her left foot, I started caressing as she slightly tittered.

"It tickles."

Putting my nose to her toes, I slowly inhaled, enjoying the natural rawness. Using both hands to massage her feet, my fingers gradually reached her inner thigh.

Sighing with enjoyment, she uttered. "Oh, it feels good. Keep going."

I sat down on the floor and rubbed her feet. Applying pressure to her foot with my thumbs, I brought my mouth to her toes and sucked. Alexia, while enjoying the sensation, slid her hand into her panties.

"Don't stop for me," she whispered in a breath.

While she played with herself, I continued sucking and lapping her beautiful toes. Extending my hand to caress her calves, Alexia's pace quickened as moans crept from her lips. She looked into my eyes, waiting for a passionate kiss.

"Cum with me tonight," she said. "I want to reach orgasm with you."

The invitation was unexpectedly sending heat to my forehead. The wetness between my legs became noticeable. I could hardly control the craving that swept through me.

I needed to stop before things got too far out of control.

"We need to cool down a bit, sis," I said.

Reaching my lips to hers, I gave her a light kiss. Then I pulled her out of the chair.

"First, we need to get in the shower," I said.

Grabbing the bottle and my wineglass, I headed up the steps with Alexia feeling tipsy. Alexia instinctively put her hand around my shoulder. I felt a soft breath against my neck as she turned her head and kissed me again. It felt warm, alluring, and pleasing as I caught the scent of her sweet perfume. All I could think about was our naked bodies together, while we ascended upon the landing. Touching and loving in a lustful session of sisterly love.

Upon reaching the bathroom door, she slid her tongue into my mouth. Accepting her without hesitation, we engaged in a romantic kiss. Relishing her taste, I did not want to let go, but the shower entered my mind. I parted lips as things were escalating out of control.

"Time to freshen up, my love," I said.

I opened the bathroom door, and we stumbled in. I felt the cold floor on my bare feet as I proceeded across the floor to the window. The cool air in the room had lost the appeal of a shower. In turning my head, I glanced at the jacuzzi. The thought of soaking in a warm bubble bath for hours immediately seized my passion. Pulling the window down shut, I locked it.

"A bubble bath would probably be better than a shower. It is cool in here," I said. "We could relax, enjoy the bubbles, and sip wine."

Alexia pleasantly agreed. "I like that idea better. Besides, we could share some quality time touching close."

Her affections heightened me like I was now her lover. I turned on the water and added a bubble bath solution. I placed the wine glasses and bottle on a table next to the tub. Alexia opened a cabinet drawer and pulled out a scented candle. She placed the candle on the table, lit it, and dimmed the lights.

Chapter 18

The Bath

The candle infused an earthy and woodsy scent throughout the room. As the wine glasses sat on the table, they dripped with condensation. Nervously, I took off my panties and unstrapped my bra. Alexia watched me intently as she slid off her pink panties. Her bareness reflected a figure of feminine distinction and beauty. Her erect nipples and hairless skin were irresistibly attractive. She peered at my finely shaven beaver, licked her lips, and swallowed.

"What do you think?" I said.

She reached down with her fingers and touched my skin in a caressing motion.

"Smooth as a baby's bottom," she said. "Feel mine."

My fingers reached for her delicate peach, caressing into the moistness.

"We are just alike," I said. "Just minutes apart."

Looking into each other's eyes, we exchanged gentle kisses. Then, a compelling moment seized our kinship as our lips locked in a spellbinding thirst for one another. Skin to skin, we hugged, desiring the fervency of sensuality. Kissing with obsession, we reached a new level of intimacy within our sisterhood. As our lips parted, the world fell silent. The ether had changed to acceptance, passion, and aching desire. Awakening from her kiss, I noticed the water level in the jacuzzi.

"The water." I said, hastily.

I reached over, turning the handles to the closed position. "Just made it," I whispered, softly.

Alexia filled our wine glasses to the top, getting us ready for an evening of affection. We stepped into the jacuzzi holding on to each other.

"Alexia, take the front. I'll take the back," I whispered in a breath.

As we sat down simultaneously, my nipples touched her warm flesh. Tingling sensations ran through my body as I spread my legs around her. I stroked her back as she grabbed the wine glasses, passing one over. We began sipping once more, enjoying the delicious taste, chatting about frivolous matters. Then, conversation drifted around idle chatting. Before long, the wine bottle was empty.

"Numero deux termine," I said.

Alexia put our glasses back on the stand. Then she opened a small drawer, took out a seven-inch dildo, and sat back in the Jacuzzi. My arms rested around Alexia as my chest pressed lightly on her back. A soft, amatory feeling emerged from the glowing candle and the soothing bubbles. Bringing my nose to her neck, I inhaled, enjoying her lush scent.

I whispered in her ear. "I could taste you all night."

"Suds me all over? You know I love your soft caresses," Alexia said, softly.

Her words were arousing and tempting. I moved her hair to one side, exposing her upper back. Taking a bath sponge, I washed her back, thinking about how many times we bathed as kids. Now, innocence has left us. Our feelings had escalated into an instinctive yearning for something much more. Falling into a consciousness of carnal desire, I felt no guilt or shame. In my heart, I only wanted to make love to her.

She tilted her head forward as I rinsed her off. I lifted the sponge over her head and squeezed. The water trickled over her sudsy body. I brought my lips to her neck, pressing against her wet skin. Her bareness was tasty. Then, I planting open kisses along her neck as my fingers delicately massaged her back. My mind wandered, thinking of the times as the beach with Marielle. The reward for giving titillating pleasure was a cone of cool, sweet ice cream. Marielle would sigh with contentment as we massaged her back with the oil. Then, we would lick the cone together, touching lips. It felt weird at first, but I desperately waited for her delicious taste after the next beach encounter. Eventually, it made me cum as I masturbated thinking about making love to her.

"You always did Marielle well. You never lost your touch, sis," Alexia murmured.

Letting go of all reservations, an unconditional liberating moment took control. Anxiety and tension had dissipated and the craving for passion ascended. She opened her legs wider while her head pushed back against my shoulder. My lips and tongue continued, arousing with deep affection. Placing my mouth upon her earlobe, I nibbled. Then, the tip of my tongue entered her canal as I left waves of soft breaths behind. She exhaled in a relieving tone, appreciating the warm pleasant sensation.

The intensity of our affections amplified without pause. Turning her body around, she brought her lips to mine. Impulsively, our mouths met with incestuous lust as our tongues deeply entwined in succulence. Her lips were full, moist, and voluptuous. My tongue sunk into her mouth and hers into mine. We sucked on each other's lips with thirst and excitement. Our enticing kisses sent trickles of saliva down my throat. I swallowed each drop of her love, only wanting more. Taking her tongue between my lips, I began sucking it as it slithered. It felt so smooth and delicious. She took my tongue playfully, enjoying the appetizing and pleasing taste.

My craving for her could not cease. Our kissing continued with substance while intermittent tongues flickered and danced. Our beautiful naked bodies were bathing in an irresistible pool of passion. Breaking our oral bond, she turned back around and washed her arms and legs as I hugged her once more.

"Tonight, we'll pop the virgin cherry as loving sisters," I said. "Nothing can stop our deep love for one another."

My mouth opened, giving soft sweet kisses along her shoulder. I began stroking her stomach with detailed attention. My fingers moved toward her inner thigh, fondling and teasing. My arousing advances quenched her with dripping pleasure. Entering the taboo world of parallel sensuality, nervousness and felicity flared.

"Fill me with love," she whispered in a steamy tone.

Her words trickled endlessly in my ears. I remembered many times peeking through the crack in the bathroom door, watching Alexia with self-love. She would never know I was there, as my fingers played right along with hers. My pussy would spasm vibrantly as I masturbated into culmination. Now, we are playing together willfully, flagrantly, and without disgrace.

My hands slowly sailed over her erect nipples, stroking, and squeezing. The soap and water created a lubrication, allowing my fingers to glide freely. Her nipples felt natural in my hands as I continued to kiss the nape with roaming lips. Her hand descended into the water between her thighs. She started playing with herself as I touched and squeezed her luscious tits. Her hand began moving in and out of the water at a hastened pace. Splashing and dousing, she dug deeper and deeper.

"Come. Time to come with me." I whispered delicately in her ear.

Savoring the moment of indulgence, she wanted me like a slave in the hands of a master. I placed my legs inside hers, spreading her wider. My cheek settled firm against her head as I placed my hand on top of hers, taking control. Then she slid the dildo into her wanton hole as my hand tamed her love button into submission. Leaning firmer against my shoulder, I could feel the pressure building inside of her as she screwed herself furiously.

Riding my pussy against her ass, my tongue licked her ear. My breath sent tickling sensations up and down her spine as sounds of delight escaped from her lips. Her body became rigid as her legs pushed against mine. Feeling every ounce of pleasure, our bodies pressed together as one.

"Don't stop. Right there. Right there," she whispered.

Reveling within our playfulness, our bodies rubbed against each other in persistent motion. Ultimate sensations were cascading throughout her body. Screwing herself in gratification, she began respiring with intensity, climbing deeper into obsessing pleasure. With her free hand, she gripped the side of the jacuzzi lifting her body while engaging in tormenting gratification. Driving into the stars of bliss like a rocket to its target, her body started vibrating into elation. Holding on tightly, she lifted herself even higher as she closed her eyes. Flashing pleasure raced in her head as she let out a scream of trembling jubilation.

Having peaked in my arms, she cried out. "Oh yeah. Ooh, Lizette? You're better than Selene."

Settling down into the jacuzzi, she placed her head between her legs for a moment. Then she turned to me as our mouths met in gentle kisses.

"Your incredible, my sis," Alexia said.

She looked deep into my eyes with desire and love. We sat appeasing each other with lips and tongues as our bodies slowly parted.

"The bath water by now had gotten cooler. Let's get out of the bathroom and head to the bedroom. The bed is nice and cozy," Alexia said nervously.

As we got out of the jacuzzi, the cool air in the room caught my attention. I blew out the candle as she grabbed the towels and tossed one over. Then we dried off in haste.

"Alexia, grab our clothes. I must take care of the bottles. Catch you in a minute," I said.

Alexia headed to the bedroom, as I wrapped a towel around my body. Then I pressed the lever on the tub to drain the water. Grabbing the empty bottle and glasses, I descended the stairs in deep thought.

Our salacious satisfaction surged like a blooming flower within the fields of kinship. Many nights, I craved to taste her succulent fruit but refrained from fear of losing a close friend. Tonight, we shattered the world of austerity by engaging in wanton, uninhibited impulses.

Chapter 19

The Next Day

Upon entering the kitchen, I pulled out a trash bag and placed the two bottles inside. I walked out into the garage and opened the trash bin. I hid the bag maliciously at the bottom.

"Evidence disposed," I muttered.

Coming back into the kitchen, I put the wine chiller in the pantry and our glasses in the dishwasher. After picking up our clothes from the floor, I headed up the stairwell. I put Alexia's gym shorts to my nose. Her feminine scent sent craving thoughts to my brain. I imagined her skillful tongue working all over my gorgeous bod.

"Patience will triumph," I thought.

I walked into our bedroom itching for deep penetrating satisfaction. Peering into bed, disappointment immediately fell upon as Alexia had fallen asleep.

"It must a have been the wine that knocked her out"

I untied my towel and placed it in the hamper with the other clothes. I sat in bed next to my sister. Drained from the alcohol, I wanted to sleep. I slipped under the sheets, placing my chest against her back. I kissed her nape, closed my eyes, and dozed into unconsciousness.

A flock of birds echoed in the distance inspiring me into the dawn. Opening my eyes, the bright sun penetrated the room, displaying a vibrant glow. My exuberant relationship with Alexia evolved last evening over a few bottles of wine. Our simple harmonious relationship had turned into one of sizzling ardor. We not only shared deep emotions but now provide each other with amatory pleasures.

Laying back on my pillow, I dragged the sheets from my breasts. As I lightly caressing my nipples, a tingly and arousing feeling came over me. Placing my fingers gently on my puss, I slowly massaged, envisioning Alexia riding the dildo into the cusp of a delicious orgasm. I spread my legs a little wider, relishing a pleasing sensation. Then my mind drifted toward Marielle. I imagined licking every drop of her soothing womanhood. I craved her soft creamy flesh, wanting to fill my mouth with its delightful goodness. Caressing myself with pace, I was feeling lusciously hot. Climbing in want, a sudden knock on our door interrupted my play. I stopped and immediately pulled the sheets over me.

Trying to calm down, I spoke, "Come on in."

Mama walked into our room.

"Morning, my love birds, brought you a little something," she said.

Her morning generosity completely caught me off guard. "Mama, breakfast, and… café. Now, that's a surprise." In the back of my mind, I wondered if mother's intuition knew what her daughters were up to last night. "How was dinner?"

"We went over to Brasserie for fish. It was absolutely lovely."

I nudged Alexia a few times.

"Wake up, sis, Mama brought us breakfast."

It took a little effort, but she finally opened her eyes into the sunshine.

Alexia sat up in bed with her tits dangling. "Morning Mama."

She placed the tray on my lap and opened the legs to set it in place. Then, she put her hand on my forehead.

"Just checking your temperature. You look a little pale."

"What have your girls gotten into last night?"

"Too much of Papa's cheap wine, but we sobered up in the jacuzzi," I said. "I feel fine. Coffee will perk me up."

"I know a healthy breakfast will take some of that hangover away. Well, I will leave you girls alone. Don't forget the tray on your way downstairs," Mama said.

"No problem," Alexia responded.

She closed the door behind her. As I poured a cup of café for Alexia, the feeling was a little weird at first. However, Mama's breakfast seemed to be the icebreaker that got us back in the family flow. It was like Mama knew that awakening after our first sexual experience would be awkward.

"I know you want cream. How many sugars?"

"The usual two."

Slicing some cheese, I spread it on my croissant with jam.

"I owe you, sis. Sorry for falling to sleep last night."

I took a bite of my croissant. The raspberry jam was delectable. A bit stuck to my lip, and I licked it off.

"I'm sure you will make it up down the road."

Alexia took a sip of her café.

"Did you take care of the bottles of wine? Papa would fire me if he found out."

"Yes. What are sisters for," I said.

I turned and gave her a quick morning café kiss. We chatted while sipping our breakfast. The discussion fully blossomed, like nothing had changed between us. We were sisters fulfilled in every aspect of our bond, but now wanting more, a different way.

Chapter 20

The Creek

Unlike Alexia, work was not on my agenda during summer vacations, unless the business really needed me for wine tastings and filling orders. My plan was to take full advantage of the warm months at the beach in the sun. The only problem was getting there. How do I get there without a car? I didn't want to bother Mama every day. So, my trail bike was the only mode of transportation left.

The main road to the beach took about forty-five minutes from our house. This route had an advantage of being a smooth, comfortable ride. However, there were some drawbacks. The traffic was dangerous and the exhaust from cars created an unhealthy ride. So, I sought an alternative route.

"Maybe I could take a back country road. The air would be cleaner and roads might be less dangerous," I thought.

In using an app on my cell phone, I rediscovered a back road to the beach called rue de pasture. I knew from experience that the local farmers use the road for transporting farm equipment, crops, and animals. Being mostly free of mainstream traffic, I calculated that the road would probably save me roughly ten minutes.

Getting on my bike early one morning, I conducted a trial run to test out the road. Heading down rue de pasture to the beach, there was farmland, vineyards, and grazing green pastures. However, the road had some drawbacks. Sheep and cow herds crossed my path, which I sometimes would have to sit and wait. The road was bumpy, hilly, and comprised moderately paved sections. Riding downhill was easy, but there was a challenge riding uphill. Steep hills would make the ride a workout.

After my trial run, I felt more comfortable taking the back road than the primary route. Besides, I could always bug Mama for a ride when I was not up to riding my bike.

Making my way to the beach along the rue de pasture during the summer wasn't without stopping. Sometimes during my bike ride, I would need to piss. Other times, I wanted to light up a joint or take a couple of swigs from my wine flask. Through these random stops, I discovered a hidden gem along the road to the bay.

In late June, the mid-morning sun penetrated my back as I peddled toward the beach. While ascending a hill, I had the urgency to pee. Getting off my bike along the roadside, I peered to the right, noticing a large oak tree.

"That's a nice hidden spot," I thought.

When I got behind the oak tree, a small thin path became visible. Not wearing any panties, I pulled down my shorts to my ankles and squatted. The warm stream of pee flowed like lava on soil.

"What a relief," I muttered.

I zipped up my shorts and looked down the trail. Exploring the narrow path leading into the woods captured my curiosity. Hiding my bike within the brush, I grabbed my backpack and began the journey inward.

The vegetation along the path was slightly dense. However, mostly, it was easy to navigate. I stopped and pulled a joint from my backpack. I lit it and took a long hit. Upon exhaling, things started settling down. After taking another hit, nature suddenly came to life with its vivid colors and native sounds. A true spiritual emergence had awakened my senses.

As my mind became inundated with the peacefulness of the woods, I continued about twenty-five yards inward. The crisp and coherent sound of running water caught my attention as I reached a large clearing. Exploring the area, it appeared the path had ended along the dense brush that surrounded the entire perimeter. I bent down and put my hand into the knee-deep creek that was at the edge of the open space.

"Wow, this is totally cool. The creek is probably coming from the bay, but where it was going?" I thought. Looking up, the sky was clear blue, and the sun was glaring. "Why go to the beach? I could catch a private tan here."

Finding a bare spot by the water, I put my backpack down. I took out a blanket and placed it on the ground. Lighting the joint again, I took a couple of deep drags and extinguished it. I put the remains in a metal cigar container in my backpack. I took off my top, unzipped my jean shorts, and unhooked my bra, crumpling them into my pack.

As I stood up naked, the marijuana had taken my mind into an incredible peaking sensation. Within the invigorating ether, the magical smells and sounds of the woods became animated. The flowing water, creaking trees, and rustling wind emerged like a hidden song in a fairytale book. The forest became alive with its colorful greens and browns. My mind became amalgamated with the divergence of flora and fauna. It was like taking a trip to 'Alice in Wonderland' while stoned out of my mind. Locked in its inner essence, I was savoring the moment of realization. The impressions of the creek had turned green and tranquil, unearthing its magical secrets. Lifting my arms over my head, a breeze crossed my body. The comforting sensation felt pleasing, indulging, and nourishing.

Memories of the past surfaced. Mama would dry my clothes on the clothesline. When dried, I put my panties up to my nose, inhaling the natural and enriching scent. Then, I slipped them on tight to my crotch. It made me feel like I was a part of the fresh, rugged outdoors.

Grabbing my backpack, I pulled out some sunscreen and a flask of wine. I took a couple gulps from the flask and set it aside. I opened a bottle of sunscreen and generously spread the lotion over every part of my body. Using the backpack as a cushion, I laid down and closed my eyes. Absorbing the warm sunlight, my mind focused on the flowing water with a keen ear.

The sounds of the creek were echoing with emerging expressions. The lexes became clearer and clearer as I listened. Coming from the bay, I could faintly hear people conversing. It was as if the creek functioned like an archaic telephone line carrying voices across the distance.

Feeling aroused, I brushed my fingers delicately across my puss, teasing myself. My other hand tenderly played with my luscious tits. I brought my nipples to my mouth, licking and tasting while enjoying the titillation. The smell of nature reminded me of Marielle and Valise making love in the backyard. Playing with my clit, I envisioned Marielle accepting Valise's open mouth, wanting her deep affections. Their tongues danced and sucked, capturing every ounce of oral pleasure. With hands buried in pleasure zones, soft whimpers of erogenous play seeped from their compassionate lips. As I stood in the window, Marielle saw my bare youthfulness like a tender fawn waiting to play its first erotic game.

I rubbed my clit in a circular motion, feeling the lustful satisfaction of self-love. The effects of the pot were driving my nerves into unescapable fulfillment. Sounds became feelings. Feelings turned into sounds. I could smell the rawness of the vegetation while reaching my first orgasm in the woods.

The heat of desire and obsession emerged as I imagined spreading my legs to their darting tongues. Stuffing my fingers in my sopping wet hole, I fingered, while rubbing my clit. On the verge of reaching a pinnacle, a pleasant rhythm shot across my flesh. With a vibrant intensity, an orgasmic adrenaline rush filled my mind with flowing seconds of exhilaration. It was like I was in space and coming down to earth. After relaxing for a minute, my mind escaped into unconsciousness.

I awoke having been asleep for some time, feeling tired and spent. I looked at my tanned body.

"I'll have to get to the other side another day," I thought.

Putting on my clothes, I took one more look around, appreciating my secret place. I walked down the path, got on my bike, and headed for home.

Chapter 21

Anna

After my first year at university, my mind shifted from studies to getting an attractive tan during the summer. On the second week in June, I was riding my bike along rue de pasture traveling in the creek's direction. Upon looking ahead, I spotted a young girl walking her bike. As I approached, I slowly braked and stopped alongside of her.

"Looks like you are having a minor problem?" I said.

"Ran into a nail about a half mile down the road," she said, in a frustrated tone.

She was five foot five, with a slim physique. Her long brown hair was bound in a ponytail. Catching my attention, her pointed nipples protruded visibly through her beige tank top.

"Where are you headed?"

Simultaneously, she looked as she pointed toward the tire. "I was on my way to the beach until I ran into this."

Peering into her brown eyes, I felt a level of displeasure.

To gain her confidence, I spoke with an air of encouragement. "I probably can help you out. Where's the problem?"

Her perky tits jiggled about as she stooped, giving indication where the nail was hiding. Bending over, I used my thumb and index finger, jimmying the nail out with a slight struggle.

"Looks like we are in luck. The damage to the tube looks minimal because of the small nail," I said.

Examining the front and back tires, I found no further damage. I pulled the repair can off my bike, unscrewed the valve cap, and squirted some in the tire tube. Waiting for the compound to take effect, she glanced deeply into my eyes, like she was looking for something. A captivating sensation swept over me as I gazed back with an avid stare.

Interrupting the moment, chirping birds in the distance diverted my attention. Then my mind gradually drifted back, focusing once more on the effectiveness of the repair.

"That should be enough time," I said confidently.

Impulsively, I mounted her bike and spun a few three-sixties on the road. Getting off the bike, I handed it to her.

"The pressure seems to hold well. But you need to monitor it. Just get a new tube as soon as you can. The compound may not hold up for very long."

She gave me a bright smile as she bent over to inspect the tire. "You seem to be an expert in this matter."

"I ran into a few problems myself over the years."

She came close and offered her hand. "By the way, my name is Anna Beaupre."

"I'm Lizette Beaufort."

"We have a couple of beautiful last names," she said, amusingly.

"Never thought of it that way," I said.

With admiration, she spoke. "Well… anyway…. Not to be too straightforward but you have a gorgeous bod."

"Thanks, I like to keep it well tanned in the summer."

Thoughts of asking Anna to the creek immediately appeared in my mind. Though I wanted to keep the location a secret, inviting Anna would give me some companionship. So, I offered.

"The beach is most likely crowded today. I know a hidden spot in a wooded area where we can catch a private tan. Would you like to join me? It's a great alternative and very close."

Holding onto her bike, she looked down, pondering over the idea.

Then she raised her head assuredly with a trusting smile. "Yeah, that would be a change. Besides, I'm still worried about the tire," she said. "Is it far?"

"Just down the road. Much closer than the beach. Just follow me."

We got on our bikes, and I led the way.

Stopping near the old oak tree on the roadside, we reached the path's entrance. There were no cars in sight, which was a good sign. When concealing my bike, I always felt uncomfortable when a car passed. Just didn't want anyone to know where my hidden spot was located.

"We have to be careful. I'm sure unmarked police cars come down this road. Questioning by the police was the last thing I need," I said.

Anna got off her bike, placed her hand over her crotch, and tugged her shorts. "That's a bumpy road, but I love the exercise. Keeps me in shape."

"We need to cover our tracks before we set forth on the trail. If you can, lift your bike above the foliage. Just be careful around the large oak tree because I like to pee there."

She slightly giggling as we lifted our bikes, hiding them deep along the path behind some bushes. We grabbed our backpacks and slowly made our way down the narrow path towards the creek. As she paced behind me, the sights, sounds, and smells of the forest were awakening my senses. Soon, we heard the crisp and soothing sound of flowing water as we entered the private domain.

"Voila, we arrived...... This is it."

Anna looked around in awe. "This place is so picturesque. How did you find it?"

"I wasn't kidding about the tree... When I squatted to pee, the hidden trail came into view. I usually come here towards the end of the week because it's when the beaches are crowded."

"Finding a reasonable spot to lie out can be a challenge within the enormous crowds. Sometimes, you need to get there early in the morning," Anna said.

"Since coming here. I've seen no one. It's a hidden gem in the countryside. Just need to cover my tracks by the entrance."

Walking over to the large open space, I placed my pack down. "I cleared more space last year to lie out. Here...... put yours down near mine."

She brought her backpack over while staring at the creek.

"The water comes from the bay but I hadn't figured out where it goes...... It's usually cool.... Wanta wade?"

111

"Sure, after walking on that hot road, I could use a cool down."

We took off our sneakers and socks and entered the creek. The water stood almost knee high. It felt refreshing as we casually made our way about two hundred yards downstream. Getting apprehensive about going further, the urge to head back came to mind.

"Let's turn around to be on the safe side. I hadn't gone this far before and don't know what to expect."

On our way back, Anna kneeled in the creek and splashed water onto her face. Standing up, she wiped her eyes as her tank top was soaking wet. Her areolas penetrated visibly through the wet material as she pulled the clinging cloth off her hardened nipples. Looking at me with slight embarrassment, she pressed her hair back with her hands.

"The cool creek is so fresh and invigorating. Almost like taking a refreshing shower," she said.

"The trees and vegetation block the rays of the sun from striking the water, especially on the other side. After laying out in the sun for a few hours, I usually like to take a long dip."

As we got out of the creek, Anna stumbled, but I grabbed her quickly. Pulling her towards me, I could sense the firmness and strength. As our bodies touched, the distance between us had broken, creating a level of comfort.

"That's the second time you rescued me."

"No worries. I usually must remind myself to be careful. No one is out here to help me. So, I carry my phone close by."

Making our way back over to our stuff, I unzipped my bag. I pulled out my towel, placing it on the ground.

Pointing to the ground. "You can put your towel over here next to mine."

As Anna grabbed a towel from her bag and placed in neatly on the ground, I secretly pulled out a joint and lighter.

I opened my hand, showing her. "Do you smoke... You know weed."

"I've taken a few puffs in my time."

"Let's light up."

112

I lit the joint and took a deep, long hit. Passing it, she took it without hesitation. As she inhaled, I looked into her eyes. They turned dark and hidden as the sun struck her face with blinding light. She exhaled, letting out a few suppressive coughs.

"Potent stuff."

"It is some of the best that I got from school."

Her eyes widened. "You go to the university!"

"I'm in the psychology program."

"That's awesome. I'm taking up art culture," she said, with a big smile.

We passed the joint back and forth, getting into a cozy conversation until the joint was exhausted. Dropping it to the ground, I pressed my heal on it. Then I picked it up and threw it into the creek.

"I'm definitely going to get more of that stuff," I said.

Then, I pulled out a bottle of suntan oil while putting the lighter away.

"Do you need some?" I said.

"No, I brought my own… raspberry scent."

She opened her bottle with absolute care and inhaled its essence. Looking slightly intoxicated, she was enjoying the pleasing aroma.

"The scent is very rousing…. It almost like having sex……. take a whiff."

Handing me the bottle, I placed it up to my nose. The sweet fragrance started arousing my senses like an aphrodisiac.

"Wow, that is some awesome stuff. I could almost taste the aroma. It's making me feel so sensual."

"Special blend my Mama gets from India. It's also edible."

I passed the bottle back to Anna, gracefully touching her fingers. As social barriers diminished, the feelings between us had gotten more tranquil and less complex. I sensed an attraction toward her. She reminded me of some of the soccer players at the lycée, firm and agile. Yet sexy in her own unique way.

"Been tanning nude since last summer. Do you mind if I take my top off?"

"That's fine. I strip down bare at the beach all the time. It's just the culture."

I dragged off my top off like a teasing stripper. I reached back to unfasten my bra.

"Let me help," she said, modestly.

I turned around as she stood behind me, undoing the clasp. I could feel her warm breath upon my neck. My bra fell into my hands as her warm delicate fingers glided over of my bare skin. Intensified by the pot, her fingers gave me a tantalizing sensation.

"Nice tan…. and a beautiful complexion."

My mind became encapsulated by her seductiveness as her fingers put me at ease. She was arousing me to a point where I felt hot and dizzy. Maintaining stillness and patience, her nonverbal communication had erupted into soft sentiments.

As I turned my body around, my tits came into view. I showed them off like a stage act, holding them in my hands and jiggling them about.

Her eyes were popping with an ecstatic stare.

"Wow, nice……. I wish I had a set like those."

"Come, touch them."

She came close and started caressing my nipples.

An almost inaudible hum escaped through my lips. "Your hands are so soft," I whispered.

"Now, let me show you mine."

She took a couple of steps back and peeled off her beige top. I became mesmerized by her slim, athletic physique and somewhat ripped stomach.

"You must be an athlete. I've seen bods like yours in the girl's locker at my old school."

Her breasts were smaller than mine, but firm and perky. Her nipples pointed upward. Watching me, she levered down her wet shorts, revealing a bright yellow bikini bottom.

"Just think. Two hot babes stoned and stripping naked in nature. It feels so licentious," I said.

She must have become aroused by what I said, because her nipples became instantly hard. Looking down, she nonchalantly touched and pinched them.

114

"It must be the wind."

"Don't feel embarrassed. It's natural."

Teasing a bit, I took off my gym shorts, leaving on my white panties. I was not ready to show her my shaven privates. Not yet anyway. In jitters, we sat down on our blankets, not knowing what to expect. I spread tanning oil across my stomach, arms, shoulders, and legs. Then I massaged my breasts, intentionally trying to catch her attention.

"Do you live around here?" I said.

"Close to the village. How about you?"

"About twenty minutes just off the rue de pasture."

She glanced over as she spread lotion on her tits. With a slight craving in her eye, the feeling of attraction between us was building.

With a sincere tone, she said. "Lizette, you have a hot, naked body. If I were a guy, I would say, you're the kind of woman to bring home to Mama. As a female, I would also say the same thing."

Her words melted me like ice cream on a hot day. They were tender, deep, and meaningful. At that moment, I knew she had an attraction to females.

"Thanks again for the compliment."

Anxiously, she asked. "Do you want me to spread some on your back?"

With sheer desire, I responded quickly. "Yeah, I could use a little help."

I handed her my bottle. She placed some on her hands and rubbed my shoulders. Her soothing fingers roamed up and down my back. Then she slid one finger slightly under my panties onto my butt crack.

"This is really a nice private spot you have here."

"It can be anyone's. It's government property."

The oil felt comforting against the warm sun. She grazed my crack once more and slid a finger in a little deeper.

"Want any in there?" she said.

"Maybe later when I strip my panties off. You can help me with that!"

Her seductive remarks had driven me into a sexual whirlpool. Highly interested, I wanted her to slip a finger inside my puckered hole and screw me crazily. I was feeling intensely wet and horny. All I could think about was roaming my hands all over her firm breasts. Then, the spirits of the forest answered my desire.

"Here, come spread some on me," she said.

She put oil on my hands, and I rubbed her shoulders.

"That feels so nice."

"Would you like a little massage?" I added. "It comes with the package."

"Yeah. My muscles are a little tight. I'm on the swim team."

"I can tell you love to work out."

Upon massaging her shoulders, the raspberry fragrance was making me feel hot and impassioned. My penetrating hands worked her sore muscles, flowing easily over her smooth skin. She began moaning, enjoying the pleasing sensation.

"Sounds like it feels good?" I said.

Her head turned around and looked into my eyes.

"Do you massage like that all the time?"

"What do you mean?"

"Are you a professional?"

"Why have you asked?"

"Because it feels so good everywhere you touch me."

"My sister and I became expert massagers years ago doing my aunt for ice cream treats."

"There all done."

Grabbing my backpack, I emptied some stuff out.

"Unpacking."

"No, I use it for a pillow."

Accidentally, my dildo fell out. She looked with sudden surprise like a fantasy come true.

"Just in case I need it."

I casually placed it back in the bag, thinking nothing of it. Then, we laid upon our beach blankets in silence, basking in the warm sun.

Chapter 22

Loving Anna

Staring upward, the clouds moved slowly across the blue sky as the sun shed its warmth upon my flesh. Feeling in the mood, I brought my fingers to my nose, inhaling the remnants of the raspberry oil. The lingering scent aroused my senses with a burning urge for sensual play. Trying to be inconspicuous, I slid my fingers under my panties, longing for salacious satisfaction. As I rubbed my puss, I became obsessed with a thirsting desire to make love to Anna. As I cautiously glanced over, she was lying on her back observing me with lustful eyes.

"Forgot to tell you. The raspberry oil contains potent sexual stimulants. The effects come on gradually," she said with a devilish smile.

Irrepressibly aroused, the oil must have taken control of my cravings. The aphrodisiac had intensified my pleasure zones, invoking a penetrating need to climax.

"I'm passionately spellbound. It's driving me crazy," I said.

".... as it lingers on the body, it works its magic," Anna replied. "You can wait it off or play it off. Most girls choose to play it off. I am all in for a game of female exploration, if you are. But first, I want to massage your ravishing bod."

Her enticing words were augmenting the pleasing sensation. I couldn't resist her offer as my passion for carnal play was at a breaking point. Falling into submission, I felt slutty, vulnerable, and kinky. I wanted to shed my juicy panties, open my legs, and have her lick my puss to paradise.

"I could use a tender touch," I said, nervously.

Placing raspberry oil on her fingers, she glided them inside her bikini, creaming her beaver. As I watched, she took her fingers out and licked them dry. Directing me to lie on my stomach, she mounted me with her legs spread over my butt. She started rubbing the oil on my back with her piercing hands.

Starting with my lower back, she moved upward, reaching my shoulders. Smothering the oil on her tits and nipples, she shuttled in a soothing motion up and down my back. As she pleasured her nipples, my fingers were in my panties, toying within my oyster. Vigorously rubbing into the escalating heat, my breathing intensified as the pleasure of sizzling satisfaction swept through me. Upon reaching an elated moment, Anna sensed my body begin to shudder. She immediately dismounted breaking my ecstatic climb.

"Not yet frisky girl," she said, amusingly.

My panties were soaking wet as I turned around and sat up slightly. Placing my middle finger in my puss, I brought it to her face.

"This is what you get for hindering my play. Now, taste my twinge?"

With craving in her eyes, Anna grasped my hand, placing my finger into her mouth. Sucking like a phallus, she accepted my feminine juices, savoring each drop. Then she puckered her lips as I slowly removed my finger with delicate force.

"Mm. Your sweetness is golden, but I definitely didn't get enough," she said.

As I lied on my back, she impulsively moved her hands onto my luscious tits. She kneaded and squeezed, seducing me into sedation. My nipples were erect, sensitive, and loving her skillful hands as she masterfully played. She put her mouth onto my sensitive nipples, nursing me like a hungry newborn. Her lips and tongue were arousing like a temptress in heat and her dexterity was gratifying.

"Let me try yours," I said.

Upon sitting up, my hands freely roamed over her chest, kneading, and rubbing. I moved my mouth onto her nipples, sucking and licking with a titillating and darting tongue. The swelter and oil on her skin was deliciously mouthwatering. I tasted and teased as she pressed her lips together and rolled her eyes back. Then I captured the dribbles of saliva that escaped from my mouth as my tongue made its way up her chest. Licking and kissing gently toward her neck, I wanted to taste her lips.

I brought my mouth to hers and we gently embraced. Her lips were moist and savory as my tongue glided between them. My long lingua flowed in and out as she tightened her lips, sucking inward. As I shagged her mouth, she responded with deep satisfying moans. Then, her luscious lingua oozed through my lips, melting me with nerve pleasing sensations. As we parted lips, our tongues flickered and danced like hummingbirds in perfect motion.

Caressing her stomach, I moved my fingers downward. I slid them into her bikini, feeling her softness. Then, penetrating her puss, I found her pink pearl. Anna glided her hands under my panties into my juiciness. Like eating sweet chocolate, she aroused my senses as I enjoyed her probing fingers within my musk.

Without breaking the urge, I hastily said, "Take off my wet panties and tongue my sweet puss."

Anna's athleticism became clear as she got on top pushing me to the ground. She slipped off my panties and untied her bottoms. With my back on the blanket, she enthusiastically began exploring my aching hole. Inserting two fingers, I spread my legs wider letting her screw me with vivaciousness. Her fingers were explosive, gratifying, and pulsating. Her carnal thrusts delighted my girl parts with progressive satisfying intensity. My head entered the clouds of joy feeling every second of her deftness. Sighs seeped through my lips only wanting more of what she was giving me.

Then, her warm pleasing tongue surfaced over my clit dancing like a ballerina on stage. She whirled and fluttered about as trickles of wetness seeped into her lips. Swallowing my juices with thirst, her lips and tongue gratified with depth. Then, she sucked me like a vacuum and the pleasure drove me senseless.

Clawing into the ground with my fingers, my breathing and heart rate escalated. Climbing to the edge of elation, my face became flush. As her pace quickened, rushing spasms surged sending me into the pinnacle of oblivion. I placed my hand on my forehead and laid back, calming myself and wanting more. Finally, catching my breath, it was her turn to receive.

With my body on hers, my fingers began probing as our lips passionately kissed with thirst and fervor. Her wetness glided my fingers easily through her puss. As I sucked and licked her nipples, my fingers found her erect clit. Upon dallying around, I found her sweet spot that immediately lit up her eyes.

She gasped, "Keep it there."

Optimizing my efforts, my fingers penetrated with gorging vigor. I peered deep into her eyes as her heart pounded faster in desire. In the heat of obsession, the blistering and quenching passion brought her to hypersensitivity. Moans of joy flowed from her lips as vibrations surged through her body. In a matter of seconds, her mind went blank, stiffening into an emulsifying climax. Then, our lips gently kissed, knowing that the oils effects had not diminished our afternoon play.

The heat from the sun drew swelter upon our bodies. With unfulfilled sensual craving, she turned her body around sliding her legs between mine. With total conviction, we joined in the unifying position of scissoring. We slowly humped as I gripped her hand tightly, augmenting the leverage. We pushed and pulled, climbing into bliss. My clit was grinding as the sound of our breaths resonated throughout the creek. The steamy ride was drawing me into incredible heights of satisfaction. Gasps of pleasure erupted from my lips as I was on my way to another peaking moment.

In the heat of passion, perspiration was dripping down my body as she milked me like a pump sucking water. Our chemistry spontaneous flowed in satisfying captivation as sounds of fulfillment echoed. With an unstoppable momentum of carnal lust, I started trembling in sheer jubilation. With the last pelvis thrust, intense titillating flared into an overwhelming sensation. I took a deep breath and lied back for a few minutes.

Coming back to reality, I joined Anna in soft, passionate kisses. Then, we fell on our blankets, exhausted, and soaked in perspiration. Holding each other's hand, we doze off into the reflecting mellow sun.

The sound of a sweeping bird awoke me as I opened my eyes. Not wanting to be out in the sun too long, I nudged Anna to an awaken state. She awoke looking at me with a deep smile of satisfaction.

"It's getting late," I said.

"Come to my place. We can take a shower," she said.

"I would like that."

We dressed, packed our bags, and started down the path.

As we got towards the road along the path, Anna joined me in a celebration.

"Cheers to your initiation into the hidden creek," I said.

We smoked some weed behind the oak tree and drank some wine from my flask. Then we got on our bikes and headed up the road to Anna's chateau.

Chapter 23

Anna's House

Stoned and partially drunk on wine, I trailed behind Anna as we headed toward her house. I pondered upon our unanticipated midday rendezvous, asking myself what transpired. The desire for a sensual companion at the creek materialized. However, just the quirkiness of our initial meeting caught me off guard. We were both headed in the same direction, but at different times. Yet, a flat tire on the road brought us intimately together. From the first touch to the last, our body chemistry ignited. We kept the oil of pleasure burning until our flame became extinguished by our culminating afternoon play. Swept away in absolute satisfaction, it was like we had been lovers for years. Yet, I really did not know her. It was only by pure accident that we became instantaneously bonded within nature's desire.

Finally arriving at Anna's home, she opened the garage door remotely, and we drifted in. The circa 1850 colonial was a beautiful stone structure containing original shutters and windows. The size looked like it was almost ten thousand square-foot. As Anna dismounting from her bike, she almost fell off but maintained her footing at the last second.

"I'm totally buzzing my head off," she said.

"I don't even know how I got here," I replied.

"Would you like some munchies or did you have enough?"

"Never enough of your stuff."

We both dropped to the garage floor impulsively, laughing. Finally calming down, our jovial rush gradually shifted as a level of seriousness emerged from our intemperance. Anna put her arm around my shoulder while my heart rate slowed to a normal pace. Holding on to each other, a level of comfort ensued, like snuggling under a warm comforter on a chilly night. Her tasty sweet lips eased upon mine. It was pure delicious candy.

Slowly parting, Anna spoke in a soft and lush tone. "Well, that was very nice. I made turkey sandwiches this morning. Are you hungry?"

"I'm starving. Hadn't eaten since breakfast."

Standing up, Anna pressed the button to close the garage door. As we walked through the entrance leading into the kitchen, the oak floor shined vibrantly off the sun's reflection. Immediately, the lavishness of the room caught my attention. There were antique maple cabinets, a large marble island, a large chandelier over the kitchen table, and patio doors leading to the pool. The table must have been decades old, made of a fine maple like the cabinets. The place settings comprised fine China utensils, cloth napkins, and glasses.

"Asseyez-vous ici," she said politely.

Sitting down, I admired the lavishness of her home that exhibited extravagant wealth. The tall ceiling made her kitchen appear unusually large and the long rooms appeared endless. Looking out the patio doors, my eyes rested on this beautiful, slim woman lounging. She was lying topless, sunbathing near the pool. She had short brunette hair and displayed large, luscious breasts.

Anna looked at me as she prepared our snacks. "That's my mom. She likes to be called by her first name, Avriel."

"Your mom is a beautiful woman."

Then Anna opened the patio door and stuck her head out. "I'm home and brought a guest. We're going to take a shower. Come and join us, if you have time. Oh... tell Jasmine that I had a flat tire. The tube needs replacing."

She closed the patio door and finished preparing the food.

"Showering with her Mama?" I thought. I did not understand the implication but only imagined that it was strange.

Anna brought sandwiches, crackers, and cheese to the table. She placed the food down, poured me a glass of red wine, and handed me the bottle. The label on the bottle showed that it was a Syrah blend from Rhone Valley.

"Help yourself if you want another glass."

She sat next to me, giving me a soft kiss on the check and brushed her leg against mine. As we ate, we discussed college, the beach, and our summer adventures. I began learning bits and pieces about her life, having grown up in Carcene. Within no time at all, we almost finished almost everything in sight. Feeling tired, I wanted to take a quick nap, but Anna's energy kept me going.

"Would you like some more?"

"No, that was delicious."

Anna took away the dishes, putting them in the sink. I got up out of my chair and stretched my legs.

With a level of domineering control in her voice, she spoke. "Come on Lizette, we have to freshen up."

She walked ahead of me as I followed her up the long elegant stairwell holding onto the antique handrail. On the second floor, she led me through wooden doors into a large bedroom. The woodwork around the fireplace immediately caught my attention. There was a king-size bed with a large ceiling mirror hanging above it. Fine art and large mirrors hung on the walls. A desk was in the corner, with leather furniture filling the room. She had antique dressers made of cherry and a large wool carpet covering the hardwood floors.

"Lizette, put your knapsack here…. in the corner."

I placed my bag down as Anna took off her clothes. She placed her bikini bottoms on the bed, but the rest of her garments went in the hamper.

As I undressed, Anna spoke. "Let me have your panties."

I handed them to her, and she threw them on the bed next to her bikini bottoms. Without saying another word, she headed into the bathroom and turned on the shower. In utter amazement, the decorative tiles completely covered the bathroom walls. Surrounding the fine marble vanity was a double sink with fancy fixtures and a large mirror. The walk-in shower could hold at least ten people.

Anna handed me a bar of soap. "Come on in. The water's fine. Let's take turns washing."

As we lathered our bodies, Anna began describing her secret family taboo in complete detail.

"My Papa, Monsieur Jean Beaupre, had passed away a few years back leaving us alone. I do not have any brothers or sisters. Since my Papa's passing, Avriel and I have developed a special relationship. I really love Avriel and cherish our female-to-female bond, but I want to be honest with you. Avriel and I slept naked in the same bed every night pleasuring until recently. We had developed a deep physical mother to daughter incestual love. We sometimes would play kinky games until wee hours of the morning. I love the smell of her body, her delicious tasty kisses, and how she makes me come. However, when we hired a maid, thing changed a bit. I was sort of …. left out of the picture."

Her juicy family stories were making me feel hot and horny. My face became flush and my puss was burning for some more loving.

"It all happened one evening. Avriel and I had been drinking wine quite heavy. We ended up in bed together, crying over Papa. Holding each other with dabbing lips, the scene suddenly turned into passionate French kisses. We shed our clothes and made love. Since that encounter, we have always been very intimate."

Anna rubbed my puss while revealing her intimate family secrets. Excited and flaming for more, I craved to ascend to yet another peaking moment. I squatted against the shower wall, opening my legs while pinching my nipples. Torching me with her skillful fingers, Anna sustained the pleasure as I imagined her words. Just the kinkiness set me in a direction that my mind had not previously ventured. A new sensuous reality had opened, and I accepted it with pleasing delight.

"When I bring someone home to have sex, Avriel sometimes likes to watch us. It makes me feel warm inside, letting her see us play around. Avriel is very open about it."

Then Anna and I started kissing deeply. Her tongue tasted delicious as it slid in and out of my mouth. Her fingers began working my clit at a faster pace. Letting myself go under the running water, I felt every ounce of her pleasure. Then, Anna instantly stopped and parted lips.

"Anna, don't stop," I begged.

"Lizette, there is something more I want to tell you. Please listen."

Looking into her eyes with a level of displeasure, she continued talking. The only thing I wanted to do was climax. "I love to have anal sex any way I can get it. Would you like to join me in an anal session after showering?"

My jaw immediately dropped to the floor as I stood there in utter speechlessness. Then, nerves shot through my flesh, right through my bowels like Mama had pushed in a mega repository. All I could think about was spasming in anal delight.

Anxiously speaking. "Anal loving is also my thing. Especially when it slides in nice and deep."

Hot and hunger for her love, we suddenly began kissing with greater affection as I wrapped my arms around her. My tongue dove deep in her mouth, licking her inner cheeks, roof, and twirling around her lingua. My head was now spinning in all directions. Then, Anna parted our lips and turned off the water.

"We can't spend all afternoon in here," she said. "We have pleasuring to take care of."

Throwing a large fluffy towel at me, I began drying off trying to contain myself.

"I have to prep up a bit. You must too?" Anna said.

Looking into the private toilet room, I saw an enema stand filled with soapy water.

"Let me go first," she said.

She walked in and closed the door. As a few minutes passed, the toilet flushed.

Opening the door, she spoke. "Now it is your turn. Want some help?"

I smiled pleasantly. "I could use some fingers."

She pulled the devise out of the bathroom and placed a new head on the tube. "Bend over and show me your puckered hole."

I kneeled on all fours, and she stuck the rubber tube up my ass, letting the water flow.

"Ok, you're filled up." I closed the door and let it go. Opening the door, "Wow, that felt so good. Let's do it again." By my last cleanout, I was feeling clean, refreshed, and re-energized.

Chapter 24

The Observer

Anna opened a drawer under the bed and pulled out a tube of edible raspberry lube.

"Stick it out," she said.

"What?"

"Your middle finger."

Extending my middle finger, she applied some gooey jell. Anna jumped on the bed getting into a doggy position with her butt in the air. With her head slightly tilted back, she reached behind and lubed her bung hole. Grabbing my soiled panties, she put them under her nose, inhaling with animation.

Letting out a long sigh, she spoke. "Lizette, I'll be coming all the way, savoring your soiled scent. By the way, the lube is also from India. Contains some delights."

Tingling exhilaration swept across my body, hearing her coltish words as I peered into the mirror. Her tits were jiggling about while displaying a mischievous smile. Anna's thrilling ride was about to start as I knelt behind her. With determination, I was going to drive her into pleasing senselessness.

I slowly circled the rim of her puckered hole with my index finger as Anna's voice echoed with the sounds of approval. After rimming around for a few minutes, my middle finger progressively slid inward right up to the knuckle. Anna's face initially cringed like she was sucking a lemon. But as I squirmed and twisted, her moans became liberated, enjoying my satisfying finger.

Then she spoke in a quick breath. "Hold it in there for a few seconds."

Firmly holding my finger in her sweet hole, her muscles contracted, squeezing my finger. She repeatedly compressed and released as I coiled about.

"Pull it out. Right now," she said.

As I did, resistance took hold of my finger.

"Now, screw me to oblivion."

127

Taking my finger, I glided it in and out earnestly, with deep penetration. Yearns of enjoyment escaped from her lips as my tempo amplified. Her sphincter muscle was working against my finger, crafting stimulating vibes. Then, I poked a few skillful fingers into her slushy hole. Dropping my panties onto the bed, Anna started rubbing her clit feverishly. Watching the visual scene in the mirror was mesmerizing. I was fingering her on one end as she pleasured herself on the other.

Picking up the pace, I rammed my writhing finger in and out, propelling her into satiated delirium. She squealed with delight as the rhythmic sensation magnified. Her body began panging as moans and groans escaped from her lips. Then, her face lit up and eyes rolled back as total pleasure swept through her love zones.

Shaking with jubilation, I pulled out my finger as Anna let loose. She rolled onto the bed, placing her face against the pillow.

"Oh my gosh," she panted.

Laying slightly immobilized, she slowly came down from her escalating ride. She turned and spoke in an easing tone. "Wow! That was so gratifying. Lizette, you really pacify me."

Not breaking the momentum, Anna quickly got off the bed and opened a drawer from underneath. She pulled out a seven-inch dildo grinning from fear to ear.

In a controlling tone, she spoke. "This is my dick. Now, it's your turn. Hop on the bed… just like me."

Wanting it badly, I obeyed her request, expecting the delights of reaching rapture. With my ass positioned high in the air, she lubed my crack and smeared some on her dick. She played with my puckered hole by making small rotating motions. Before long, my hole gradually opened like a budding rose.

Sliding the dildo incrementally in and out, she pushed her dick all the way. With my cavity relaxed and longing, I was now ready for some female tinkering. As she began screwing me with a steady stride, the heat was coming on strong. Playing with my clit, my body quivered as Anna's oozing sensation felt so deliciously satisfying.

Anna spoke lasciviously, "Come on, my gorgeous babe, fill Mama's diaper."

Wanting to release it so badly, a vibrant sensation palpitated throughout my body as the smell of sex infiltrated the air. Then, unexpectedly, she stopped and came around the bed. Her lips met mine in a delicious kiss as our tongues snaked in pleasure. Then, I watched her disappear curiously into the bathroom. With complete shock, she walked out wearing a black rubber strapon, getting me nervous and shaking.

"I've got a better idea. This is Mr. Slinky," she said.

Her cock was long, thick, and hung. It must have been nine-inches and dangling like a man's ready for penetration. She walked over to the edge of the bed.

"Suck Mr. Slinky. He enjoys being sucked and slurped," she said.

She took the dick in her hands, got on the bed, and put it on my lips. I opened my mouth and began nursing it like a hungry child. At that moment, Avriel walked to the edge of the bedroom door.

"Don't mind Avriel, she wants to play with us."

Avriel stood in the doorway bare chested. Her amazing torpedo shaped tits displayed hardened nipples. Her fingers were under her bikini, playing with her puss. I continued sucking on the enormous dick as saliva oozed from my mouth. Anna grabbed my panties and threw them over to Avriel. She took them off the floor and brought them to her nose. While fingering her clit, she inhaled my trace with sensuous craving. Then Anna got behind me and inserted her long dick into my vagina. As she pumped, my tummy felt a warm, loving sensation.

Avriel untied her bikini bottom, letting them fall to the floor. Sliding into a sitting position, she spread her legs wide watching every inch of Anna's dick screw me. Avriel continued to grind her minge as Anna was pleasure sailing my pussy with firmness. As I watched through the mirror, Anna's bowlegs reminded me of a cowgirl breaking in a horse. Her tantalizing maneuvers were pleasurably ascending me into multiple sensations. Continuing to penetrate with fervor, I bit my lips firmly. My mind slipped into a world of delight as the pleasure had insurmountably escalated. Feeling the heat of sex, Anna reached down, toying with my clit. Blood was flowing through my veins as my checks were glowing rosy pink. Breathing deeply, tremors shot with feverish felicity. Then, a burst of vibrancy overtook my mind as delightful seconds of orgasmic bliss drove my mind and body into ultimate satiation.

Trying to catch my breath, Anna got off the bed and approached Avriel. She put the long cock next to her mouth.

"You loved her scent, now taste it," Anna said.

"I'm throbbing for pleasure. Put Mr. Slinky deep in my ass," Avriel said softly. "I'm aching to get it deep."

"Not yet," Anna replied in a domineering tone.

Anna pushed the dick into Avriel's mouth as she melted into glory. Avriel's eyes were tearing with desire as she relished it with splendor. Then Anna pulled it from her mouth.

Avriel started begging for more. "Let me taste her juices. Give it to me," she whimpered. "Lube my ass."

Avriel took the cock in her mouth and started sucking on it once more. She choked a little as she wanted it badly deep inside. Then Anna jerked it from her mouth.

"Did you like my cock? You'll have to wait. Manners… our guest must come first," Anna said. "You can watch me while you finger your ass and play with your clit. Get on all fours like a nice doggy for your daughter. Show me your nice shaven puss and brown hole."

Avriel turned around, showing me her feminine bits and pieces as Anna brought Mr. Slinky over to me. I began sucking it again as Avriel got on all fours playing with herself. Anna gave me Avriel's bikini bottoms.

"Hold them to your face and enjoy Avriel," she said. "Now, my long dick is going right up your ass. My nine inch will screw you better than a man can. I going to ride you like the girl you always wanted."

Soaking wet and ready for some more action, Anna took the big cock and lubed it with plenty of jell. With her finger, she put a glob on my puckering hole and pushed some deep inside. Pressing the tip against my anus, she teased around as the pleasant sensation was dousing my pleasure zones. Then, she slowly inserted the monster centimeter by centimeter until it was working in a smooth, pleasing motion. Anal nerve endings lighted up in tantalizing delight as she rode me with mounting momentum.

Avriel sat on the floor watching intently while furiously masturbating with my panties to her nose. Immersed in the pleasurable flow, the satisfying sensation was pushing me into irrationality. Drilling me into anal orgasm, I was squealing like a pig, wanting more of her hungry cock. Gushing sensation swept through me while guttural sounds escaped from my lips. Anna reached around and found my clit as she pumped me into a frenzy. I could barely take it much longer as she played with my oyster like a guitarist to strings. Shaking in delight, I reached the edge. My mind went blank enjoying the seconds of euphoric palpitations. Rolling on the bed, I gasped while pushing my head against the comforter.

The intense sweetness finally settled down. Anna laid down beside me and placed her lips on mine. We began gently kissing and hugging. Then Avriel walked over and joined us. Our lips, tongues, and mouths shared in my taste of an incestuous journey.

Chapter 25

Avriel Invitation

Walking out the bedroom door, Avriel's head turned at the last minute. "The chef's preparing dinner for us soon. Lizette, why don't you join us? We are having escargot and salmon. It's very informal," she said eloquently.

"Sounds delicious. I just have to call home to let them know."

"Then we'll see you at the table."

As Avriel left, the mood in the room mysteriously transitioned from one of prurience into one of sophistication. Anna walked over and gave me a warm hug, enveloped with a sweet kiss.

When our lips parted, she said. "Thanks for staying for dinner. But first, I need to take a shower. How about you?"

"I definitely could use one."

Anna took me by the hand, leading me into the shower. She grabbed some fresh towels and a bar of soap.

After getting the water just right, she called. "Lizzette, the water's perfect."

I stepped in, feeling the stream of warmth against my skin. It was so relaxing after our little escapade. In sharing thoughts, a level of intimacy emerged like we had been friends for years.

"As you experienced, Avriel and I love to role play. Particularly, when we have nothing else to do. It's fun. Sometimes we dress in sexy and teasing outfits. Having a guest over always makes it even more...... you know...... stimulating."

"I understood that support and comfort are essential in a family relationship. Especially when a love one has died unexpectedly. However, incestuous kinky behavior is pure taboo. I never thought you and Avriel would be involved in such an erogenous relationship," I said. My thoughts instantly gravitated toward Alexia. "Well, my sister and I have passionate moments," I said, rationalizing.

"I will have to meet her. Especially if she is like you," she said. "What's her name, again?"

"Alexia. We're fraternal twins."

"She has an exquisite name."

With a final rinse, Anna turned the water off. She handed me a couple of fluffy bath towels from the rack. We dried each other off and walked into the bedroom.

I looked around the room. "Anna, did you see my underwear? I can't find them."

"Avriel must have taken them to the wash. Mama has extra pairs that might fit."

Anna walked out if the bedroom, coming back with a pink thong in her hand.

"Try this."

The silky-smooth material had a subtle touch. Putting the thong to my nose, I inhaled. Then, I pulled the thong up to my crotch feeling the comfort.

I gazed into the mirror. "These are really nice. What do you think?"

"Lizette, you absolutely look hot in pink. It makes your luscious nipples stand out."

My body felt very sexy as Anna inspected me with a craving stare.

"By the way, you can keep them. Mama has plenty," she added.

Deciding to go braless, I zipped up my jean shorts and put on a spare white tank top that was in my backpack. My large breasts fit snuggly into the top, leaving my nipples and dark areoles penetrating.

"I'm going barefoot. You should too," Anna suggested.

"I'm with you," I said.

A woman in a French apron walked into the bedroom as we finished dressing.

"This is Jasmine, our maid," Anna said.

Jasmine was a slim Spanish woman with brown hair and a dark complexion. Her hair was in a bun. Her crème white fingernail polish stood out. Then, I intently focusing on her bare feet. Her toenails had the same delicious crème color. The beauty of her olive skin tone and youthful facial features captured my attention. I felt my nipples getting hard staring at her. I began feeling submissive. The compulsion to lick and suck her toes mysteriously entered my mind.

Breaking my trance, Anna spoke. "Jasmine, you can pick up later. It's about dinner time."

Pacing down the stylish stairwell, Anna filled me in on a few family details.

"After we hired Jasmine, it only took a few weeks for Avriel and her to become passionate lovers. That's why Mama hired that flaming woman. Avriel sort of left me out of the picture wanting something different. You know, family probably. So, Avriel and Jasmine sleep together in the master bedroom like some type of secret marital union. Avriel fills the needs of Jasmine with perpetual stimulating delight. Jasmine worshipped the way Avriel could make her reach a cliff hanging orgasm."

Upon reaching the bottom floor, my eyes popped out. The elegance and design that surrounded me was fascinating. The décor comprised fine art on the walls, antiques on wooden pedestals, original oak flooring, wool rugs, and historic leather furniture. Things I hadn't noticed when we initially ascended the stairwell.

"Those paintings must be worth a fortune."

"Papa was an antique collector."

As I walked with Anna toward the dining room, it was almost like stepping back in time. In the center of the dining room was a large cherry table, surrounded by matching hutches that sat along the walls. An enormous chandelier hung above the dining table. French style doors led out onto a patio where a flower garden surrounded the jacuzzi.

"You can sit here. Next to me," Anna said. "Mama will join us in a few minutes. She usually sits across from me."

The table settings comprised lace and fine linens. Then Jasmine appeared with a tray of appetizers and wine glasses. Setting them on the table, there was cheese, fruit, nuts, and crackers. The chef followed behind, leaving a fresh hot baguette with butter.

"Help yourself," Anna said.

I put a couple of slices of bread, some cheese, strawberries, and a knife full of butter on my plate.

"Give me a minute to text my Mama," I said.

"Take your time Lizette," Anna replied.

While enjoying my plateful of appetizers, Avriel arrived.

"Lizette, glad you stayed for dinner."

"Thanks for the wonderful offer."

Avriel was wearing a sexy open back mini dress without a bra. The color was black and came above her knees. She wore silky nylons with no shoes. She came over giving a warm, luscious kiss. Then, the chef brought out a bottle of Cabernet Sauvignon from Chateau Lafite aged nine years. He uncorked the bottle, handed it to me, and gave me a sample.

"Lizette, give us your expert analysis," Anna said.

After taking my time inspecting, I gave my opinion. "The correct branding appears on the cork. The cork is moist and not tainted and it tastes delicious. "

The chef generously filled our glasses.

"You know your wine, Lizette," Avriel said.

"Yes, not as good as my sister. My Papa is a well-known merchant throughout Europe. We have a well-stocked wine cellar at home."

"I want to raise the first toast to the roman goddess of Voluptas," Avriel said. "It was her that brought us together."

We all lifted our glassing clinking them together. I really did not know the god but wanted to be courteous.

"Finally, I like to give a toast to Lizette for helping Anna today," Avriel said.

Giving cheers, I spoke. "No problem at all." I set my glass on the table. "It was odd that we found each other. Ended up being quite an enjoyable afternoon."

We settled down, enjoying our appetizers. I had some cheese and bread as Anna talked with Avriel about household matters. Then the conversation drifted over to me.

"Lizette, I understand you go to University," said Avriel.

"Yes, I am going into my second year studying psychology," I said.

"Did you know Anna is on the swim team?" Avriel said. "She has such a nice, firm body."

Anna looked over to her Mama with a hidden smile.

"Mama, you are embarrassing me," she said.

As our conversation continued over wine, Anna took control. "My Papa was an executive for one of the largest innovative technology firms in the world before he passed away with cancer. He left us quite a fortune. I used to go to a private school in Italy. Since his passing, I wanted to be close to Avriel. So, I attended the local university and keep active in sports. However, I miss Italy."

Avriel's softly glided up and down my leg her foot. Her fine nylons were silky smooth, having the sensation of tingling feathers. Anna had rested her hand on my thigh. She began tenderly caressing while I began sinking within their soothing advances. Then, Avriel started skimming her toes across mine with long, delicate brushstrokes. Accepting her invitation, I caressed my bare foot against her sleek nylons. Our sensual play was making me feel pleasant, appreciated, and accepted.

"Lizette, stay the night and keep us company. We are alone and you're welcome to sleep in the guest bedroom," Avriel said.

Anna looked over at me. "We could spend the night in my bed enjoying each other's company."

"I'd really like that," I said.

Avriel settled her feet next to mine as the chef brought out the appetizer.

"Escargot, my favorite," Anna said.

In tasting the snails, the melted garlic butter was amazing. Dripping a piece of bread into its juicy essence, my tongue twirled in delight. I loved the taste of garlic butter with herbs.

"The escargot is scrumptious," I said.

"Our chef has received many awards for his culinary expertise. We pay him well."

Avriel continued caressing my feet as Anna was feeling me between the thighs. When we finished the appetizer, the chef brought out the main course comprising herbed salmon, garlic mashed potatoes, and fresh vegetables. He filled our wine glasses once more as we idly chatted and touched under the table. With no time at all, we finished the main course. Jasmine brought each of us a small glass of dessert wine to complete our meal. In one chug, it was gone. I was thinking about asking for a second round, but hesitated.

"Avriel doesn't like heavy desserts. It puts on weight," Anna commented. "Did you like the wine?"

I looked at Anna. "Sweet and savory."

Jasmine came in to pick up the dishes. She placed them on her cart and headed for the kitchen. She soon reappeared without her apron and a mischievous smile on her face.

Chapter 26

Under the Table

Wrapping her toes over my bare feet, Avriel massaged, putting my mind into easing calmness. Relishing her pleasing advances, I returned the pleasure as we simultaneously engaged in stimulating arousal. Then, I peered into her dark eyes, becoming fixated and submerged. Her gaze gradually drew me into a mesmerizing state of want and submission. Feeling tangled and seduced, my mind wanted to escape, but the force of her magnetism was overwhelming. As seconds passed, her magical spell dissipated like a fog had lifted between us. Coming back to a state of unrestrained sobriety, my will to resist her exploitations had weakened.

"Lizette, you look a little tired," Avriel said. "Jasmine, why don't you give Lizette a special treat?"

Jasmine stood behind me, placing her hands upon my shoulders. I could see her movements through a wall mirror positioned directly in front of me. Pressing and pinching, she massaged my tense muscles as Anna stroked my inner thigh. I relaxed in their pacifying advances, feeling deliciously intoxicated.

Anna's fingers slid over my zipper with a penetrating rub. She turned, positioning her moist lips very close to mine. My mouth touched hers as our tongues opened in a delicious embrace. Our passion unfolded as she slid her glossa between my lips. Tasting and teasing, she unsnapped my shorts and pulled at my zipper. Her fingers worked their way under my thong, touching my soft skin. She pushed deeper and deeper while my mind became lost in her pursuit of driving pleasure.

"Anna, why don't you give Lizette a special topping for dessert," Avriel said.

Jasmine jimmied the chair away from the table. Then, Anna slowly stood up and stripped naked, revealing her tanned naked body. She finessed her way in front of me and knelt. Her hands began caressing my legs with affection, sending chills up and down my spine. Gliding her fingernails along my inner calves, she tickled and tantalized. Then she started yanking at my shorts. After tugging for a few seconds, they easily slid down my legs and over my bare feet. Anna reached in, feeling my pink thong. Slowly opening my legs. She kissed along my inner thigh, savoring, and licking within my musky scent.

Avriel was sitting across from me staring into my eyes, licking her moist lips. Her gape was deep, mysterious, and wanting.

"Feels nice, Lizette? Want a little more?" Avriel said.

There was a surreal undertone, as though her amiable words reflected a divergent meaning. Standing up gracefully, she unzipped her dress, letting it fall to the floor. Her tanned bare chest glimmered off the chandelier light. She played with her erect nipples as I stared in captivation. Squeezing and pinching, I couldn't keep my eyes off her beauty. Slowly, she peeled off her nylons displaying a pink thong. Running her nylons across her face, she inhaled, enjoying the scent. Then she slid one hand under her thong and began caressing in circles. My hunger for her flesh was on the edge of eruption. I wanted to lick her while enjoying the dripping goodness. I wanted to feel every part of her body as we played within the realm of female passion.

Temptingly, she brought her hand up to her mouth and sucked. She slowly peeled off her thong like a stripper, exposing her bareness to a fascinated audience. I was melting in my chair, watching with thirst. The seductress has brought me into her playpen. Her playmates had taken command of my body. Hypnotized into submission, all inhibitions escaped like a sex slave allowing her master to take full control without resistance.

Anna took her fingers from her puss and placed them in her mouth, savoring the taste. She played with her puss once more and pushed her fingers into my mouth. I began sucking fervently as the salver dripped from my lips.

Then, Anna gripped my wet thong leisurely and gradually pulled them off. Unbound with emerging pleasure, I spread my legs wider wanting her love. Her tongue danced up and down my inner thigh as her soft hands glided over my sensual legs. She lapped, kissed, and nibbled every portion of my flesh like a flaming feast. Her mouth was impishly leading me into a pinnacle of delight. Titillating vibrations were driving me senseless. I wanted more of her as I gripped onto the chair.

Jasmine pulled off my tank top, leaving me completely bare. Under their power, Jasmine massaged my upper body, finally reaching my breasts. She fondled and pinched my bare nipples, making me feel pain and pleasure as she licked and sucked my earlobe. The mounting satisfaction melted my dripping pussy into obedience as the carnal craze amplified. Then Jasmine strapped a leather collar around my neck. I accepted it as though it was part of their evening play.

Anna's satisfying tongue was getting closer to my shaven puss. She was teasing me crazy licking my thigh with enthusiasm. Then she placed her lips and tongue directly on my vulva as I slightly jerked with total acceptance. Her other hand caressed my legs with delicate passion. Within seconds, her fingers parted my lips, revealing my precious oyster. Placing her moist tongue into my sweetness, the sensations multiplied tremendously.

My body was draining into a state of hypnotic euphoria. I leaned backward, absorbing every ounce of their passion. My eyes drove to the back of my head, feeling the immensity of pleasure. The taction amplified, sending my mind into nirvana. Ready to explode, she moved her tongue and licked my inner thigh, tormenting me with patience and anticipation.

As I gazed into the mirror, Jasmine unzipped her dress. It fell to the floor, revealing her bare chest. Avriel approached, placing her hands on Jasmine's back touching and fondling. She started kissing her neck. Jasmine continued fondling my tits as Avriel fastened a chain to my collar. Pulling on the chain to get my attention, Avriel put her thong to my nose.

"Enjoy my wonderful scent," she whispered in a breath.

Anna's sportive mouth moved back into my pleasure zone. Her darting tongue and sucking lips were furiously French kissing my clit. Gripping the chair, the pleasure bourgeoned as Jasmine pinched and rubbed my nipples. Holding onto the intense satisfaction, my breathing became quicker. In unrestrained satisfaction, I was ready to scream in elation. Vibes swept throughout my body as my mind became engulfed in obsession. Avriel slid her thick tongue between my lips, pleasing

140

my mouth. With determination, Anna continued licking me into bliss. With eyes closed, I let out a wail of joyful gleam, finally seeing bright lights in my head. I closed my legs as my body relaxed, having enjoyed another playful session.

Jasmine unfastened the leather collar from my neck. Somewhat relieved, I realized we had been in the dining room, engaged in a lustful family game.

Then Jasmine whispered in my ear. "If you want some more, we can toy around in secret. Dominant kinky play is my game with plenty of satiating moments. You can be my sex slave."

As she spoke, a mysterious and alluring aura drew me to her. I turned around, wanting to see her nakedness. She flaunted olive skin, pointed breasts, and a slim waistline. She positioned her mouth over mine, giving me a luscious kiss. As our lips touched, nervous excitement swept through my body like a bolt of electric stimulation. I peered deep into her dark eyes, seeing an endless world of sensual fascination. Now it became apparent why Avriel wanted her as a lascivious playmate.

Silence broke as Anna spoke. "Hope you enjoyed the special after dinner treat."

"It was absolutely unexpected," I remarked.

"You girls can stay in my bedroom tonight. Jasmine and I could sleep in Anna's room," Avriel said.

"I would like that very much."

Holding onto Avriel's thong, I unconsciously put it to my nose, relishing her scent once more.

"You can put them on if you like. Of course, to keep warm," Avriel said.

As I looked into her eyes, I slowly slipped them on, watching Avriel observe me with wantonness. She licked her lips, becoming aroused by my subdued act.

Slipping her hand over her wetness, she spoke with elegance. "Lizette, you look so hot wearing my thong."

As my fingers were caressing the soft material, I said. "Our feminine scents will make me feel more at home with you,"

Avriel picked up her black nylons and tossed them over.

"A souvenir for tonight's playful event," she said.

"We will have to invite you to dinner again," Avriel said.

Avriel walked over and gave me a warm hug. Placing her arms around my neck, we traded soft, gentle kisses. Her lips were moist and delicious as we grazed our nipples bringing on a pleasant sensation.

"The host is generous and beautiful. I would love dinner again," I whispered.

Spellbinding love had emerged from lustful play. Her body chemistry attracted me like a magnet as it felt comfortable being close to her. Then, I noticed Anna watching with questionable, envious eyes.

"Mama! Lizette please," Anna spoke. "Isn't Jasmine enough?"

"Such a covetous daughter," Avriel said.

Avriel picked up her dress from the floor. "I think you girls deserve a couple of weeks' vacation. So, I'm planning to send you to Paris for a week around the end of June. You'll stay at the Four Seasons Hotel. All expenses paid, including money for shopping. Then, you can join Jasmine and myself in our home in Italy for another week of pleasuring. How does that sound?"

Anna became excited. "Mama, that would be fantastic. Lizette, would you join me?"

"I will just need my Mama's approval," I said.

"I am sure she will approve. So, it's all settled. I will arrange everything. But for now, it is time you girls get to bed."

With that, Avriel and Jasmine gave us a goodnight kiss.

We proceeded upstairs, holding hands. Upon reaching the entrance to the master bedroom, heavy double doors stood before us. The doors must have been two-hundred years old. Anna pulled them open, and we walked in. The room's appearance immediately struck me with admiration. The immense room had classical paintings on the wall, wool rugs, hardwood floors, antiques, and a wood-burning fireplace. There stood a large picture window with a full view of the enclosed, heated pool below. The moonlight pierced through the window onto the bed. The light appeared mysterious and ghostly as it gleamed off the comforter. Then, the smell of logs burning and the sound of the crackling caught my attention.

"On cool nights, Jasmine would carry the firewood to the bedroom. She would keep it going for their night session of lovemaking," Anna said.

"Do you miss sleeping naked with Avriel?"

"She connects with me from time to time during the day. But I miss her scent and warm cuddling during a cold winter's night. Mama has found a more suited lover. I care for her a lot. So, I cannot be selfish."

The bed was a contemporary style but much larger than a king-size. It could hold four people comfortably.

"Jump on it," Anna directed.

I hopped on. "You can get lost in it. It is so comfortable." As I laid down, it felt like resting on a cloud. I took a pillow and put it to my nose and inhaled. Anna jumped on the bed and looked at me.

"Let's sit in the middle and prop up some pillows. I'll turn on a video for us to enjoy."

There was a large screen television across for the bed. As Anna turned it on, three women were fondling and kissing.

"Lizette, I loved sucking on your pussy today. It is so sweet. I could taste your juices for days and still be thirsty. Are you a little sore after today's activities?" Anna said.

"Yes, but I could still use a light nightcap."

"Then, it's time for some lez play. Tease yourself with Avriel's thong on while I play with myself."

With fluttering tongues, we began meticulously rubbing our clits. The erotic sounds of pleasure coming from the video augmented the sensuality. Anna masturbated irrepressibly as I watched her face gleam of pleasure.

"While licking you under the table, I played with myself. I've been waiting to cum all night long," Anna said.

She reflectively fantasized about this evening's exploit as she was stimulating herself to climax. Her fingers began hastening with a pace as our tongues were vibrantly engaged in a steady rhythm. Then she moved her mouth from mine. I stopped playing with my clit and massaged her breasts. I put my mouth on her nipples and sucked. Moans were extracting from her lips.

143

The smell of her feminine scent was deliciously sexy. Her heart rate increased with deeper recesses. Her checks were getting flush as a warm feeling generating throughout her body. She closed her eyes and pressed back against the bedspread. Expressive twinges encapsulated her body. She moaned in deep fulfillment, achieving a creamy orgasm.

"I'm tired and need some rest. I'll turn off the video," Anna said.

I lied back on the comfort of the bed. The sound of the crackling fire echoed throughout the room. As I listened, I fell asleep thinking of the arousing words that Jasmine whispered in my ear. Then, a thought entered my mind from nowhere.

"All were welcome to taste and please within the taboo of feminine love."

Chapter 27

The Morning

I felt the cool morning air upon my face as I came into consciousness. Propping a pillow to support my back, I sat up and gazed at the fireplace, thinking about Alexia. We'd fallen asleep many nights watching the fire as the sounds of crackling wood echoed throughout the room. Within its glow and warmth, we snuggled, caressed, and kissed. Sometimes we stayed awake until the wee hours of the morning talking about anything and everything.

Anna was laying asleep naked under the covers. We slept close like a loving couple savoring each other's comfort. Her natural scent was enthralling and desirable. Her subtle skin felt sensual and sedative. Reaching down, I took off Avriel's thong and put them to my nose. I inhaled the intricate fusion created by our aromas. Its essence pacified my senses as I thought about our brief encounter last evening.

Her lips and tongue embraced me with serenity and acceptance as I became absorbed by her luring charm. Her penetrating eyes put me into a mesmerizing trance. A fervid craving drove my inner being into her mystery. Then, Anna became overtly envious, interrupting our sensual moment.

I clearly witnessed how hiring Jasmine created a separation between their incestuous bond. Lingering feelings of betrayal and resentment emerged as Anna vented in discontentment. Maybe that's why Avriel was so generous to offer a week's vacation in Paris. Perhaps, Avriel realized how her daughter must have felt about hiring Jasmine not only as a maid but a lover. All this, after losing her father to cancer.

Anna opened her eyes and lifted herself to a sitting position. Using her fingers, she attempted to comb her tangled hair.

She kissed me on the cheek. "Morning love. I treasured sleeping with you last night. Our bodies comforted well for our first time."

We glanced at each other while purposely avoiding a morning breath kiss.

"Did you enjoy last night's festivities," Anna said.

"The whole day was one magical pleasure trip from the raspberry oil to the dining table. How about you?"

"Well, I had your company.... and that's what made it exciting.... and now, you know I love anal. Can't get enough."

There was a sudden knock on the door. Jasmine peaked her head in the room.

"Breakfast for the college girls."

She walked in wearing white panties and an apron tied to the back. Her bare tits were slightly hanging from the sides. Her crème white fingernails once again captured my attention. I licked my lips thinking how much I wanted to suck her fingers and toes. My mind could not escape her penetrating words last night, suggesting dominant play in a game of satisfying moments.

"How did you sleep, Lizette?" Jasmine inquired.

"It was cozy. Your bed is so soft," I said.

Jasmine had prepared a morning breakfast tray filled with muffins, eggs, fruit, sparkling waters, and espressos.

"Hope you had a good evening as well, Anna."

Jasmine looked at Anna with complete servitude.

"I prepared two double espressos. It's just how you like it. Where would you like the tray?"

"I'll take it here." Anna replied. Anna took the food and set it between us, propping the legs of the serving tray.

"Wow, breakfast looks great," I said.

"By the way, there is sugar in the espresso. Now, I will let you love birds enjoy your meal. I have things to do."

Then Jasmine quietly left the room.

"Must be nice to have a live-in maid."

"It has some benefits.... especially when she prepares a warm breakfast like this."

Anna loved a double espresso in the morning to get her energized. She preferred it with heavy cream, a large cup, and an orange peel smeared along the rim.

She handed me a cup. "Here, Jasmine prepared a double for you too."

146

I stirred the cream into the dark liquid and added a splash of heavy cream. Anna drank some sparkling water to clear her mouth. She stirred her espresso and began sipping the hot liquid.

Anna looked at me. "Avriel seems to like you more than I expected. She had her hands all over you last night. What do you think of her?"

"Her hospitality was welcoming and unexpected," I said with a smile.

"You seemed excited about sleeping all night with her thong."

"Come on. Her body chemistry is likes yours natural and fresh. That's why I like her. She's just like you."

"Mama would have dragged you into bed with her all night, if I didn't say something. She likes the young colleges girls. Especially the ones with gorgeous bods like yours. There are many things you do not know about her."

"Like what."

"It concerns some rumors with different ladies in the upper class. But not only in this city. She has friends around the world."

"Well, why does she want us to go to Paris?"

"Since Papa's gone, she wants me to create an amorous female affair. She feels it would take my mind off Papa. So, she wants us to spend every waking moment together. She drools over the idea that her daughter being intimate with another girl. Besides, she probably feels guilty about kicking me out of bed."

"Well, I'm sure she has good intentions. However, it doesn't matter what your Mama thinks or wants. Being with you for an entire week in Paris is something I want." I brought my lips to hers, giving her a quick pecking kiss. "I'm having feelings for you. The best parts in that our friendship it that it just begun."

Silence fell between us as I put butter and jelly on my croissant and took a bite.

Anna looked at me with a sense of brilliance. "Well, since we are getting to know each other, let's do something kinky. Something unique that would set us apart within our generation.

Something that would be a lifelong remembrance of our journey into Paris as college students."

We sat there for a few minutes, sipping our espressos.

As I took another bite of my croissant, Anna spoke with an enthusiastic tone. "How about not wearing panties and bra's while we're in Paris?"

Almost choking, I wiped a bit of jelly from the corner of my mouth. It took a minute to get my words out.

"What!" I said, somewhat shocked.

Anna swallowed with immodesty in her eyes. "That would really be make our trip sensually exciting. After we get to the hotel in Paris, let's totally forget undies."

"Almost naked in Paris together," I said. "Well, it would be a once in a lifetime kinky sort of thing."

"We could even pretend that we have a committed relationship like an engagement. Just likes Mama wants... or we could even pretend that we are sisters. I'm sure Mama will get us a premiere suite."

"Easy access anywhere and every way possible," I said excitedly. "Even in public. Waxed all the way."

"In public without the pubic's," I said.

We sat there laughing almost falling out of bed as the anticipation surrounding our little erotic venture escalated. I became quite fond of Anna as we chatted in bed, sipping our espressos and eating breakfast. There was contentment in our relationship as she was getting close to me. I just savored her lush life-style and how she thought of the world. It was opening my eyes up to new erotic adventures.

Chapter 28

After Breakfast

Finishing my espresso, I placed my cup on the breakfast tray. I got out of bed and walked over to the picture window. Looking down at the Olympic size pool, the early morning sun sparkled off the blue water. Anna got out of bed and placed the tray on the bureau. Picking up her cell phone, she scrolled through several text messages and made some replies. Then, she came across the room and put her arm around my waist.

"The water is warm. I usually do my routine laps in the morning. Take a dip with me?"

"Is your Mama home?"

"Avriel sent a text. She and Jasmine went to do some shopping. Looks like we are alone."

Anna went over to the linen closet and grabbed some towels. Naked, we headed down the long stairwell into the kitchen. However, the corner of my eye caught family pictures on a bureau. As Anna was opening the patio door, I stopped to examine them closely.

"Come on, Lizette. We have some privacy before they get home."

"Go ahead. Be there in a minute."

Looking at the family photos, the three of them looked happy together. Monsieur Jean Beaupre was a tall, thin man, slightly bald, standing with a cane. His stature displayed boldness as he wore a fancy suit with a colorful neck tie. There were a few photos that depicted Anna with her classmates at school in Italy. One photo showed them all standing in front of a house by the water.

"Wow, a house on the water," I whispered.

Walking outside, I closed the patio door behind me. Anna was already in the pool concentrating on her stokes moving quickly from side to side. Her slim body moved effortlessly through the water like a squirming fish. The double espresso must have taken effect because she seemed fully motivated.

Picking a corner spot along the pool, I sat down and put my feet into the warm water.

My thoughts pondered over Avriel's generosity. Since leaving her friends in Italy, Avriel probably wants Anna to bond with new friends in Carcene. But maybe Anna is right. Avriel loves sex with young female college students.

Hanging onto the edge, Anna took a short breather. "Are you coming in?"

"No, but I could use a shower."

"Let me do a few more. I'll need a rinse off too."

As I watched Anna complete her last few laps, I grabbed the towels from a lounge chair. Anna got out of the pool and I threw one at her.

I watched her dry off her firm, naked body. "Your dad is a handsome man."

"Thanks."

"By the way, nice house by the water… in the pictures."

"It's in the province of Bari, Italy. It's one of our vacation homes. We will be flying down there after Paris."

"I have only been to Rome," I said. "With my family."

"The seafood is absolutely the best in Bari. My Papa conducted a lot of business in the city. He bought the house out of convenience. Did you see my school in the pictures?"

"Yes, do you miss your friends?"

"We'll probably visit some of them when we get there."

We headed up to the master bathroom. Anna placed some bath towels at the end of the walk-in shower. She turned the water on, playing with the handles to get the right temperature. I opened my bag and took out a pair of shorts and a tank top.

"Lizette, the water's ready."

Walking into the bathroom, there were double sinks, a private toilet, and a large walk-in shower. The mastery of the tile work was amazing.

"It must have cost you plenty for this bathroom."

"Papa liked to get the best as Mama was always pushing."

As the water ran over our heads, we began instinctively kissing. Then Anna took her lips from mine and looked into my eyes.

"Is there something on your mind?" I said.

"Do you think we're soul mates?" Anna said. Her mood changed from a sexual nature to one of sensitivity. "There's a lot more that comes with this rich package."

Our nipples were touching as I was enjoying the feeling between us. "We are sensual lovers. It's natural between us. Let's not get too serious."

Instinctively, my fingers touched her stomach, feeling her gentle skin. Our eyes focused with affection as my lips pressed against hers with endless want. French kissing, our tongues tangled and swirled with craving. My hand glided down onto her hairless genitalia. Her skin melted away in my fingers as I toyed with her delicate pearl. Then, her hand gently touched my clit, teasing me with playful penetration. Our mouths were tasting as fingers stoked delicately. She was loving me with immeasurable passion and intoxicating skillfulness. My breathing became more intense as we passionately pleased. Our clitoral play endured in oneness as our fingers moved in the chorus of pacifying delight. Flushing with conscious impulsiveness, I felt a strong magnetic bond pulling me inward. I gripped the shower door as a light flash struck within an elated plateau giving me extreme gratification. As Anna finished herself off, silence fell upon us. While relaxing in the stream of water, Anna gripped the handles turning off the shower. Desiring to get home, I quickly dried and dressed. We gave are farewell kisses and I was on my way.

Heading for home, I felt a bit empty having left a newly formed friend behind. Anna differed from Alexia, especially in the way she loved me. Her body was so unlike mine, but we connected in chemistry and passion. "Paris," I thought. The anticipation began building as I wanted to fall in love within the city's historical ambience.

Chapter 29

Check-In

A fortuitous meeting along a country road led us into the creek's seclusion. Engaging in affection, craving, and exploration, the intensity of our sensuality was unstoppable. Our quest continued within a plush setting where seduction, thirst, and satisfaction took on an amplified level of desire. Skin to skin, we brought on many blissful moments within the obsession of feminine love. The endless game of self-satisfaction continues like an unscheduled train running without a stopping point.

A couple of months had passed since the dinner party at Avriel's. During that time, Anna and I engaged in many erotic moments at the beach, the creek, and her home. However, I saw very little of Avriel because of her out of town social engagements. So, when I came to visit, we were alone, absent of Jasmines company. In spending time with Anna, we learned how to satisfy our emotional and spiritual needs. We revelled in our similarities and compromised our differences. We explored intimacy within the innocence of our youthful desires.

The beginning of July had brought on temperate summer weather. We arrived at a rail station near Carcene with Paris as our destination. Jasmine helped us unload our luggage from the trunk of the Mercedes. We gave our last kisses and hugs.

"Do you have your tickets?" Jasmine said.

Anna checked her purse. "Have them here."

"Ok...then...I'll see you in Italy."

"Tell Mama thanks. I'll call you when I get there."

We grabbed our luggage and waved as we walked to the platform to catch our train. The air around the station smelled of diesel fuel, electrical smoke, and tar. There were sounds of rail wheels rolling, squeaking brakes, and announcements of arrivals and departures. My thoughts pondered about the expectation that lie ahead within our Paris excursion. I envisioned shopping in the fashion district, partying within the social highlights, and becoming immersed in its history and elegance.

As we boarded the train, Anna selected our seats. We placed our luggage in a compartment and sat down. Fatigue had caught up with me from the anticipation of our journey.

"Mind if I nap on the way?" I asked.

"I don't mind. I'll keep an eye out for the ticket collector. But first." Anna pulled me close. "I think you're absolutely hot. Before you doze off, let me taste you."

She brought her mouth to mine and slid her tongue between my lips giving me a probing kiss. Her lingua felt tingly, full, and delicious. As I savored her pleasurable advances, I felt her hand caressing my thigh. Realizing that children were on board, I casually released my lips.

"We're in public. Manner's playgirl! Let's wait until Paris."

"Your so delicious. I could suck your mouth for hours and never get bored." Anna placed her head back against the seat. "Just think…… Mama paid for one week at the Four Seasons Hotel in Paris. We have one hundred-thousand-euros to spend on just about anything we can get our hands on."

"That's a lot of cash. Must be nice to be rich."

"Money is not everything. It's the only thing."

We broke out in a playful giggle while the last passengers boarded. Settling down in our seats for the trip, I put my head on Anna's shoulder as thoughts about the venture filled my mind. It seemed like a whole new world of autonomy and exploration was awaiting upon our arrival. Then I thought about Alexia, Valise, and Papa.

I thought, "This will be the first time that I will be without my family visiting a large city." I gradually closed my eyes and dosed off as the train sped away from the station.

After what seemed like minutes, Anna shook my shoulder, waking me up. As I opened my eyes, the train arrived.

"We're here sleepy head."

"That was fast."

"That because you were in la la land all this time."

We grabbed our luggage and followed the crowd to the transportation pickup. Then, we hunted down a taxi. As we got in, the driver took our luggage and placed it in the trunk.

"Where to, ladies?"

"The four seasons hotel," Anna said.

On the way, we snuggled in the cab's corner passing affections while holding hands. As we kissed and teased, the driver kept looking at us in his rear-view mirror. That was until Anna stuck her tongue out when he peered a bit too long.

"I think he got the message," she said, whispering.

Then, she nibbled on my earlobe, sending warm sensations throughout by body. Anna learned how to optimize stimulation during our lovemaking sessions. Her skilled lips and tongue escalated me into many pleasurable moments. Our chemistry interconnected with fluency. It felt like our friendship was eternal.

When we arrived at the hotel, the driver set our luggage on the curb. "Hope you girls have a pleasant stay in Paris."

Anna paid the driver as a chubby bellhop with a funny hat greeted us. His suit was tight, and he wore a large colorful tie.

"First time in Paris at the George."

"It's my first. My girlfriend has been here before," I said.

Anna started giggling, looking at the man's hat as he took our bags to check in.

"Lizette, wait in the lobby while I check in. The line looks long," Anna said. "By the way, I got a little surprise for you later on."

Walking into the lobby, I noticed a table with complementary coffee and a variety of brownies. I took a cup from the stack and placed it under the spout. I filled it with coffee, added creamer, and selected a brownie. Then, I sat down on a black leather sofa, enjoying the sweet taste of chocolate while sipping my cafe. Minutes later, a junior employee wheeled a cart containing freshly brewed coffee. She had a pretty face, silky long blonde hair, and a slim figure. Her uniform comprised a beige blouse and a short brown skirt. Her breasts jiggled in a teasing manner as she cleaned the table. When she bent over, her white panties became visible under her skirt. Easily replacing the empty container, she struggled a bit getting the container into place.

Accidentally, she knocked over a pile of white napkins that scattered all over the floor. Putting my cup down, I walked over to help. When I approached, I could smell her sweet perfume that had a delicious scent of berries. Picking up the napkins, my hand slid over her slender, long fingers. Turning my head, I stared into her clear blue eyes. The magic between us melted like butter on a hot biscuit. Our fingers touched for what seemed like hours. My stomach filled with yumminess and my knees felt weak. Her alluring attraction sent passionate flames throughout my body. Thoughts of running my tongue up and down her feminine tenderness entered my mind.

"Anna," I thought. "Focus girl!"

Standing up, she held out her hand formally. "I'm Cher. I'm a new hire in the kitchen as a server."

My hand accepted hers and we gently shook. "I'm Lizette. My girlfriend's is Anna Beaupre. We're staying in the hotel for a week...... on vacation."

"By the way, thanks for your help. I'll probably see you around." Then she wheeled her cart away. My heart suddenly sank with the feeling of a lost love.

Sitting back on the sofa, I had a desire for her like soft vanilla ice cream.... Looking at the front desk, Anna finally made her way to the clerk.

"Reservations for Anna Beaupre," she said.

"Ok. Let me check," he said, typing into the computer. "Give me a moment...... I will need a credit card and identification."

He read the information on the computer screen. "Mademoiselle Beaupre, you're upgraded to the suite viewing the Eiffel tower."

"I just need you to put your initials here, here, and here and sign there," the clerk said.

Anna initialed and signed.

"Here's two electronic keys. Have a pleasant stay. Anything you need, call us."

Giving a room key to the bellhop, Anna approached me with a big smile. "Looks like we are in for a treat. Mama paid for a suite viewing the Eiffel tower."

The bellhop took our luggage as we accompanied him up the elevator to our room. He opened the door and handed Anna the key. Leaving our luggage, Anna tipped the bellhop, and he scurried off. My eyes immediately widened, taking in all the elegant features of the suite. The exquisite chambre had a kitchenette, bar, a king-size bed, and an elegant lounging area.

"Avriel knows how to treat a dinner guest," I said.

"Mama is always generous. You just need to be careful or she will have you in the palm of her hands."

"You don't have to worry about that...... Do you mind if I take this dresser?"

"Not at all."

Placing my clothes in the drawers, I noticed a bottle of red wine on the bar.

Going over to the bar, I picked up the bottle and read the label. "Cabernet! Well, I am going to start our vacation off on the right foot? Want a glass."

"I could definitely use one. I just have to make a quick call to Avriel, letting her know we made it to the hotel."

After unpacking, I found a corkscrew and opened the bottle. Taking two glasses, I filled them and handed one to Anna. I strolled over to the window, pulling up a sofa chair. Sipping the wine, I peered out into the cityscape. The Eiffel Tower was a golden wonder, putting on a brilliant light-show. Sitting back in the chair's softness, I couldn't believe that we were in Paris at the George.

"Paris, a city that never sleeps," I uttered. "Anna, come relax with me."

"In a minute. I feel gritty and want to take a shower."

I got up, dimmed the lights, and sat back on the soft cushiony chair. Savoring the wine, my mind fell at ease. Just think, two kinky females enjoying a week in Paris and then Italy. How did I end up in Paris enjoying this wonderful view? As I stared out the window, the sky was dark, allowing for the lights of the city to stand out. I took another sip and looked at my nails.

"I will need to get a pedicure and manicure by the end of this week. I have to look good for Avriel," I thought.

I poured another glass as Anna pulled up a chair wearing a white fluffy robe.

"Looks comfy," I said.

"There's one for you too."

Anna sat looking out the window.

"Been here before."

"Many times…. that was when Papa was alive."

"Must have been hard."

"After leaving Italy and getting back to Carcene, I never really knew how much I missed him. He was always there for me. I just took it for granted. Mama seems to be the one that expresses little feeling. She rarely talks about him. So, I question her sincerity. She is with so many women in those secluded upper-class clubs. I can see why it might not be such a significant loss. Besides the inheritance."

"What types of clubs?"

"Actually, they're very exclusive. Jasmine knows, but keeps it a secret. Every time I ask, she avoids the topic."

"Avriel has such a mysterious aura about her. She can seduce me in a second."

"Avriel can easily seduce anyone. She has a certain way around females by hypnotically alluring them into her arms. Just like she did with you. Well, it wouldn't be surprising if she and Papa even had sex after me."

"Papa," I said.

"Probably hidden mistresses in many European cities. A wealthy man can get around easily. Money attracts the most beautiful woman for a night out on the town. You can get anything in secret…. if you have the cash."

I poured Anna another glass.

She looked up at me. "Lizette, you definitely fulfill my burning desire. Thanks for joining me."

"Wouldn't miss it for the world." With her sensual words, I got up from the chair and kissed her. "Shower time before I collapse in bed."

"Could you turn off the lights? I like to see the city in the dark."

"Not a problem."

I turned off the lights and walked into the bathroom. Turning the shower on, I took my clothes off and stepped in. The cool, flowing water elevated my senses. Feeling clean and refreshed, I was in the mood for pleasuring. Getting out of the shower, I toweled dry and blow dried my hair. I dabbed a little perfume on my body. I went to the bed thinking Anna had slipped under the covers. However, she was not in bed and nowhere in sight. Then, a hidden voice caught me by surprise.

"Time for our first night of fun and games. Close your eyes. Don't peak. Now, get in bed," she commanded.

Hearing her voice in the playfulness of darkness, I anxiously obeyed. Closing my eyes, I gradually felt my way onto the bed. Within seconds, I could feel her close to me.

"I have a gift for you. Open your eyes."

My eyes immediately popped out of my head. She was wearing a black veined nine-inch strap-on dildo. I never thought our first screwing session in Paris was getting it on with Anna wearing a monster.

"My cock wants to love you. Come on. Suck me off, my love."

Without haste, I got down on my knees, positioning my mouth over the orifice and began sucking for desire. I desperately wanted that big thing stuffed in me.

"I'm going to shoot my goo all over your pretty face."

Having put edible berry lubrication on the cock's surface, it tasted sweet and fruity. Savoring and slurping every ounce of her black dick, my mouth was working the shaft like a girl who hadn't had sex for months. In my mind, I was only thinking of one thing.

"Now be a good little girl and get on the bed with your ass high in the air," Anna said nervously.

She took some more lube and coated her cock, putting extra on the tip. Getting behind me, she played with my puss, getting it nice and juicy. I felt the delicious pleasure of her probing fingers as she rubbed and toyed, bringing me into dripping wetness. Then, she positioned the cock to my vag and slowly eased it in inch by inch. Having entered all the way, she escalated the pace, moving her hips back and forth as I felt a finger feeling my bung hole.

"I know you like it there, too."

"Oh yeah, take charge commando, give me some heat."

"I'm firing my rockets. You're going to get multiple explosions."

Anna had placed some lube on my anal crevice and slowly inserted her finger. She was screwing me with the thick dick as she poked me with her squirming finger. Letting myself become absorbed in the thrilling ride, her strokes were flowing like gravy on hot potatoes. Screaming for joy, she propelled me with that black rod like lightening into ecstasy. Her nails dug into my back as I was crying for more. Within a matter of minutes, it was like gold. I shuddered and shook as my mind ascended into the zenith of ultimate pleasure. She pulled out her finger and slowly dismounted. Taking off the strap-on, she got out of bed and placed it in the drawer. Then she turned off the lights.

Sliding next to me, she whispered, "I love getting you wet. Remember, no panties tomorrow."

We gently kissed and fell asleep in each other's arms.

Chapter 30

Waking in Paris

Opening my eyes to the welcoming morning sunlight, the sounds of the city resonated in the distance. This was my first time in Paris without my family, as a sense of independence led me into slight nervousness. The realization that I will need to financially support myself in the future materialized. Mama and Papa won't be around forever giving me handouts. Maybe, I should think about working in the family business. The income is stable. Besides, Alexia always bugs me to help her. So, I know there's plenty of work.

"Oh…. must text Alexia," I muttered. "With all the excitement, I had forgotten to contact her."

Forcing myself out of bed, I dragged myself to the coffee machine and got a fresh pot brewing.

"Where is that cell… on the dresser?" I thought. Upon grabbing it, I texted Alexia.

'We arrived in Paris safely. Tell Valise and Papa all is well. Love you very much.'

Sending out the text, a sense of relief came over me. "Safe and well in the sweet arms of Anna," I thought. "With a lot of money to spend."

Walking into the bathroom, I turned on the shower and stepped in. The cool flowing water enkindled me into the new day. As I fidgeted with the knobs, attempting to get a warmer temperature, thoughts of today's adventures brought about curiosity, anticipation, and inspiration. Last time I was here, we stayed in a cheaper hotel for only a few days. We didn't get around too much because Papa was working during the day. I stepped out of the shower and grabbed a towel to dry off. The fresh aroma of coffee had carried itself to the bathroom. Inhaling that morning scent, it was getting me motivated for the start of a brand-new day, in Paris.

I put on a robe and sauntered to the coffeemaker pouring a cup adding cream and sugar. Pulling up a cushioned chair, I sat back sipping my coffee, gazing out the large picture window. I fell silent, looking at the bustle of the urban landscape. The city's progress moved like an unstoppable frictionless machine. Its intricate parts were fluid, vibrant, and captivating. Yet, each component served a distinct purpose and destination. Then, there's Anna and I adding to its complexity with our own fated function and purpose. What will we explore? What will we do? We never really planned anything.

Getting up from the comfort of the chair, I poured another cup.

By now, Anna awoke with a smile on her face, rubbing her eyes. "Up already, my love," she said.

"Shower energy… and the city's wakening call."

"I need some of what you got."

"There's plenty of it. All you have to do it listen to the sound of the city."

In a daze, she walked into the bathroom, turned on the water, and got in.

Last night's performance was unexpected and electrifying. She quenched my female thirst as a skilled partner with nothing left to be desired. That's the benefit of having an athlete for a sensual lover. Whatever time of day or night, Anna could turn on my switch. She could flip me like a pancake and do me any way she wanted. Not returning the favor was selfish, but she planned the surprise to be a one-way pleasuring session.

Wearing a towel around her head, she walked out of the bathroom and greeted me with a warm kiss.

"No laps today."

"Didn't get up early enough. The cozy bed was like a magnet that kept me dreaming."

"Want some coffee. Made extra."

"Thanks, but no thanks. I'll wait for breakfast. Double espresso will be my wake-up call."

Then I looked at Anna with deep sincerity. "Thanks. I truly embraced the passionate ride last night. Mating in Paris for the first time felt so wonderfully beautiful. Just letting myself go drove me quickly into ecstasy. I've never screamed so loud."

"Glad you enjoyed yourself. I enjoy giving surprises because they make me feel good."

We joined lips and started tonguing around a bit. The lusciousness of her kiss was incessantly mouthwatering. Her orifice was very moist and fresh, as her taste was pleasantly appeasing. Not getting enough of her, we slowly parted lips.

"Very sweet, my love," she said. "There's more where that came from. But we need to get moving or we will end up in bed all day making love."

"That's not an awful choice."

"Avriel paid a lot of money for us to enjoy Paris and not ourselves."

She got up and blow-dried her hair while I finished my second cup.

With the last drop gone, I needed to get myself moving. So, I placed the cup on the dresser and opened the dresser drawer. Pulling out some clothes, I tried to narrow down what to wear.

"Miniskirts… let's wear miniskirts," I said.

"Good idea. Mine are teasingly high and a perfect fit."

"So, why not wear skirts and sneakers? Did you bring yours?"

"What an athlete without sneakers!"

"I love it. Sneakers, a miniskirt, no bra, no panties, and my white top," I said. "It's going to make me feel licentious and erotically naked."

Putting on my white tie-back crop top, I looked in the mirror to straighten it. My nipples and areoles were piercing through the material. I turned to Anna, cupping my tits.

"Do you like?"

"Your tits look gorgeous…. of course, in that top."

Anna came near, feeling my nipples through the fabric. "Nice," she said.

Then, a quick sensual excursion came into mind, but I realized time was of the essence.

"Let's get breakfast before I ask for more," I said. "By the way, where is a good place to eat?"

"Dumont's café. It's just a short walk away."

"I better get some makeup on."

"Don't be too long."

"Out in a flash… promise."

Within no time at all, I finished applying makeup. We grabbed our purses and heading out the door.

When we arrived at Dumont's, we sat down outside with Anna sitting to my right. We placed our orders as the waitress came around. When the café arrived, I put two sugars and added cream. Anna ordered a double espresso just the way she liked it.

"What's the plan for today?" I said.

"Let's visit one of the city's popular fashion districts first. Then, play it by ear."

"Anything in mind."

"Le Marais has some great shops. I need to buy Avriel a thank you gift. Have you ever been?"

"No, this will be my first in that area."

"You'll love walking down the cobblestone streets and visiting the old square," she said. "It's a Jewish community. You got to try the pastries."

I nudged Anna while whispering down towards the table. "Those boys are looking at us."

A few tables down, two college age males were staring like they wanted to pick us up.

"Bet they can see my legs under the table," I said. "It's playtime. Put your hand on my leg. Go ahead. I will open my skirt a bit."

Anna caressed my thigh as I spread my legs just wide enough for them to get a quick peek at my puss. Their faces lit up like a bolt of lightning. Within seconds, I closed my thighs to their dissatisfaction. We started giggling and passed quick kisses, adding our tongues. When they looked away, my skirt opened wider, then closed, catching them off guard as they peered back. We were having a grand ole time at the coffee shop playing hide and seek.

"Too bad there weren't a couple of hot chicks sitting there," she said.

"Anna, you're turning into your Mama."

163

"Not by a long shot. But one on three would really be deliciously appetizing," she said. "All we have to do is open wide for lunch."

"Anna, you're a dirty little girl."

Before long, the boys had gone on their way. Asking for the check, we finished breakfast prepared for a day of shopping.

"Let's walk to Le Marais and take our time. We can get a taxi on the way back," Anna said. "It's less than an hour away. Besides, I need the exercise."

As we swaggered down the street showing off our booty, Anna was enjoying the workout. We sporadically stopped to fondle and kiss, not caring about who was watching. It felt so natural as we pleasantly touched in public. I loved that firm, athletic body of hers. In rubbing her ass, I enjoyed exposing it to the world. But what I liked best were the warm breezes that swept through my legs.

"Glad we brought sneakers," I said. "Now, I can enjoy Paris from the ground level and embrace the outdoors."

A billboard caught my attention as we proceeded to our destination.

"Hey look, a Venus lingerie show. Holdup, I want to read it. It's two days before we fly to Italy," I said.

Anna got behind me and started feeling my bare butt as I read the details. Then she turned and kissed me as a tickling sensation flowed across my body.

"Later on, my love. First, let's call and see if tickets are still available. Are you into it?"

"Sounds like an adventure."

Anna called the number on the sign and started talking with customer service.

"It's an exclusive woman's show. Tickets are still available."

"How much for the best seats?"

Anna inquired about front row seating. "The catwalk is selling for five thousand euros per seat."

"Let's do it Anna. We got the cash. The card will still have plenty of money on it."

"It sounds like fun. I'll get their location."

She took out her cell phone from her purse, pulled out the stylus, and wrote the address on the note. The street was full of taxi's running back and forth. With ease, we hunted one down.

Getting in the cab, Anna said, "Rue Jean Jaures, merci."

When we arrived, Anna told the cab driver to wait until we got back. We walked up to the center's ticket booth. There were six cat walk tickets left; we purchased two.

"Great, up front in high fashion," I said. "Now, let's find some topnotch fashions of our own."

Getting into the cab, Anna asked the driver to drop us off on rue Pavée at Le Marais. Upon arrival, Anna paid and tipped the driver. Being my first visit to Le Marais, I was feeling very spirited. Anna anxiously led the way, searching for something.

"Where we headed," I said.

"I need a midday energy fix. My brain requires sweets and caffeine. After, we can shop at the local boutiques."

Arriving at Anna's favorite pastry shop, she devoutly acclaimed that they have the most delicious pastries in town. As we stood outside, we gently kissed in a moment of bubbly excitement. She grabbed my hand, opened the door, and we walked in.

Peering at the baked goods sent my mind into sugar and butter land. The pleasant scents lured my salivary glands into pure, dripping desire. It was a tough decision, but I made one as Anna selected what she desired. We added two coffees to the order and paid for it. Upon looking around, I noticed there were no seats in the bakery or outside.

"Where are we going to sit?" I inquired with a blank stare.

"There are plenty of benches in a beautiful nearby park. It's about one block away. Follow me."

We left the shop and approached the park. There were well-trimmed trees, hedges, and pretty flower beds scattered in the landscape. As we sat down on a bench, I could smell the pleasant fragrance of the flowers and the fresh cut green grass. I walked over and picked a tulip and placed it in Anna's hair.

"For my beautiful lover and playmate."

Her face fell to a little embarrassment as a couple watched from a few benches down from us. I gave her a soft kiss and sat down to enjoy the delicious treats.

Then Anna pulled the cell phone from her purse. She pulled the stylus out and opened a note. "Let's plan a shopping route for this afternoon."

In opening the map app on my cell phone, I began searching for local shops in our vicinity. By the time we finished the last sip of coffee, we had carefully mapped out our afternoon shopping route.

"How about we end up for a glass at the wine bar close to the hotel? Then, we can have dinner at that popular Italian near the restaurant," I said.

"I'm all for it," Anna said.

Enjoying the silence of nature, we sat contented about our plans. The fresh air of the park reminded me of the creek. Turning her head, Anna looked at me with that kinky face of sensuality. I knew what she was thinking before the words flowed from her lips.

"How about a quicky before we shop? I know a public bathroom in the park."

I raised my eyebrows, giving her a signal of acceptance. Anna led me down a narrow path to the public restrooms. We threw our trash away and securely locked the door behind us. Without hesitation, we embraced in a warm hug, holding hands and gently kissing. I nervously trembled, holding her close, knowing our intimacy had reached a level of dependency. Every time we were about to make love, the realization became more vivid. There was submission, mixed emotions, and ambiguities. Then, our absorbing desire overcame all uncertainty, leading me into selfless satisfying pleasure.

She removed some anal lube from her purse. Removing each other's clothes quickly, we stood naked in the heat of desire. She lubed her anal cavity, wanting me to pleasure her. I could feel the caffeine augmenting my erotic drive. My finger reached down, feeling her anus as our mouths meshed in a strong bond. Her taste was delicious as she drove her tongue into my mouth, lapping my inner cheek. Then our lips parted as tongues fervently flickered and licked with thirst. We caressed and pinched nipples, getting ourselves aroused and wet. I brought my lips down to her nipples, sucking and lapping while working my finger. Encircling with tenderness, my finger pressed inward, pushing, and pulling as she gasped, craving the sensation. I brought my lips down to her clit, licking as I penetrated her love canal.

"Don't stop, Lizette. Give me your love," were the words breathing from her lips as she wiggled in desperation, wanting more.

Within a matter of minutes, she tensed up and came as I sucked her dry. Slowly, I slid my finger out of her back hole as I kissed my way to her lips.

I put one hand around her neck and the other over her puss. Anna did the same. Sliding my fingers over her vag, I leisurely glided, feeling her smooth skin. Finding my erect oyster, her fingers probed pacing in tempo. Rubbing each other with electrifying gratification, I felt each stroke vibrate through my body. With every bit of energy, our fingers brought on escalating animation. Our whimpering voices became shallow within our deep, penetrating kisses. We held our ground in abounding felicity as our hands worked with pleasing skill. Gripping each other tight, my mind escaped into space as my breathing intensified. I gripped her neck as trembles awakened me into the blissfulness moment of rapture.

Anna spoke in a relieving tone. "Kinky in the bathroom. That was absolutely tremendous."

In complete nervousness, we washed up and put our clothes on quickly. Upon unlocking the door and walking out, I felt totally fulfilled by our little escapade. Like a romantic couple, we held hands strolling out into the sunny afternoon inhaling the vegetation of the park.

"Where is our first shoppe?" I said.

Anna reached into her purse, grabbed the cell, and opened her notes. "Let me see. Looks like the first stop is Moiselle. It's near Rue Normand."

As we chronologically progressed through the many clothing shops trying on the latest styles, we either liked the styles or hated them. Some clothes were hot and trendy while others were not quite our style. Time seemed to pass quickly as we kept busy shopping in the La Marais district. Then I looked at my cell phone.

"Anna, it's nearing five o'clock. Some of the remaining stores on our list are almost closed. We have all day tomorrow why rush. How about we end the shopping day and head up for a glass of wine? We can always have an early start in the morning and finish up. Beside my legs are a little tired."

"I could use a glass of wine. Let's call a cab. Then we can also have dinner at that Italian restaurant."

We departed the La Marais district with the cab, dropping us off in front of the hotel. Being only one block from the wine bar, we first brought our shopping bags to the hotel room. Then we quickly showered, changed clothes, and putting on loafers.

Next, we stopped and had a couple of glasses of wine, chatting about our day. Having gotten a good buzz, we proceeded across the way to the Italian restaurant.

"A booth for two," I said. "Right this way," the attendant said.

Sitting across from each, we took our loafers off. Anna put her feet on mine, giving me a foot massage. I returned the favor as we caressed under the table. The server came by and we ordered a glass of wine and some food. Then, I put my foot between Anna's legs, slipping it under her skirt. Anna closed her legs slightly.

"Wow, that's nice and warm," she said. My naked foot rubbed against her minge as I curled my toes inward. Then Anna's phone rang. It was Avriel.

"Yes, mom everything is fine. We stopped off at an Italian restaurant for dinner. Ok, I will. Talk to you later," Anna said. "That was mom checking in."

Upon finishing dinner, we ended up relaxing at the hotel pool with a bottle of wine before heading to bed.

Chapter 31

Claudia

Morning had arrived too early. Peering at the alarm clock, it was seven o'clock. Anna had already left unnoticed for her morning swim. Getting out of bed, I called room service and ordered breakfast.

"It should arrive by the time Anna gets back," I thought.

Getting a fresh pot of coffee brewing, I stepped into the shower. I washed under the tepid pulsating stream with a soft, soapy sponge. Upon rinsing, I dried off and put on a white downy robe. Progressing to the coffeemaker, I poured a cup, adding cream and sugar. Then I plopped myself on the cushioned chair, holding the warm cup in both hands.

Peering into the dawn of Paris, my mind wandered thinking about the Venus models parading on stage wearing sexy lingerie. I really didn't know what to expect, never attending one before. But it was something that I always wanted to do. It was so odd that we ran into the billboard on the street as we strolled to La Marais. Then, I thought about my tight budget and their expensive line of clothing.

A knock on the door startled me.

"Breakfast…. that was fast? Coming," I said, snappishly.

As I opened the door, it was the girl that I met in the lobby at the coffee station.

"Cher!" I said, looking surprised.

She stood there with her hands on the cart, peering into my eyes with a sense of desire.

"Mind if I come in."

Hesitating for a few seconds, I responded. "Yes…. sure… let me get out of your way."

The smile on her face was flirtatious as she wheeled the cart into the room with a modish swagger.

I pointed to the big picture window. "Place it there on the table next to the sofa chairs." Standing like a speechless statue, I watched her gorgeous body strut across the room. My heart rate escalated and my puss felt tingly warm. Putting down the tray, she smiled and looked straight into my eyes. Unexpectantly, she boldly stripped off her panties, placing them on the tray. My eyes lit up as I swallowed impulsively, catching a glimpsed of her soft shaven peach.

As my knees weakened, she spoke in a soft, sensuous voice. "Lizette, enjoy your sweet treat." Then, in a captivating saunter, she glided out the door while pushing the cart ahead of her.

As she disappeared, Anna returned, heading straight into the bathroom.

"Morning love, have to pee and shower."

Craving confusion ran through my head.

"Did I just imagine what happened?" I whispered.

Pulling myself out in a state of disbelief, I finally came to my senses looking at the white fringed panties sitting on the tray.

Knowing Anna was under the water, I spoke in a piercing voice. "Breakfast is getting cold."

"I won't be long," she shouted. "Just need a quick rinse off."

Taking the pair of panties off the tray, I put them to my nose, inhaling her feminine fauna. Her scent melted me away in the zone of burning obsession. Realizing that Anna will be out shortly, I quickly dashed to the dresser and hid them deep inside a drawer.

Almost breathless, I sat back down in my chair and picked up my cup of coffee. Anna finally strolled out of the bathroom drying her hair as I sat there like nothing happened.

"Just in time. Breakfast is still warm," I said, anxiously.

"I'm starving. My workout was intense. Ran on the treadmill after my laps. You should join me."

"I just lack the motivation. Sometimes, it's hard getting up at the crack of dawn. Especially after a night of drinking wine. I don't know how you do it."

Anna sat on the chair next to me, propping her legs up in a lotus position. She picked up the cup of double espresso from the tray, smelling its deep flavor.

"Nice and strong. Just the way I like it," she said.

Anna sat staring into space while taking small sips of her hot drink. Seemingly, her thoughts were reflecting upon something pleasant because she had a big smile on her face. Putting the cup down, she pulled her plate close. She cut into the omelet with her fork and took a bite.

"Mm…. the food in the hotel is scrumptious. The omelet is just the way I like it."

After swallowing a mouthful, I spoke. "The service is also awesome. I think we should order breakfast here for the next few days."

"Great idea. It is so convenient. This way, we can be right on our way in the morning without having to stop."

Enjoying my omelet and toast, the atmosphere in the room was quite relaxing as I intermittently peered at the tower. Then, an idea popped into my mind.

"Anna, I was thinking about a change of plans for this morning. Why don't we get a tour of the Eiffel Tower first thing? We have all afternoon to complete our list at La Marias. Besides, I always wanted to observe the city from the summit."

Her mind seemed to have drifted elsewhere as she took another sip. "Taking a tour of the tower… first thing… would be quite interesting. I like to check it out."

My thoughts couldn't escape Cher as we were quietly finishing our meal. Cher's unexpected actions just kept coming back to my mind as I yearned to pleasure myself. Putting my fork down, I stood up in a state of bewilderment.

"Well, that was a splendid meal. How about you?"

"Breakfast was really tasty," Anna said. "I'm full."

"Let me take the tray out," I said.

Anna pulled her second cup of expresso from the tray. I lifted it off the table, opened the hotel room, and placed the try on the hallway floor. As I came back into the room, Anna had already gone into the bathroom to blow-dry her hair. I began picking out some clothes for the day's adventures. Then I noticed Anna's blue workout top on the floor. Picking up her top, I inhaled the material, desiring to elate myself in her oils and swelter. To my surprise, the scent was not hers but that of an unfamiliar perfume.

171

"Is that why she ran to the shower so quickly?" I thought. My mind went blank thinking about her with another female. Then, I remembered breakfast the other day when she mentioned the desire for two hot babes pleasing her.

Coming out of the bathroom, Anna spoke, "Well, we better get moving or we will miss the morning train."

With my mind in confusion, our conversation fell silent. We finished dressing and headed out the door.

It was another lovely shopping day in Paris. The morning was cool as we made our way to the tower. Upon arriving, we bought two tour tickets at the entrance. In no time at all, our guide showed up and the tour began. The guide methodically discussed the history and legends of the tower as we stopped at the various levels. Upon reaching the summit, the panoramic view of the city was spectacular. We saw the Basilica, Golden dome, Arc de Triomphe, Seine River and much more. Next, we proceeded to the second floor to the restaurant to catch a quick bite. Then, we called a cab and headed back to Le Marais, beginning where we left off.

Gradually working through each shop on the list, we tried on a ton of clothes but just made a few minor purchases. Before long, it was late in the afternoon. The next store on the list was a boutique known for younger lady's called JFTP. As we walked in the double glass doors, a loud beeper went off, startling me. Slightly nerved from the sound, a lady with a welcoming smile greeted us.

"Good afternoon. My name is Claudia. By the way, sorry for the loud noise. Sometimes, I'm in the back storeroom."

"My name is Anna. This is Lizette."

"If there is anything that you need, please ask," she said politely.

Claudia seemed pleasant and easygoing, giving us plenty of space to enjoy our shopping experience. A woman in her mid-thirties, her hair was dark red, falling well below her shoulders. She had a pretty face, a slim physique, and medium-sized breasts. She wore a V-neck split mini dress that displayed her long silky legs. The lingering fragrance of her alluring perfume caught my attention as she came near me.

Casually looking around, my interest started peaking. The fashions in the store were more inclined toward my taste. In picking up a skirt from the rack, I felt the material and fancied the design.

"Anna, what do you think?"

"I like the pattern," she said.

"I agree. Why not take our time?"

"I'm ok with that."

Gradually searching through the racks, I accumulated an armful of clothes. Claudia, noticing my accrued selections, casually approached.

"Looks like you're needing some help."

"Yes, I'd like to try these on."

"Follow me. The dressing room is right over here."

I followed Claudia to the dressing room, and she unlocked the door. Turning around, she curiously began eyeing my physique.

"Would you mind if I take your measurements?" There was a slight pause, as though she was waiting for a quick response. "This way, I can find clothes that fit you to perfection. Believe me, I will not disappoint you. It will astonish you at what we carry."

Hesitant at first, I nodded in agreement. "No one has ever asked me. I guess it wouldn't hurt."

We stepped into an unusually large fitting room. Being embarrassed about the lack of a bra or panties, I slowly took off my clothes, placing them on a bench. Her eyebrows raised slightly as I stood completely naked in front of her.

"Here… hold your arms up toward the ceiling so I can get around you," she said.

Raising my elbows above my shoulders, Claudia glanced up and down my body with an unfulfilled look in her eyes. She gently licked her lips and swallowed. Without hesitancy, she moved behind me. Reaching around with her arms, she measured. Immediately, I could feel nervousness as her fingers gently glided over my skin, creating a soft and inviting impression. Her soft hair brushed affectionately against my cheek while her fingers accidentally grazed my nipples. The warm emanating sensation from her movements sent chills up and down my spine. My nipples hardened as her breathing intensified.

Adding a layer of divergence to our intimate contact, she spoke in a sharp, professional manner. "There, all set. I think I have a few ideas that you may like. Let me bring out some clothes from the back." Then she spoke in a tender voice. "By the way, you have a very sexy body. Be back in a flash."

Standing naked, moments of sensual warmth lingered. Realizing that my heart rate was above normal, I reached down and breathlessly touched my sweet twinge. Feeling inadvertently seduced by her actions, I took a relaxing breath inward. I looked at my body in the mirror, caressing my nipples. I thought about her grazing fingers that unconsciously brought me into a state of arousal.

"Wow, she got me really excited," I whispered. It was like someone had unconsciously seduced me.

Anna was still up-front shopping as I heard wheels rolling down the hall. Claudia was pulling a rack full of fashions. Picking up my top from the black cushioned bench, I pressed it against my chest. Stepping out of the dressing room, Claudia placed the rack in front of me.

Speaking in a sophisticated tone, she said, "These are just some of my eye-catching styles designed for a girl of your age and stature. Pick what you want…. there is more to come."

Looking through the rack, I picked a few dresses that looked appealing as Claudia pulled some from the rack. Then, I slipped a dress over my head.

"Claudia, could you zipper it up?" I asked, nonchalantly.

Her fingers tenderly touched along my back as she pulled the zipper to the locking position. Then she stared at my body with fascination.

"Wow, you look hot in that."

I immediately blushed, sensing a powerful chemistry that had emerged between us.

"Thanks," I said, softly.

Suddenly, Claudia became enthused. "You know what? I'm going to close the shop. We would normally close in half an hour, anyway. This way, I can concentrate on your needs more efficiently."

Claudia walked to the front door and turned the sign around to indicate the store was closed. She pulled the blinds down and locked the door.

"Anna and Lizette come here. I have a special treat for you. We have a special room in the back with plenty of mirrors. Come this way."

Anna had a handful of clothes picked out and followed along.

Claudia rolled the rack to a large curtain that was hiding behind a set of double doors. Pulling the curtain away, she opened the doors. After turning on the lights, she rolled the rack to the center of the room.

"This is the VIP room for our special customers. Clients love it in here. We have mirrors that surround the walls, a plush carpet to keep your feet warm, a bar for entertaining, leather couches for lounging, and a private bathroom with a shower to freshen up."

She walked over to the bar and pulled a couple of chilled bottles from the refrigerator. "Would you ladies like a glass of champagne?"

Anna and I were absolutely astonished by the setup. I've never seen a special dressing room with all the amenities to serve customers. Especially with champagne.

"I'll take a glass," I said.

"Yes, please," Anna replied.

"Sit, relax, and enjoy. We'll take our time through the lineup."

She uncorked a bottle, filled two large glasses, and handed us each one.

"These are not your normal size champagne glasses," Anna said.

"We like to be generous to our VIP guests. We had those specially made at a glass blowing factory in Paris."

Filling a glass for herself, she took a large sip. Making ourselves comfortable on the couch, we sipped champagne, learning about each other. We discussed what we liked to wear and even informed her of the Venus show. As our glasses became empty, Claudia filled them once more.

"Now that I know what you like, let me pull some designs out of our special inventory. But Anna, let me measure you up before I pull from our special stock."

Anna took off her clothes, and Claudia measured.

"By the way Lizette, feel free and try anything from the rack that you like. If you run out of interests, I'll fill it up again from the back. By the way, we have styles that are only for our VIP guests. You will not find them up front. We keep them in a special place in the back."

Claudia got up from the couch and disappeared, carrying her glass. There was a round wedding stand in the middle of the room with a large chandelier above it. Anna and I took turns trying on clothes while displaying them to each other. Claudia just kept bringing clothes out while carrying the rejected ones back. Making our final selections, we set them aside to purchase.

"I know some clothes are dusty. Why don't you ladies take a quick shower and meet me on the couch? The bathrobes are hanging in the bathroom closet. By the way, I'm throwing in a nice discount."

"Thanks," Anna replied as she gave Claudia a credit card.

Completing the transaction, she bagged our merchandise and placed the bags by the back door of the store. We took a quick shower, ending up on the couch drinking champagne while wearing pink bathrobes embroidered with the store's logo.

Claudia came back into the VIP room. "Finally, business is over for the day. I hope you don't mind me getting naked and joining in on the fun? But I must take a shower first and put on some perfume and fruity lipstick."

"We have plenty of time," Anna said.

"Help yourself to more champagne. There's another bottle in the fridge."

Claudia nervously took off her mini dress in front of us, exposing a luscious slim body. In wanton captivation, she unsnapped her bra and stripped off her black stockings and white panties. In a matter of seconds, the sound of water flowing caught my attention.

Placing our champagne glasses on the table, I brought my lips to Anna, giving delicious kisses. Our lips became engaged as tongues continuously tangled and twirled. Minutes had passed as I noticed Claudia out of the shower, drying off. Watching our licentious play, she seductively dropped the towel to the floor. She started pleasuring herself with one hand, petting her luscious hairy beaver and the other caressing her nipples. Parting lips from Anna, I opened my legs, giving Claudia an invitation to join our amorous play.

Claudia sauntered in our direction, setting her gorgeous naked body on the coach between us. She placed her hand on my thigh and stroked my skin with the tips of her fingers. As I turned towards her, Claudia leaned inward with pleasing aspiration and surrendering lips. Touching her lips with mine, her long tongue eloquently sank into my mouth, liberating a warm, savory, and succulent sensation. While reveling in oral satisfaction, Claudia's fingers were playing between my thighs, grazing my minge, and arousing me to prurience.

Inadvertently, Claudia turned to Anna, giving a luscious mouthwatering kiss. With darting tongues, the sounds of lush pleasure echoed throughout the room. In moments of spontaneity, we faced each other in a triangle of aching thirst. We brought on the heat of feminine sensuality, exchanging lips and tongues. As pulsating passion escalated, Anna broke from our lips and opened my robe, exposing my bareness. I slipped the bathrobe off as Anna let hers fall to the floor.

Anna, kneeling to the floor, lifted Claudia's foot off the plush carpet. She cherished each of her toes as smiles of enjoyment surfaced over Claudia's face. I brought my tongue to Claudia's erect nipples, feverishly licking and sucking. Claudia legs opened wider, feeling Anna's tongue inch up her leg. In reaching her thigh, a trickle of wetness dribbled down as Anna delectably consumed each droplet. Then, Claudia began tensing as Anna was inches away from her minge with a slithering tongue.

Enthusiastic and unyielding, Anna's placed her mouth onto her vaginal lips diligently focusing her tongue along her sweet spot. She lashed incessantly, begetting every ounce of nerve ending pleasure as I continued sucking and teasing Claudia's savory nipples. Gasping sounds of pleasure erupted from Claudia's lips as she fell back. Then, Anna eased two fingers into her wet hole, screwing firmly as she devoured her sweet nectar. Climbing into elation, the intense pleasure lit Claudia's face as her eyes rolled to the back of her head. With legs spread open like a butterfly, she became breathless in satisfaction with two tongues teasing her flesh into ecstasy. Anna's ceaseless penetrations climbed Claudia further into the enriching pleasure. She stiffened with a radiant smile, letting out gushing sounds of climatic satisfaction.

Anna's flesh was on fire, wanting an explosive culmination. She immediately got down on all fours with her ass facing Claudia.

"To complete the sale, lick my puckered love hole with your long, pleasing tongue," Anna whispered.

Claudia got behind her with a willing desire to taste her bung hole. Laying down on my back, I opened my legs in front of Anna as Claudia dribbled saliva on top of Anna's puckered hole. Her anal cavity now glistened, ready for Claudia's slick tongue.

Lapping her crack with driving strokes, Anna's hole gradually blossomed. Then, her tongue slid into her crack, churning, twisting, and pleasuring. Taking her fingers, Claudia penetrated Anna's dripping pussy as her long darting tongue flayed Anna's luscious anus. Anna started moaning in sheer delight, receiving the satisfaction that she was yearning. Within a matter of moments, she started flaring on the verge of an explosion. Anna's lips moved from my puss as her head lifted in the air. In pure spatial bliss, shockwaves dispersed through her body as Claudia masterfully climbed her into climatic bliss.

Then, Claudia moved her mouth to my pussy, penetrating my clitoris with long cavernous stokes. Within a matter of seconds, she finished me. As I came up for air, her lips approached mine, and we gently kissed.

Slightly dazed and buzzed, we gathered our clothes and slowly dressed, grabbing a last glimpse of our naked bodies.

Breaking the silence, Claudia spoke. "I can let you ladies out the rear door."

Then, we all sort of giggled, realizing what Claudia said. She led us to the back door, where our merchandise and purses were waiting. Claudia handed us each a business card as we both kissed her goodbye.

"If you're ever back in Le Marais, call me," she said.

We grabbed our bags, saying our final adieus. We called a cab and journeyed back to the hotel.

After dinner at the hotel, we ended up in the jacuzzi recapping the day's events and planning for tomorrow. Sneaking a bottle of wine, we sipped until after midnight. Going back to the room, we quickly fell asleep, fulfilled in every way with the sensuality of Paris.

Chapter 32

The Show

It was two days before our departure to Italy. Anna left early in the morning for her usual workout. Having difficulty falling back to sleep, Cher suddenly appeared in my thoughts. Going to the drawer, I found her stained laced panties and laid back in bed. Inhaling her natural scent, I caressed my nipples and puss while closing my eyes, enjoying a titillating fantasy.

Grabbing Cher by the hand, I imagined leading her into the shower, sinking into a stream of passion. Our mouths and tongues savored as her delicate fingers worked along my bod. Not able to let go, my flesh felt magnetized by her venereous attraction. Pleasing each other in a bubbly manner, we tasted into a moment of rapture. Feeling wet and unsatisfied, I lifted my head from the pillow, gradually coming out of my daydream. Then, I realized I haven't ordered breakfast.

Getting out of bed, I hid her panties back in my drawer. I called room service, ordering a double espresso, bottled water, potatoes, vegetable omelets, and English muffins. Then, I made some fresh coffee and sat in my usual spot observing the Paris landscape. From nowhere, thoughts of Avriel entered my mind. I reflected on her generosity and compelling charm. She had a mysterious ambience, like being a part of a hidden underground cult. Her impression carried an unfathomable secret that fell subordinate to her towering fervency. Captivated by her hypnotic trance, my compulsion grew in magnitude and strength as she kissed me after our dinner escapade.

Anna was unlike her mother, or was she? Anna seemed like an honest, down-to-earth girl compounded in innocence. She apparently nurtures her love by sharing time, transparent expressions, and sensual intimacies. I gradually grew accustomed to her ways as we socialized, engaged in folly, and slept bare.

But what about the unfamiliar scent that remained on her work-out clothes? Another athlete may have seduced her into a lustful game in their playful sweat. Maybe her true amatory compulsions lean towards someone that appeals to her physique, strength, and agility. Beginning to feel paranoid, I felt used as a travel playmate while she frolics without my knowledge. So, why shouldn't I feel the same? There are no boundaries established in our relationship, except for companionship on a vacation arranged by Avriel. Anna entered my life with her aphrodisiac, kinky tactical lures, and taboos filled with pleasures. Leading me into obsessive cravings, there was Cher. Out of nowhere, a touch of her hand has led to these intricate sensual incidences.

The door opened abruptly, awakening me from my deep thoughts. Anna had come back from the gym sooner than expected, leaving the door slightly ajar.

"Morning love. Room service is right behind me in the hall." Anna said. "Could you take care of breakfast while I shower?"

Anna stripped off her clothes quickly, threw them onto the bed, and disappeared into the bathroom.

"Come on in," I said.

Cher wheeled a cart into the room with an unbuttoned blouse, a black leather skirt, and shoes that matched.

"I'll put the tray on the table like last time," she said cheerfully. Her tits jiggled with every stride as she strutted across the room with confidence.

I fell silent, watching as my nerves were ready to shatter into pieces. She turned and stared at me with those deep blue eyes, adding a warm pervasive smile. As she bent over, her blouse opened wide, displaying a set of gorgeous tits. Placing her hands under her skirt, she slowly peeled off her panties and rubbed them vigorously against her minge. Heat flowed across my forehead, becoming very aroused by her display of lewdness.

"Do you want anything else?" she said. "I can do wonders."

"Tomorrow.... I'll order tomorrow," I said. "Are you working?"

"No, but I will be back the following day. Call me by name when you order. This way, I can get things done quickly... and serve you just the way you like it." She dropped her panties into my open hands as she strolled out the door, pushing the cart.

Inhaling her raw scent once more, I became obsessed with her feminine assets, suaveness, and persistent behavior. The flow of running water had stopped immediately, catching my attention.

"Anna...... must dispose of these before she comes out of the bathroom." I whispered anxiously.

Scurrying about, I hid them in my drawer intending to save them as a souvenir. While turning around, I noticed the pink top that Anna threw on the bed after her workout. Picking it up, I inhaled the sweaty cottony material. There it was again, the scent of the mysterious perfume. I sat down near the breakfast tray in total confusion. My mind spun in circles, thinking of Anna's top and Cher's panties.

Finally, Anna came out wearing a robe sitting next to me. She immediately began picking at the meal as I sat there in complete bewilderment, sipping my cup of coffee.

Looking at me with a sense of reservation, she said. "Are you going to cherish that coffee all day long? There's plenty and I not eating it all."

She snapped at me for the first time while a look of contentment filled her face.

"Just thinking," I said in a calming tone.

I buttered a muffin, cut into the omelet, and began enjoying breakfast. The vegetables were fresh and slightly crispy. I licked a bit of cheese that stuck to my upper lip.

"Have you thought of anything to do before the show?" she said.

"Well, it's two days before flying out to Italy. Why not take it easy? This week's been an adventure," I said.

"It definitely went by too fast."

"We certainly took full advantage of using our time well. Don't you think?"

Anna was looking down at her cell phone, scrolling through some texts. Being unresponsive, her mind was focusing on something else. She looked up at me with bright eyes.

"Avriel just sent me a massage that the flights leave from Paris to Italy at 3:00 pm. By the way, she will not be there. She needs to take care of some personal business. However, Jasmine will be there to accommodate our needs. Let's pack the night before. This way, we can get up and go after my workout."

"Ok...... but how about walking around Champ de Mars Park before noon? There are plenty of vendors out. Then, we can take in Thai for lunch," I said. "We hadn't eaten any Asian food since we got here."

"We'll put on sneakers," she said. "The show starts at two, so we have plenty of time."

Anna looked at me with a quirky smile. She began massaging my toes, making me feel good.

"Do you want to suck on my toes?" she said seductively. "Your lips are so luscious and tingly. My body could use some of your skillful pampering."

As I looked into her eyes, Cher was in the back of my mind. "Love, if we do not stay focused, we'll miss the show. We have all night."

We continued with breakfast as my infatuation with seeing Cher again was building into frustration.

"Breakfast is scrumptious. Don't you think?"

"I found out that one of the top chefs in the world runs the restaurant," she said.

"Top rated and convenient. Ordering again is a definite must."

There was a brief pause of silence with no disapproval. Getting that out of the way made me feel at ease as I wondered if Cher will work on the morning of our departure.

Thinking of Anna's sweaty top. "What's good for the goose is good for the gander," I muttered.

"What was that?"

"Thinking about dinner at a French restaurant. Hadn't had duck in a while," I said.

"Too soon for that. But I've got a kinky idea for today," Anna said suggestively.

"Another one," I replied with interest.

"Let's wear butt plugs during the show. We'll get the lube with the warming sensation."

With a devilish smile, I thought about the sensual experience while attending the lycée. I missed that nerve ending feeling that brought me into an escalating vibrant culmination.

Anna giggled. "Then, we can play around while the models display the newest fashions," she said, amusingly. "Not to be rude, of course."

The level of excitement between us heightened.

"Now that's free reciprocity. Unsuspecting voyeurs displaying their stuff as we show ours," I said, sniggering. "They do not even have to tip us."

We immediately broke out in one of our elongated giggling sessions, almost falling off our chairs. Upon calming down, our fun-loving thoughts had sparked the day into one of adventure.

"Let's get the strawberry lube at the adult store. I love the sensation. We can insert them at the show," Anna said.

"But we need to wear thongs," I said, insistently.

We finished our meal, dressed, and called a taxi to meet us in front of the lobby.

With tickets in hand, we left the hotel and walked within the Champ de Mars. After spending the morning at the park, we grabbed some Thai. Then, we took a taxi to an adult store to buy some strawberry lube, telling the driver to wait for us. After our purchase, we got into the cab and headed to the show's location.

Feeling a bit embarrassed, we told the cab driver that we bought a gag gift for a friend. When we arrived, the thrill and excitement began building. The thought of sitting at the Venus lingerie stage was unexcelled. Anna paid for the taxi ride as I became charmed by the signs along the entrance. A handful of photographers were taking pictures of models within an enclosed area.

Anna gripped my hand, dragging me along as we walked to the entrance. Handing the tickets to the attendant, she tore them, handing back the stubs.

"Girls, don't lose your stubs. There will be a drawing at the end of the show. There will be four cat-walk tickets randomly selected to party with the models back stage. They are serving Champagne, hors d'oeuvre, and other tidbits."

"Partying with Venus models. That sounds exciting. Thanks for letting us know," Anna said.

The anticipation was driving me crazy as we entered the building, trying to find a private restroom. Anna spotted one around the corner. We entered and locked the door behind us. Fumbling nervously through my purse, I pulled out a pink plug with a tube of warming strawberry lube.

"We're going to smell like sweet dessert," I said. "You first. Let me see you bung hole. Remember, it's going to heat up a bit."

Anna bent over, lifting her skirt. She yanked the thong down to her knees. Her puckered hole looked sensuously inviting. Swallowing my oozing saliva, I wanted to please her with my long naughty tongue. Putting some lube on my finger, I rimmed her hole until it glistened. Then I slowly inserted a finger and maneuvered it in and out. Reaching a smooth rhythmic pace, sounds of enjoyment surfaced from Anna's lips.

"Ooh, yeah, keep going," she said.

"Not now…. in the show," I said.

I withdrew my finger and dabbed a little lube on her hole. In a winding pushing motion, the plug glided easily all the way to its circular base. A sound of relief emanated from Anna's lips.

"All in," I said.

Pulling up her thong, she stood up straightening her skirt.

"Oh my gosh, the feels tremendous fulfilling."

I pulled out a purple plug from my purse and handed it to Anna, along with the lube.

"Now, it's my turn to play doctor," Anna said. "Bend over like an obedient patient."

I pulled down my thong, bent over, and drew my skirt, revealing my anus. Anna put a glob of lube on my crack and circled her finger around the rim. Then she gradually pushed inward with penetration. At first, the sensation was icky, but I soon loosened up feeling more comfortable. My bod started heating up as she screwed me with her middle finger. The sensation swept through my love canal and along my vaginal

185

outer wall. She added a little more lube to help ease the toy inside me.

"Here I go," she said. She pushed the plug inward in a coiled manner and jittering it around. Finally, it slipped in all the way in.

"All done," she said.

I pulled up my thong and straighten my skirt. The warming sensation swept throughout my abdomen like lightening. I felt invigorated and ready for an afternoon of fun. Putting the lube in my purse, the room smelled like a fresh strawberry patch. We leisurely made our way into the hall and headed toward the seating area.

"Anal plugs are just like taking an energy shot with no side effects," I said excitedly.

Chapter 33

The Cat Walk

Walking to the information booth, the warming effects of the lube circulated through my pleasure zones. There was a young girl standing behind the counter that greeted us. She wore a vibrant pink thong and a matching bra. Her name tag read Maria.

Smiling, she said. "Looks like you girls need some help."

Anna pulled the stubs from her purse. "We're lost," Anna said. "Could you help us find these seats?"

She gazed at the tickets for a moment and looked up.

"No problem. Follow me to the catwalk. I'll take you using a shortcut through the business offices."

As we proceeded to our seats, I noticed the Venus ushers were wearing very provocative outfits. As we passed an office with a door wide open, I hesitated briefly, looking in. Two gorgeous models were fully engaged in an intimate encounter. Their hands were inside each other's panties, fingering as they passionately kissed.

Anna pulled my hand. "We need to get going. The usher is waiting ahead."

As we caught up to Maria, she showed us our seats. "Here you are, girls. Have a nice show."

"Thanks," Anna replied.

Our seating was much more than expected. The chairs were oversized leather recliners with tall circular backs and high elevated arm rests. The positioning of the recliners along the runway was spacious and close to the stage, allowing for total privacy.

"Let's push our chairs together. So, we can hear ourselves talk," I suggested.

"Good idea," Anna replied.

Struggling to move the chairs, a stage hand passed by.

"Having trouble, ladies," he said. "Let me help you."

The man slowly jimmied the chairs together.

"Thanks," I said.

I sat back buried in the chair's softness, feeling relaxed and comfortable. The scent of the leather added to the ambience teasing my senses. Turning to Anna, I blew lightly into her ear, wanting to tease her before the show got underway.

"Anna, lift your butt. I want to touch." My hand moved across her crack as she squirmed. Noticing an usher approach, I quickly removed my hand.

"Would you girls like drinks or appetizers…. They come with the ticket price. Here's, the menu. Take your time." she said.

Handing us the menu, we examined the food and beverages. Having eaten, we both agreed that a bottle of champagne was enough. I called the usher and ordered. Then, the waitress placed a table in front of our chairs.

The stage was above eye level, not allowing us to see the other attendees. So, I stood up and looked around the large room. There was a spacious gap between the regular seating and the catwalk. Security guards were standing close by observing the audience. At that moment, the waitress appeared with the chilled champagne bottle. She poured two glasses, handed me one, and set the bottle on the table as I sat back down.

"The best seating in the house," I said. "… and quality drinks."

"A toast to our first fashion show," Anna replied.

We raised our glasses and started enjoying the bubbly taste. As Anna and I slowly sipped and chatted, the expectations of the show augmented the excitement. Then, soft music played in the background as the host welcomed the audience to the event.

One by one, the models strutted down the stage. They displayed the newest Venus fashions as the host described their styles. Many models were tall and thin, with long silky legs and tanned bods. Models that presented thongs and panty lines walked down the runway topless. As we watched judiciously, models would stop almost in front of us and turn around in a three-sixty. Then, they gave the audience winks and smiles before moving on.

Anna reclined back in the chair, spreading her legs like a butterfly. Getting in the mood, I casually set my glass down.

Reaching over, I glided my fingers under her thong. She was already soaking wet watching the hot sexy models strut their stuff on stage. Rubbing delicately, her face gleamed with pleasure. A model stopped in front of us, observing my fingers paying with her puss. She gave an approving wink as Anna's head pressed against the back of the chair, enjoying the pleasurable sensation.

Anna mumbled, "The plug feels so good. Oh...."

With stimulating fingers, I was stroking her as she was approaching cloud nine. Then, another model came by, watching us with lustful eyes. Anna suddenly gripped the arms of the chair, made a relieving sweet sound, and peaked into a gratifying orgasm.

Feeling anxious and excited, I peeled off my thong and placed it in my purse. Putting my feet upon the chair, I spread my legs to the armrests. My fingers gliding through my wet puss like melting butter. A model with deep tanned skin, a pretty face, and large breasts came towards me. She looked Mediterranean. She wore a purple strapless outfit, looking very hot and sexy. Seeing my bare slit, she watched me masturbating as she licked her lips in desire. Desperately wanting to achieve an orgasm, she squatted in front of me, opening her legs. Soaking wet, I furiously fingering my oyster as she teased me even further.

She turned around slowly, displaying her lush butt. Like a stripper, she slowly peeled off her panties, revealing her shaven delights. Bending over, her salacious lips and puckered hole gained the audience approval. She stood there for what seemed like hours, giving me an extended show. She flexed the elastic band and threw them at me. My energetic play had climbed to the edge of fulfillment. With nerve endings blazing in fulfilling pleasure, I squeezed the anal plug with my sphincter muscle. Within seconds, I exploded into spasmatic sizzling orgasm.

Coming up for air, I realized, I climaxed in front of that gorgeous model. As I regained my composure, the Mediterranean woman had left as another model came down the runway. Wanting to get another souvenir, I quickly put the woman's panties in my purse.

Anna was drinking champagne like it was water. Her voice echoed, cheering the models like a man in heat. Absorbed in the gala, we completely forgot about the drawing for the party. Then, a hot-looking female got up on stage with a microphone.

"Now it's time to see who gets to go backstage for the party. If you win, stand up and let us know. Raise your hands high and shout," she said.

Calling the numbers one by one, the winners stood up and gave a cheer. Then, she called the numbers on my ticket.

Totally surprised, I got up from my seat. "Hey, I won. I got the ticket."

There was a lady sitting close by that also bellowed.

It was the finale. All the girls came out to give a last bow. We stood up, clapping and cheering. The show had suddenly ended as the echoing sound of the attendees dissipated as they left.

I looked over at Anna. "What a way to blow ten thousand Euros. Only one ticket for the party...... I can try sneaking you in."

"We really do not have to go," she said, disappointedly.

The lady next to us over heard us and approached.

"I see you are together. I come to these often. Here's my ticket. This way, you can both enjoy the party as a couple."

"Wow, that's very generous of you," Anna said. "Thank you very much."

An usher approached us from behind, asking. "It looks like we have some winners."

"We both have winning tickets," I said.

"Follow me, ladies. Just to let you know, the backstage fashion show can get a little wild."

In approaching the entrance to the party, two huge security guards stood in front of a large security door. Mean faced and muscle packed, they reminded me of NFL defensive tackles. As the usher showed her credentials, one man pressed a button and the door opened automatically. Upon walking in, we met an attendant at the podium that greeted us.

"Welcome to the party! Chilled champagne is at the bar and hors d'oeuvres are circulating around. Please, help yourself," she said.

The room was spacious, comprising models and the winning guests. The music was loud as the dimmed illumination added to the ambiance. Most models were completely naked, sipping champagne and celebrating a successful show. Some girls were dancing together on a stage among the multi-colored lights.

Anna interjected, "Going to the bathroom. We'll catch up later."

Making my way to the bar, I asked for a glass of champagne. The Mediterranean model saw me, waved, and approached. I felt flush and fearful, realizing that my behavior was probably unacceptable. The thought of the two muscled men escorting me out entered my mind. Trying to avoid her, I attempted to step away in the opposite direction, but it was too late.

"Hey," she called. "Remember me."

She came near me, touching my shoulder. I turned around. Getting an upfront view, her dark skin, perky nipples, and a well-shaven vulva were picturesque and alluring. Having watched me climax, the feeling of embarrassment magnified as our conversation materialized.

"My names Colette. Congratulations on being a winner… How was the show?"

Then, total relief escalated throughout my body as her welcoming words implied a conditional approval.

"It was very exciting."

"Did anything turn you on? Well, you know…. the lingerie."

We smiled together as a sense of serenity emerged.

"That purple outfit you were wearing was very sexy."

"It should fit you comfortably. We have a private room out back. Want to try it on?"

She took a wipee from her tiny purse and swiped the perspiration off my forehead. "It gets a little warm back here after a show," she said. "That's why the models usually shed their clothes. It makes them feel more comfortable."

Her mannerisms and voice transformed into a seductive and persuasive tone. She touched my skirt, feeling the material with her fingers.

"Everyone loves being naked backstage. No one really cares. Besides, many of the winners strip down with us."

In looking around, everyone was laughing, smiling, and naked, putting me more at ease.

"Come on. Let yourself go."

Peering across the room, Anna was already naked and talking with a few models.

"I guess it's alright," I said, questionably.

Collete helped me take off my top and unzipped my dress.

"There, that's better."

"You have an exquisite body. Did you ever think about being a model?"

"No, going to school for psychotherapy."

"That's crazy," she said.

We looked into each other's eyes and laughed. The chemistry between us blossomed into pure sweetness. Her flesh was no longer at a distance but radiantly warm with the sense of goo girlishness. She stared into my eyes, getting me aroused. I wanted to suck her tongue as it danced while she spoke. Then, our conversation completely changed.

"By the way, you turned me on. I couldn't contain myself when I got backstage. You know…… my girlfriend licked me with her crisp tongue as I thought about you climaxing with your legs spread."

She totality caught me off guard. I never thought that Colette had become aroused observing me masturbate in front of her. In fact, I thought the opposite.

"Many of the models fool around at work. It's just the thing. Besides, I love to watch too."

Within a matter of minutes, all the social barriers had become vanquished. She was expressing herself flagrantly with compassion. Absorbed in my desire to be with her, I impulsively revealed my true feelings.

"Getting into you watching, the sensations just amplified like multiple sparks flying everywhere. I came instantaneously as you took off your thong."

Colette drew me into her flesh as she craved me with obsessing urges. Her lips met mine, and we kissed spontaneously. Our nipples touched, and I wanted her in the most stimulating manner. She caressed me as we savored our intertwined tongues.

In parting lips, she softly spoke. "We have a back room. Come join me for some fun. I just need to book it for a few hours."

"I'd love that," I said.

Colette got on her phone and scheduled the room. Another model approached us from behind, holding a champagne bottle.

"This is Leas. My girlfriend and the manager. Leas this is..."

"Lizette," I said.

Leas touched me on the shoulder, sending chills through my spine.

See gazed at me, looking up and down. "You have a gorgeous body. You could easily be a lingerie model."

"This is the beautiful woman I was telling you about in the audience while you were...."

Leas interrupted. "... Collete is a scrumptiously sweet girl any time of day. I can definitely attest to that."

Leas was skinny, with large breasts and pierced nipples. She looked much older, probably in her late thirties with a tattoo of a hawk on her back. Her ears had three layers of piercings, which reminded me of a domineering biker.

"Do you smoke," Colette said.

I hesitated a bit. "Yes."

"Come on," Colette said.

"Wait, I need to get Anna."

"Don't worry. She having some fun with the other girls," Colette said. "You can catch up with her later."

Then, she led me by the hand down a back hallway to a large door labeled 'Playtime.'

"This is the model's break room," Colette said.

"Playtime," I said, questioning.

"Models love to relax, play around, and watch," Colette said.

Colette called security. After verification, they opened the door remotely. As we walked in, Colette turned on the lights and locked the door behind us. A large circular bed stood in the middle of the room that could accommodate a group of girls. There were mirrors on the walls and a large circular mirror above the bed. The furniture comprised massage recliners, leather sofas, large projection screens and a kitchen table. Many sex toys, including bondage paraphernalia, hung on the walls and shelves.

"Quite a collection," I said.

"Wait until you see our humongous walk-in closet," Colette said with an impish smile. "The models like to.... play a lot in here."

"Colette and Lizette, let's freshen up before we toke," Leas said.

Leas opened the bottle of champagne and poured it into three glasses. Then we walked into a large shower in the back of the room. Colette took out linens from a closet and handed me a couple of towels. Within no time at all, we soaped up, rinsed, and dried off.

As I bent over drying my legs, Colette spoke. "Relishing a favorite toy,"

"Oh, forgot about it getting caught up in all the excitement. Perfect time to pluck it out," I said.

"Let me help you," Colette said. Bending over, she felt me crack with her probing fingers. Taking her fingers, she jarred the plug from my love hole.

A relieving tension crossed my body as it eased out. "Oooh, that felt so good," I said. "I like it in and out."

We all smiled as I started to image the expectation of our small gathering. A private room with toys and our naked bodies aspiring some female affection.

"Time for a little afternoon fun," Leas said.

"Girl-girl games," Collete said. "I was waiting for this moment when I saw you in that leather recliner self-pleasuring."

Colette turned on the air filter as she lit up a large joint.

"Play acting is what we like best," Collete said, exhaling.

"Play acting," I said.

"Leas likes to be a dominatrix. We play act for fun," Colette said. "You should join in. Nothing serious. We fall into our roles easily when we get stoned. You'll see."

I took a large hit from the joint, held it in, and let a long stream of smoke out. Colette handed me a glass of champagne. It cooled my throat as I sipped on it. The joint came around again. I inhaled the warm smoke once more and felt a strong buzz coming on. I took a few more sips of champagne as the pot put me in a state of compromise.

"This stuff is pretty potent," I said.

"The best in Paris," said Leas.

Collete handed me the joint. "Finish it, Lizette."

While taking the last few hits, I walked around the room looking at the various toys. Leas put on a pair of leather gloves, boots, and harness, looking like a dominatrix. Colette got into a leather harness and fastened a leather collar around her neck. Leas attached a long chain to the collar.

"Colette likes to play submissive. Don't you?"

"Yes, mistress."

"Get down on your knees for me," Leas said.

As I finished the joint, their game had begun as serious roles emerged.

"Look, we have a new playmate. Lick her feet for me."

Colette, guided by Lea's chain, crawled to my bare feet. Colette licked and sucked my toes. It felt nice having them pampered. I lifted my feet as she savored them. She was nourishing me like a juicy piece of fruit.

"Come join us," Leas said. "Grab a leather harness while I place metal clamps on Colette's nipples. You like clamps, don't you?"

"Yes, mistress," Collete said, slightly whimpering.

Searching the wall, I found one that fit. I fastened the leather harness over my neck, breasts, and around my thighs. There was a ring on the neck section missing a chain.

"Looking hot Lizette. Grab me the leather whip on the wall… near you," Leas said, casually.

I turned around and took the leather whip from a hook and handed it to her.

"You would look nice in a chain," Leas said.

Without warning, she fastened a chain on the ring and pulled down. The feeling in the room immediately changed to lewdness. My mind was confused and spellbound by Leas domineering approach. She automatically assumed that I wanted to play and I couldn't refuse.

"Our little pet wants to party," Leas said. "Now I am your mistress. What I say goes. Call me by my proper name."

"Yes," I said.

"Yes what," Leas said.

"Yes mistress," I said.

"You are a fine, obedient girl. You will obey me or undergo punishment. Now, get down on your knees pet," she said. "Or I will put nipple claps on those luscious tits of yours and place you in our medieval rack with a vibrant whipping session."

I immediately got down on my knees, not wanting to undergo her punishment. "Yes, mistress." Totally under Lea's control, I started playing the role in submissiveness.

"Let me parade you around a bit like a tamed animal."

As I crawled on all fours, she stuck my butt with a leather whip. Harsh stinging sensations seesawed throughout my body as I felt her leathered glove on my puss. With every snap of the whip, pain and pleasure escalated to a new level.

"That will teach you not to masturbate in front of my girlfriend. You'll have a nice pink butt before I finish with you. Collete, grab a nine-inch strapon and put it on."

Colette walked over to a shelf and strapped on a pink cock. It limped and jiggled as she walked to a table drawer, pulling out some lube. As she sauntered, I watched her meticulously drooling while sensations swept through my anal cavity.

"You and Lizette are going to make love in bed. Lizette got on the bed like a nice pet and spread them wide."

Immediately, I got on the bed spreading my legs, waiting for her cock to enter me.

"Beg her Lizette," Leas said. "Beg like you want it bad."

"I'm your little sissy muffin, needing your lovely cock stuffed in me," I said.

"More, beg for it with meaning," Leas said in a demanding tone.

"Give me that big, luscious dick. Screw me like a bronco wanting to come home to Mama."

"Colette, eat her out," Leas said, commandingly.

Leas got behind Colette and was striking her butt pink.

"Eat that pussy."

Her tongue was digging deep, licking me with a fervent satisfying force.

"Now, tongue her ass."

I moved my butt higher off the bed. Colette was working her tongue along my slit and anus. Feeling her lusciously hot tongue was getting me nice and wet.

"Do her now."

Colette got up and spread some lube on her well-hung cock. She mounted me slowly, pushing it into my wet hole. My puss felt the gratification as she picked up the pace. It was like she was trying to fill my insides with her cum. Huffing and puffing, my mind escaped within an ozone of penetrating pleasure.

"Oh yeah Colette," I murmured.

"Ride her like a hungry bull Colette," Leas commanded.

I did not see Leas put on a strapon, but she got on the bed while Colette was doing me. The thought of filling my rear hole with her deep penetrating love sent me into furor.

"Open wide my pet and suck me until I come," she said.

She stuck it in my face. My tongue licked and danced around like there was no tomorrow. Then, she glided it into my mouth, right to the back of my throat. Wrapping my mouth around it, I sucked her cock like a thirsty girl. Saliva was oozing down the corner of my mouth as Leas pulled it out. Lubing it up, Leas ordered me to get on top of Colette while she got ready to penetrate my behind. The anal plug I was wearing made my hole nice and loose, which allowed Leas to ease her cock inside me. As Colette was riding me in one hole, Leas slowly screwed me in the other. Soon, I had the two cocks simultaneously giving me nookie in both holes.

"Ride her. Ride her home," Leas said.

Within no time at all, there was a simultaneous feeling of heat, pressure, and pleasure. It felt like a wave of sensuous fever was sweeping through my body. Respiring at a faster rate, they worked their cocks with intensity. I was screaming in crazed jubilation, making sounds like a hungry pig wanting all the pleasureful feast. My body was in sheer bliss as electrical vibrations swept through me, elevating me closer to the threshold. Screaming and shaking with intense quenching fulfillment, my mind went into a euphoric state of delirium.

I grasped for sheer joy, holding on to my head like I've been to nirvana and back. Then, the girls slowly dismounted as I sat up, feeling the stinging sensation on my butt. Their lips approached mine in a three-way kissing session until everything seemed to calm down.

"Wow, that was amazing," I said.

"Hope you got your money's worth," Leas said. "We are going to stay here longer. Go. Meet your friend."

Taking off the paraphernalia, I put on my top and zipped up my dress forgetting to put on my thong. Thanking the ladies for a wonderful time, I walked back in the party and noticed many of the models had left. I approached Anna at the bar. Now dressed, she greeted me with a pleasant kiss as the scent of the mysterious perfume drifted from her clothing.

Chapter 34

Cher

Struggling to get out of bed, traces from Lea's strong pot still lingered in my brain. With much effort, I yanked the covers off my body and set my feet on the floor. I switched the coffee maker on to getting a half pot brewing. Like a typical European, I loved my morning java in any form I could get it. As it dripped, the aroma infiltrated the air, making me feel at home. After pouring a cup, I sat in my favorite chair viewing the emotive city one last time.

Resting in front of me was the epitome of historical perseverance and culture uniqueness. Through wars and battles, many remnants, stood with great pride. Melancholy seized my spirit like someone had taken something special from me. In leaving Paris, I wondered if there would be a return to its astounding marvels and amorous adventures. But the duplication of experiences can never be the same within time and space. Subsequent journeys would be different as the next.

Taking another sip, I reflected on my new destination, Italy. Complex emotions of unfamiliarity, anticipation, and curiosity emerged like the day we boarded the train to Paris. Then, Anna took me by surprise by getting out of bed like a jackrabbit. In a fluid motion, she put on her exercise clothes, white socks, and sneakers.

"Working out longer today. Be back about nine. Don't forget to order breakfast." She grabbed her swimsuit and was off to the pool.

Being our last day in Paris, I assumed she would skip her morning workout, but suspicion drew me in further. Our last sexual episode together was at the show in the plush leather chair. Then paranoia took hold of me. I wondered if she would be late because of the desire to have sweaty sex with her mysterious acquaintance. Returning to the room, I'd assume she would almost immediately jump in the shower. Well, it would be interesting to have sweltering sex when she got back. But sloppy seconds? Unlike men, it's quite different in the world of feminine love, because seconds can be the absolute best. Smiling, I realized what I needed to do to return to a surprise.

"Yes, salty seconds," I whispered.

Finishing my cup of coffee, I stepped into the shower. The cool refreshing water flowed onto my face, making me feel energized. I soaped my entire body and rinsed off. Then, a sensual mood came upon me as I pleasured myself, thinking of Cher. My head immediately spun in circles as I vividly remembered what she had told me.

"She's working!" I said, anxiously.

I quickly dried off, put on a bathrobe, and called room service. "Is Cher working today," I said. "Great, could you have her bring me two espressos right away? Then, at nine bring us our usual breakfast. Yes, the Beaupre's...... like last time. Yes, she told me to ask for her. Great!"

I opened the door and placed a rubber jam, leaving a small crack. Sitting down, I waited in complete nervousness, counting the seconds while visualizing erotic thoughts. Then there was a knock at the door.

Hopping out of my chair, I said, "Come on in."

Extreme heat flowed across my forehead. Cher walked in wearing a black leather skirt well above the knees with her white blouse fully unbuttoned. Braless and ready for amatory exploration, her luscious breasts wiggled about as she ambled in. My mouth dripped with saliva viewing her striking figure.

"I hope my appearance is not too straightforward. I just saw your roommate in the pool swimming laps," she said playfully. "Looks a little tied up. I'll place these on the table?" Upon placing the cups down, she turned toward me, pressing her tongue against her upper lip. "Is there anything else I can do for you or are you well served?"

"If you are asking me, I just need a little more help..." Slowly opening my bathrobe, I let it drop to the floor, revealing my nakedness.

Her eyes popped out of her head.

"Now I need you to service me right here!"

Without hesitation, she pulled off her top and unzipped her skirt, letting it fall to the floor. Her erect nipples pointed upwards and drooped like round balls. Not wearing any panties, she displayed a well-shaven mound of beauty.

"I was waiting two days for this moment," she said. "I'd hadn't yet...."

I approached, putting two fingers on her mouth silencing the inception of our erotic play. Taking her hand, I led here to the foot of the bed and laid down on a pillow facing her. Spreading my legs wide open, she looked at me with a salacious focus and a rapturous smile. She slipped out of her shoes, kicking them aside. Lifting my foot, she vibrantly sucked my toes. One by one, she slovenly relished as my lips wanted to desperately taste her flesh. Then, inching her tongue up my legs to my thighs, her lingua slithered, reveled, and satisfied. In reaching my sensitive breasts, her mouth nurtured my nipples as her tongue teased. Then, she pinched and tugged while mounting me as we bonded in burning obsession.

Moving her lips upon mine, we connected with unstoppable feminine desire as our affections ignited explosively. Craving each other with wanton fervency, we savored in succulent oral satisfaction. Sliding her tongue deep into my mouth, she filled me with tantalizing vibrancy. Her lips were sensually gratifying and tasted lusciously appetizing. She sucked, lapped, and swallowed while I indulged with a torrid compulsion.

Pressing firmly against my vulva, our osculation's intensified. She pumped her pelvis against my minge like a man in heat, bringing me into a dripping orgasm. Sounds of pleasure escaped from my lips as total arousal filled my feminine parts with escalating pleasure. Maintaining the momentum of passion, she spun around, entering the lures of a sixty-nine.

Easing her vagina gently onto my face, I teasingly opened her lips with my penetrating fingers. Then, my long tongue penetrated, danced, and flickered around her erect pearl. I licked and sucked her juices, basking in her lush sweetness.

Cher's lips fell upon my puss, lapping into the moistness. She inserted two fingers in my sopping hole and began screwing me into a flaming fever. Her tongue was skillful and untamed as the pleasure became ceaseless and intense.

Sucking her clit passionately, I rubbed her anus with my middle finger. Moans of pleasure seeped from her lips as the intense stimulation was incessant. My finger slipped into her anal cavity, wriggling in and out as I sucked on her pussy like a vacuum on full power. Without noticing, her body tensed as she let out a cry of pure felicity.

"Oh, that's so good," she breathed. Falling to the side of the bed, she rested momentarily.

Gaining her composure, she turned her body around placing her mouth onto my craving minge. She worked on me with penetrating fingers and a furiously lapping tongue. I firmly gripped the comforter, coming closer and closer to culmination. Moaning like there was no tomorrow, I was on the edge of bliss. Within seconds, my body shook with elation as I exploded into a breathtaking orgasm.

Slowly her mouth ascended onto my lips, kissing with tenderness. Our tongues gingerly melted with appreciation, and I didn't want to let go.

"I definitely could use another go," I said.

"I have to force myself to get back to work," she replied with determination. "I'm on call."

Getting off the bed, she picked up her clothes as I rubbed my puss watching her dress. While buttoning her shirt, she put on her skirt and slipped into her shoes. She waved and left as silence filled the room. I got up from the bed, put on my robe, and sat in the cushioned chair. Another unanticipated sensual escapade in Paris has filled my fancy. Sitting back, my mind wondered as I finished a cup of expresso.

"From a touch to a fulfilled fantasy. Now, that's love in Paris," I said. A knock on the door took my attention away from my sensual thoughts.

"Who is it?"

"Room service," she answered.

Casually, I opened the door, but it was not Cher. The server pulled the cart into the room.

Pointing at the window, I said, "Please, put the tray on the table over there by the chair."

She placed the tray down, scurried off with the cart. Walking over to the tray, I noticed a card. I opened and read it.

"I just wanted to add a sweet treat to your breakfast," love Cher.

On the tray there were two chocolate-covered strawberries. My mind could not escape her sentiment. I could still feel her tongue craving every ounce of my pleasure zones. Then Anna unlocked the door and entered the room. She was dripping wet with sweat.

With haste, I said. "Don't say a word. Let me help you."

Walking over to her, I helped her out of her clothes, almost ripping her panties off. Her perspiring body was intensely desirable. Wanting to bathe in her swelter, I took off my robe. Pressing my naked body against hers, she intermingled with my flesh. My lips kissed her salty delicious lips with sheer happiness. Taking a chocolate-covered strawberry, I put it between our lips. We tasted it until our lips touched.

"Mm, that tastes so good," she said.

Then, I dragged her on the bed as she lied with her legs spread open.

"Wait here," I said. "Don't move. Keep them wide open."

I went into the bathroom, coming out with a warm facecloth and some strawberry lube.

"Something to soothe your tension," I said.

Placing the cloth between her legs, I wiped her puss nice and clean. She squirmed like a worm stimulated by the titillation.

"Oh, that so good Lizette," she said.

I lubed my middle finger and slowly felt along her crack. Playing around, I slid my finger slowly into her anal cavity. As I was sliding in and out with a pleasing pace, my fingers rubbed, getting her nice and wet. Bringing my mouth to her pussy, I licked and sucked.

Finding her sweet spot, she panted. "Keep it right there," she said breathlessly.

Keeping up my pace, she was moaning in absolute fulfillment. As I felt her body vibrate, my tongue vigorously penetrated her erect oyster like fire. The sensation climbed her into a moment of rapture.

"Yes, yes," she screamed. "Do me like ice cream!"

Putting forth every ounce of energy on the tip of my tongue, she screamed in satisfaction, reaching the pinnacle of sensual love. Bringing my lips to hers, we kissed deeply and passionately, melting into each other's arms.

Slowly, my words escaped from my mouth. "Did you like my surprise?" I said.

Her face was smiling ear to ear. "Yes," she said, softly. Bringing her lips to mine, we softly kissed once more, calming into the peacefulness of the room.

Then, I took her hand, leading her into the shower. I washed her body from head to toe with soapy lather. We rinsed, dried off, and put on some clothes.

Walking over to the breakfast tray, the silence between us broke. "It was my turn. I needed to return the favor from our first night in Paris."

We shared breakfast almost in silence. When we finished, I placed the tray outside the door. We packed our bags, checked out of the hotel, and flagged down a cab to the airport.

On the way to the airport, I thought. "There wasn't a trace of that mysterious perfume."

Chapter 35

Italy

We arrived at the airport before our flight was departing and checked in our luggage. Patiently dragging ourselves step by step through the tedious customs procedures, we finally headed to the gate. While walking through the airport, our fervent intimacy unraveled itself amongst the diverse crowd. Without constraints, we held hands like passionate playmates. We kissed, embraced, and laughed as others gazed at our playfulness. Our fingers touched and caressed, only wanting more of each other. Upon reaching the gate departure, Anna placed her arm around my shoulder as we sat like no one else was around. She whispered erotic words in my ear as she caressed me to pacification. Becoming aroused by her advances, I intermittently gave her sweet kisses. Breaking our intimacy, the attendant called our rows. Showing our tickets, we boarded the plane to Bari International Airport. Anna took the window seat, and I sat in the middle.

Once in the air, Anna fell asleep, resting her head on my shoulder. As the airline stewardess came around, I requested a hot coffee with cream and sugar. Giving me a wink and smile, she stirred the contents and delicately handed me the hot drink with a napkin.

Taking small sips, I listened to the aerodynamic noise of the plane, thinking of the fun time we had yesterday. Without a bra and panties, we played like adult children within the Paris streets, lost in the irresponsibility of innocence. We lightheartedly teased boys, allowing them a glimpse of our private anatomy. We shopped for souvenirs, bought pastries, and fine cheeses. After a site-seeing tour of the right bank, we ended the day by savoring some of the best wines in France. Quite inebriated, we went back to our room and collapsed into bed.

Being college girls, Avriel would have expected our light-heartedness. She would have applauded the accomplishments we achieved in such a short time. Looking at a woman reading next to us, my thoughts shifted toward the fall semester at the university.

Anxious and lacking clear forethought, I began wondering about my future and reflecting on my past. Paris taught me that creating my destiny in life gave me a sense of freedom and choice. I desired to be an aspiring, independent business owner in human sensuality. But my decision was something of impulse not thinking comprehensively of the risks involved. At the creek, I became aware that people are very much a part of nature. Yet, social constraints separate us from our instinctiveness and places us in a confused state of denial. Erotism is not purely an evil thing that we must hide, but something we must explore to become self-actualized.

Finishing my java, I passed my empty cup to the stewardess that came around collecting trash. Then, Anna's eyes opened as the pilot announced our descent.

"The angel has come to life."

"I didn't mean to fall asleep, but was quite tired from the workout."

"It was your turn, anyway."

"You look flustered. What's on your mind?" Anna said.

"Thinking about Paris and school." I said, turning my face toward her. "Can't wait to experience Bari." Then I gave her a soft kiss and kept my lips close to hers. I whispered, not wanting the other passengers to hear us.

"Without Avriel...... did it disappoint you when you heard she was not coming?"

I kissed her again. "Not really."

"I'm glad. You only know one side of my Mama. Well known in the upper circles of society both in the France and Italy, she has mastered the language and the social skills because of Papa's position. I've heard rumors she has a dominatrix style around her secret female acquaintances."

"She definitely had a hypnotic power over me. I melted in her arms like ice in the desert...... and she is very generous, which makes our relationship highly appealing."

"Well, you must be very cautious next time you come over to the house. She will control you like a master to a slave."

Giving her one last kiss before the plane landed, I turned, looking straight ahead gripping the arms of the seat. I've always hated landings. There was this inner terror that always struck me while realizing what was transpiring. Within seconds, an almost frictionless coast took us on top of the runway. Looking out the window, the speed of the plane against the passing terrain added a level of stress as I held tight. The tires bumped a bit before settling into a quick slowdown as my back pressed firmly against the seat. Immediate relief came across my body as the anxiety left me in a quiet sigh of refuge.

"Down at last," I said. "Bari. Made it."

Getting off the plane, we made our way through the airport. Anna looked at her text messages.

"Jasmines waiting for us."

We picked up our luggage and proceeded to the passenger pickup area. As we walked outside, Jasmine was standing against the Bentley. We approached, greeting her with warm kisses. She opened the trunk, helping us with the luggage. Then we both climbed into the back seat and drove off.

"Hope we are not rude," Anna said.

"It's, ok. I know you girls want to be together," Jasmine said. "I hear that your trip to Paris was exceptionally exciting. Even a fashion show."

"It was a total adventure," Anna said.

We talked with Jasmine about the many things we accomplished in Paris during the ride to their Bari home. As our conversation dwindled down, we pulled up to the house. Jasmine helped us take the luggage out of the trunk and parked the car in the garage.

The Beaupre's casa had an elegant and classy style, just like the picture on the bureau depicted. Characterized as more contemporary, it was much smaller than the one in Carcene. As we carried our luggage inside, I walked through the front doors as affluence filled the air. There was an open floor plan with a large island separating the kitchen from the living space. We placed our bags by the stairs that led to the second floor. Settling down, I took a relaxing breath staring through a window.

Jasmine spoke. "Lizette, let me give you a quick rundown so you know where everything is. There are bathrooms on all floors. The lower floor comprises a finished basement and a private workout room. There is a set of patio doors leading out into the sea. The floor above us are the bedrooms with baths. The top floor comprises an additional dining and living space. It also includes a large office. We have a food elevator in the kitchen that sends up meals right to the top floor. Of course, it stops in the master bedroom. Finally, there are plenty of towels and guest robes in the bathroom. You girls head downstairs to the bar while I put your luggage up in your bedroom."

As we walked downstairs to the finished basement, thick panes of glass covered the entire wall facing the sea. Stained cherry wood separated the large panes. The bar was in the corner, having an excellent view of the landscape.

"Let's grab a seat at the bar," Anna said.

"A wood fireplace," I said.

"The fireplace definitely comes in handy when the weather gets cold, damp, and rainy during the winter months. Papa designed a special mechanism that dissipates the heat evenly throughout the room. So, it stays nice and toasty."

As we sat down, the gorgeous view comprising an azure blue sky, the deep blue sea, and a green yard struck me in awe. I could see a white open picket fence along the edge of the cliff. In the distance, a few yachts glided across the water.

"The luxury of the sea is at your backdoor. What else would you need from life?"

"You probably hadn't noticed, but the window panes shade electronically. When we turn on a switch, no one can see inside, but we have a clear view looking out. It's one of my Papa's cool inventions. You will see it when we head outside. We also can change the colors and even work in Christmas lighting. Yachts on the water can see our light display during the holidays."

"Your papa is an inventor?"

"He actually has many technological patents that my mama now owns. That's where most of the family wealth is buried."

Jasmine came down stairs gliding behind the bar like an experienced bartender taking control. She was wearing a stripped crop top with a V-neck that was sleeveless and bowed. In not wearing a bra, her tits jiggled as she was trying to arrange some bottles below the bar. I could almost see her nipples as she bent over. She stood up and looked directly into my eyes. As we gazed deeply at one another, I felt animated and mesmerized.

Taking her eyes away from me, she gripped a bottle. "Well ladies, after a long day, how about a glass of wine?"

"I have a Cab," I said.

"I'll take a glass of Barbera," Anna said.

With an effortless technique, Jasmine opened the individual vintages, poured our wine into glasses, and recorked the bottles. Then, she placed the wine glasses and the bottles on the bar in front of us wearing a big smile.

"I have things to do in town. Make yourselves at home. If you get hungry before dinner, there's some cheese, vegetables, and dip in the refrigerator. If you need anything, just call me."

Jasmine went through a side door leading into the garage. We could hear the garage door open and close as the Bentley sped off.

"Let's have a little party outside," Anna said. "Grab both glasses. Jasmine probably won't be back for a while."

Anna grabbed the two recorked bottles of wine and a corkscrew. Then she grabbed an additional bottle of Cabernet behind the bar. Leading me through the patio doors, we strolled toward the sea. I looked back at the large picture windows at the back of the house.

"Anna, that is so neat," I said. "The windows appear covered like there are blinds."

"But it only gets better. I will show you a few more of papa's inventions, but not tonight. I want to catch a pleasant buzz and settle down. Plane rides always throw me into a state of disarray."

Reaching the lawn furniture at the edge of the cliff, we placed the bottles and glasses on a table. I brought the wineglass to my lips, sipping the bold taste.

"Mm… this Cab is dynamite."

"Probably a ninety-nine pointer. Mama only allows the highest ratings in the house."

Sitting down enjoying the view, warm breezes surfaced from the sea as we drank and chatted with spontaneity. Within no time at all, the sun gradually set as the full moon illuminated the surrounding area. The sound of the water on the shores brought me into the pleasing venue as the night unveiled a dark color around us. Staring upward, an aircraft's lights blink across the sky. My eyes then gazed deeply into the bright stars filling the vast space. Observing and speechless, peacefulness surrounded us while we consume the last bottle of wine. Coming to reality, I felt very buzzed desiring to collapse in bed.

"I need some food," Anna said.

"That was exactly what I was thinking."

"We shouldn't have drunk wine on an empty stomach. Let's get inside to see what Jasmine had prepared."

We grabbed our glasses and bottles and tumbled across the yard to the house. Making our way into the kitchen, Anna picked up a note on the island and read it.

"Gone to bed. Your dinner is the refrigerator. Just needs heating… Jasmine."

Anna took out the plates, placed them in the microwave, and served. We ate like we hadn't eaten all day. After finishing, Anna put the plates in the sink and led me up into the bedroom. We stripped naked and fell fast asleep under the warm covers.

Chapter 36

Friends

The sunrise shined brightly throughout the room, waking me into the dawn. Looking around the room, the bedroom was plain when compared to their house in Carcene. There was an oak desk, a large closet, a pair of dressers, and two leather chairs with a table. Thinking to myself, a bathrobe and a cup of coffee were all I needed to get the morning started. Pulling the covers to one side, I slowly got out of bed. I walked into the bathroom and the bright floral colors of the tiles were to much for my hangover. I noticed a private toilet that stood off to the side with a private door. Taking a white robe off a hook, I placed it around my body and tied a knot. Then, I walked over to the leather chair and sat down, looking out into the deep blue water.

The panoramic view was distinctly the opposite of Paris. The soundless and almost motionless landscape had a distinct stillness that displayed many vivid colors. There were no people, cars, trains, or buildings but a beautifully colored sea with plenty of boats. Catching my attention, a faint smell of freshly brewed coffee drifted within the room.

"Jasmine must be up and around," I thought.

Craving a cup, I descended the stairs into the kitchen, letting Anna sleep. Upon reaching the bottom step, I paused and looked around. Jasmine was sitting at the oak kitchen table staring out the window, enjoying her coffee.

"Go morning," I said.

Upon hearing my voice, she became slightly jittery.

Then she looked at me with a bright smile. "Up so early. I bet it was the sunrise…. This is the best part about the Beaupre's. These beautiful sunrises never go away. The architect put a full set of windows on the seaside walls throughout the house."

"The entire house must have cost plenty," I said.

"The Beaupre's can afford anything… anywhere."

Jasmine went over to the espresso machine and turned it on. A half pot of hot coffee rested on the marble island next to a bouquet of fresh red roses.

"A special occasion."

"No, I just like roses."

Carefully pulling one out of the vase, I smelled the spicy and fruity scent.

"You know they're not just any flower but designed by nature for a meaningful purpose."

"What do you mean?"

"The flowers' structure contains the essentials of life, comprising pleasure and pain. Vibrant, they blossom beautifully while carrying a pleasurable scent. However, the protective thorns can cause pain and even spill blood. That's if one is not careful. Just like our existence, pleasure and pain unite in a special bond to make us whole."

Jasmine's mysterious comparison of a rose to ourselves had a certain level of substance. As I put the flower back into the vase, the pleasant sound of the creek entered my mind, bringing me into a state of peacefulness. Nature had brought me to Italy. Thoughts of meeting Anna on the back road to the beach emerged. However, our special bond seemed to be slowly drifting apart like something else was trying to take its place.

"Well, I regular cup of coffee with cream and sugar will do me fine. Save the expresso for Anna."

Jasmine opened the cupboard door. "Large or small mug."

"I'll take a large mug."

Pulling out a large white cup, she poured the coffee, filling it almost to the top. She walked over and placed it on the table.

"Sit here," she said. I settled in my chair, looking out the large glass panes. There were birds on the picket fence, white cumulous clouds in the sky, and waves crashing upon the shore.

Jasmine's hair touched my face as she placed the cream, sugar, and a spoon next to the cup. The scent of her sweet perfume lingered as erotic feelings emerged between us. It was as if Avriel had awakened our spirits in some unifying field of sensuality. Recollections began creeping into my stomach. I felt the desire to caress Jasmine's olive skin, suckle her nipples, and taste her moist lips.

Unnoticed, Anna had descended downstairs into the kitchen.

"What have you two been up too," she said, sitting down next to me.

"Double espresso." Jasmine said. "Coming right up."

"Yes, please."

"What would you girls like for breakfast?"

"I've prepared home fried potatoes with onions and peppers. I also diced fresh fruit. Omelets are a go, if you like."

"Those are one of Jasmine's specialties," Anna said. "I'm going for a vegetable omelet with cheese."

"Make that two," I said.

Jasmine served a double espresso to Anna as she swung back into the kitchen. "Ok, two vegetable omelets with cheddar cheese coming up."

"Did you want to have lunch in town?" Anna said. "Jasmine will drop us off this morning."

"Yes, let's walk around town and see the sights. Maybe we can plan some tours," I said.

"The area is a tourist paradise," Jasmine said.

"It has been a few years since I've been on a tour," Anna said. "What time is dinner…"

"Seven… dinners at seven," Jasmine said.

Anna swigged the expresso down. Then, her fingers were texting on the smart phone as she clenched it.

"Texting is impolite at the table with guests," Jasmine interrupted.

She looked up. "Sorry. It's my friend from school, Aurora. She would like me to stay in the dorm overnight to visit. I told her that my friend was visiting me this week."

"Anna, I'll be alright with Jasmine tonight. Visit. I'm sure you miss them. Besides, we have the entire week ahead of us."

"Lizette, you're the best. I promise…. I will make it up to you."

213

"Jasmine, could you give me a ride to campus around six?"

"No problem, but only one night. You have a guest visiting."

"Ok, thanks," Anna replied.

"Lizette, we will figure something to do tonight," Jasmine interjected.

She put the hot plates in front of us and pulled some silverware from the drawer. She gently touched the back of my hand, setting the utensils down. Chills went up and down my spine as sensual nervousness erupted.

"Anyone for English muffins."

"Yes," Anna said. "With loads of butter."

"Not for me," I said.

My fork cut into the omelet, and the melted cheese flowed like lava. The taste was delicious as I took a scoop of potatoes into my mouth.

"The potatoes are better than some of the best restaurants around," I said. "Jasmine, you must have been a professional cook."

"I went to culinary school, but that was years ago."

We sat there indulging in our breakfast as Jasmine cleaned up behind us.

"Jasmine, are you going to join us?" Anna said.

"Already had breakfast. Before I forget, put your dirty clothes down the chute. I am sure you have a load from Paris."

After we finished breakfast, we walked upstairs to the bedroom and dropped our dirty clothes into the laundry chute. Anna went into the bathroom and turned on the water.

"Come on in."

I entered the shower and sat down. Anna gave me a razor and cream. I shaved my legs, thinking of Jasmine. Then I shaved my vulva clean.

"You missed your armpits," I said. "It looks odd,"

"What! You never seen girls with hair under their arms. None of us do it at school," Anna said.

"It actually looks different. Like a man." I giggled.

214

We soaped and rinsed off under the warm running water. Our eyes met as we began French kissing. Then, a draining sensation filled my stomach. Something was missing as our fingers simultaneous probed. Avoiding the feeling, I slowly began indulging within the delicious pleasures as the warm water flowed freely over our bodies. Our fingers playing diligently to bring about savory and sensual sensations. Within a matter of minutes, blood rushed to my face and my heart rate increased. My mind drifted off as she teased me into a delightful creamy climax.

"Are you almost ready?" Jasmine yelled from downstairs.

"All set Jasmine. Just getting out of the shower," Anna said. "What is the temperature today?"

"Twenty-seven degrees Celsius."

We dried off and put on light summer clothes and scurried down the steps.

Jasmine opened the garage and pulled out the car. She took us to the center of town and dropped us off.

"Call me when you are ready," Jasmine said. "I'll pack some clothes and toiletries for tonight."

As we were walking around the center of town, I noticed the narrow streets and stone buildings. Anna began describing the city and its surrounding areas.

"Bari is a metropolitan city with a prosperous economic center. The seafood industry is an important aspect within its vast seaport."

She also detailed other industries and the must-see tourist attractions. Then, an idea surfaced that interrupted her stream of thought.

"Let's do something completely different today. Instead of sitting down at a restaurant, we could sample the street food around town. A small nipple here and there."

"That would be quite different," I said.

"It would also make our site seeing a little more interesting. Besides. I could use the exercise," Anna said.

We started feeling into the mood of the city. The people seemed to be inclined toward a more relaxed and friendly atmosphere than bustling Paris. So, we spent most of the day enjoying the city while sampling the street food. Then, in mid-afternoon, we tried some of the local wines.

We had gotten a good buzz realizing that the time was approaching five-thirty. Anna called Jasmine to pick us up at the wine shop. After picking us up, she dropped Anna at the dorms.

While driving us back to the vacation home, Jasmine spoke. "Are you hungry?"

"I am absolute stuffed," I said. "I got a surprise when you get home. It's on the kitchen table," she said. "If you need to clean up theirs one in the bedroom."

"What was she talking about?" I thought.

When we arrived, Jasmine left me outside and parked the car in the driveway. I walked into the house and looked on the kitchen table.

Chapter 37

Jasmine

A leather collar, long chain, and a pink stained thong was on the kitchen table with a rose. Next to the items was a white sealed envelope. Putting the envelope to my nose, I inhaled Jasmine's sweet perfume. I opened the envelope, drew out the note, and read it.

'Mistress desires you to fall into the world of total amatory submission tonight. If you desire an ultimate ride of boundless satisfaction, follow the instructions below. Otherwise, I will see you in the morning for coffee and breakfast at dawn.

'Think back to our sensual sweet dessert at Avriel's. Peering deeply into your eyes, an endless bond stood between us. A mysterious and alluring magnetism drew your bare flesh to mine. You submitted to obedience as I strapped my leather collar around your neck. You accepted me like a subservient lover, wanting a mistress to fulfill your every desire. Tonight, my domination will awaken you with the dripping wetness of surrender. Climaxing twice today wearing the pink thong, you will put them on to start of this evening's festivities. As our juices blend deliciously, you will melt away in the obsession of blissful sensuality.

'First, take a shower. Then, strap the leather collar in place, fasten the chain, and put on the thong. Go to the bottom floor. I have opened the secret passage behind the bookcase. This is Avriel's secret playpen. Once inside, the door will shut. Bow down on the floor in obedience. Our playful game will begin. Our encounter and location must be an eternal secret kept from everyone even Anna. After tonight, never speak a word to anyone!'

Concentrating became difficult as I nervously thought of her controlling power. I went to the bathroom and took a long shower. Looking in the private toilet area, the enema bag was full and waiting. Anxiously, I purged myself, wanting to feel her inside me. Putting on a few dabs of alluring perfume, I went down into the kitchen, completely naked. Extremely anxious, I slipped on the leather collar, fastened the chain, and slid on the thong. Reaching the bottom floor. A secret door behind a wall book case was open.

"Wow, this was something out of the movies." I thought.

I entered the dark room. The door immediately closed behind me. I bowed down in submission as the lights slowly turned on.

In the center of the room was a king-sized bed with bondage paraphilia hanging from the walls. A lady stood fastened to a whipping rack with arms spread and wrists tied with leather bands. She was thin, small-breasted, and wearing nipple clamps. Her legs spread wide open with a leather strap tying her ankles to the rack.

Jasmine appeared completely naked, displaying her olive skin, voluptuous tits, and erect nipples. She held an eight-inch ribbed strapon. On the other side of the strap-on was a four-inch vibrator that would snuggly fit in her puss while she screwed. Jasmine walked over and pulled my chain as I laid there in submission.

"Look at me, my slave."

Staring deep into her eyes, I was shaking and waiting for the unknown.

"This evening you are under my command. Do not mind the lady tied to the rack. Your flesh shall join hers in an evening of erotic play. Bonding with women is all you need in your life to achieve sexual gratification."

She fastened leather restraints around my ankles and wrists to a twelve-inch neck chain. Then she picked up a whip.

"Lick my toes, my pet," she said. "Like a dog does to her master."

I began sucking on the white polished toes as she struck me hard in the ass with her whip.

"Lick me. Lick and suck." She struck me again. "Lick it up to my thigh and enter my minge with your slithering tongue."

Sucking and savoring her toes, I gradually inched my way up her silky legs. I licked and kissed until I reached her inner thigh. Feeling the sting from her whip, my tongue danced and flickered, not wanting to feel the pain much more. I inhaled her feminine scent and tasted her dripping juices.

"Now, devour my hot pussy, place your lips around my vagina, and suck me off while vigorously working your tongue."

My mouth covered her erect clit. I sucked like a vacuum pump while my tongue darted and twirled.

"Make me come, slut." She snapped the whip again.

My efforts sent pulsating surges through her flesh, putting her on the edge of peaking pleasure. "Keep your tongue working," she said. "More, more."

She immediately became rigid. I could feel her shake as moans escaped from her kips. Shivering convulsively, she let out a muffled scream having culminated upon my lips. Taking deep respirations, she stood with her eyes staring at my flesh.

She walked over to the shelf and pulled out a latex girdle.

"Quickly, put these over your pink panties," she ordered.

I immediately put them on. The latex fit extremely tight with a large cup like device that covered my vagina. Then, she put clamps on my nipples separated by a heavy chain. Opening her hand, she displayed a remote control. She pulled my chain as I started crawling on the carpet. Then she reached down and pulled the nipple chain. My sensitive nipples felt the painful pinch as I crawled to her reigning voice. She pulled on the nipple chain again. I took a deep breath inward, not wanting her to hear my cry of pain.

Then, unexpectedly, she clicked the remote. An intense venereous vibration swept through my pussy. The pleasure of potency spun my brain into pure ecstasy. Gripping the carpet with my fingers, I was struggling to endure the delirium. Then she stopped it.

"Oooh, oooh," I whimpered.

My breathing heightened, never experiencing such penetrating pleasure. The sensation was absolutely mind blowing. The lady in the rack watched meticulously, licking her lips as Jasmine clicked on it again.

"My gosh. Please mistress, please. The pleasure is unbearable."

I was screaming at the top of my lungs with tears running down my checks. The pulsating stimulation flooded my brain with intense rushes of towering ecstasy. Unable to control myself, I rolled onto my back. Then she turned it off.

"Get back in the crawling position," she commanded. Coming back to reality, I wanted more and more and more. This technological stimulant was like an addictive drug. Within a few minutes, she clicked the control again. Each millisecond of pleasure was driving me like a savage animal in raging heat. My eyes rolled in the back of head.

"Specially designed for girls that like to climax instantaneously," she said.

Jasmine struck me with the whip multiple times, turning my butt pink. I could not take the pleasure any longer. Then, I shivered fiercely and let out a cry of aggravating cry having orgasmed in her thong. She turned the devise off.

"The devise drives females insane, if they have too much. Now, peel off the latex."

My body was shaking from this mind exploitation. I barely slipped the latex off, still feeling the intensity the device.

"Reach under your thong and bring your fingers to your mouth to taste our blended juices," she commanded.

Sopping wet, I rubbed my ultrasensitive clit and brought my fingers to my mouth, tasting with pleasure. She looked into my eyes as she fastened the strapon, putting the four-inch section into her hole. She tightened the belt around her waist. Her cock hung down as my mouth opened in thirst. She stoked it like a man as I watched with extreme detail.

"You only love woman. I'm your woman. I am going to make love to you, just how you like it. You will soon fall deeply in love with me," she said in a mesmerizing tone.

My mouth watered in anticipating of getting the cock inside me.

"Now, come close."

She undid the arm and ankle restraints. Then she grabbed the chain around my neck.

"Get on top of the bed on all fours, right here."

She put her ass close to my face.

"Lick me out. Send your tongue deep into my bunghole and lick for wanton pleasure. If you do a good job, I'll drill you crazy like an animal."

I peered over at the lady on the rack. Jasmine pulled my chain.

"Concentrate on me."

Her wanton puckered anus was waiting for my tongue. Smelling the mustiness, I spit saliva on her crack. I moved my mouth over her hole and licked. With the tip of my tongue, I rolled and reamed. Sounds of delight seeped from her lips. Reaching around with my hand, I grabbed her shaft. I began jerking it slowly, pushing it into her hole. Wanting to make her cum again, my tongue probed inward with force. Twirling and twisting, she moaned with great delight. Then, I placed my mouth over her hole, driving my tongue as deep as I could. Loving it in absolute gaiety, I jerked her with force. She panted harder, pulling my chain as she felt my sensuous pleasure.

"Lick me. Lick hard."

My slippery tongue did its wonders as she was peaking within the felicity of anal love.

"Give it to me, my slave."

The shaft rubbed against her clit as the vibrator was probing her vagina with pleasure. Started to tense, I put more force on the shaft and worked my squirming tongue as far as it would go. Her anal muscle tightened as I lapped viciously. Deep, guttural sounds flowed from her lips. She let out a big gasp and bucked like a male horse having spewed the last bit of cum in the mare. Then, she settled down, gaining her composure. She looked at me as I was craving her enormous cock.

"I enjoy delicious anal. Good work, my slave," she said in a soft voice.

She brought her lips to mine. Then, we embraced in a deep, meaningful, mouthwatering kiss. My tongue entered her mouth, and she filled mine with hers. We sucked, slithered, and sank within the oozing slaver. We could not stop loving each other through our passionate osculation's. Our deep longing for one another had come to fruition. I fell in love with her flesh and dominance. She was the woman that I longed. She loved my submissiveness as our tongues flickered and played pressing and driving endlessly.

She tugged on the chain and undid the nipple clamps. My sensitive nipples felt the easing of pain as I let out a sound of liberation. Getting behind me, she put some cherry lube on her middle finger and felt around my bung hole. Her finger was prepping me for an anal ride as it slid in and out of my wetness.

Within seconds, the pleasing sensation felt gooey good. Then she placed the tip of her cock on my puckered hole and teased around. As my hole flowered, she gradually being moving the cock inward as she pulled it back. Repeating this motion, she gradually slid the eight-inch all the way in. I grabbed the comforter on the bed, feeling more pleasure than discomfort. Her pace began flowing in a rhythmic pattern. The smell of cherries filled the air as she ravished my anal cavity. Enjoying each stoke, the world of nirvana opened its floodgates.

"Ooh, ooh, ah," I muttered in pleasure.

She was riding me like a tamed horse, holding on to my chain like it was a bumpy trail. Probing at a faster pace, the sensations intensified. I bent my ass inward to gain maximal pleasure. Then, I began screaming and squealing like a pig as she gave me a buckaroo ride. My big tits swayed back and forth, bouncing around as her pelvis stuck my ass cheeks. I tightened my sphincter muscle as the ribbed dildo was sailing. My breathing increased with every thrust as my head got extremely hot. Within a matter of minutes, my face got pinkish red as I achieved a lustrous euphoria sensation. Immediately, I dropped to the bed with my head on the comforter. The screwing session was something I never experienced before. Then, she got on top of me bringing her lips to mine. We passionately kissed for minutes but what seemed like hours.

Getting off the bed, she spoke. "I hope you enjoyed our kinky game. I want to give you something special." She walked over to the rack and undid the straps of the lady.

"This is Maria. She is Italian and speaks some English. She will take control of your chain."

Jasmine took out another strapon and tossed it on the bed with some lube.

"This is for both of you to enjoy each other till dawn."

"Maria loves to play with college girls. All night long. You find that she also has a very pleasing tongue. She is one of the best in Bari, as you will soon find out."

Maria gave Jasmine a sensuous kiss.

"I will close the bookcase for good measure and be up early to open it. There is an emergency exit behind the curtain against the back wall. But I do not think you will need it. Enjoy each other."

Jasmine left the room as we began our lovemaking session. I did not utter a word, but started to tongue and kiss Maria passionately. We never stopped making love until the wee hours of the morning. Then we fell asleep in each other's arms.

Chapter 38

Maria

After our amorous adventure that lasted until dawn, Maria and Jasmine influenced my commitment to feminine love. Maria fulfilled my softer sensual appetite by the way she pleasantly kissed, licked, and teased. Her expertise in love making pierced my inner soul. Her luscious lips, pleasing tongue, and graceful touches instilled a feeling of passion, yearning, and obsession.

Jasmine satisfied my deviant side of licentiousness, filling me with submission, kinkiness, and indulging satiation. Through these diverse experiences, the transient feelings that I had for Anna had dissolved into one of toying friendship. Our high-spirited relationship that built its dominion upon innocence and excitement had collapsed into the awakening sunrise. Becoming intimate with feminine diversity had now risen as a primary means within my reality for sexual satisfaction.

In the early morning, Jasmine opened the secret door as fresh coffee filled the air. Maria and I got up from bed and proceeded to the shower in the master bedroom. As the water flowed, we kissed passionately, with animated feelings that flared into paradise. Tongues tenderly pleased with compassion, tenderness, and sensitivity as our lovemaking session continued. We enthusiastically played until the water ran cool over our unsatisfied bods. Descending naked into the kitchen, we were in gaiety to see the master of seduction greet us with a pleasing smile.

Jasmine was only wearing an apron over her naked body. We joined in a three-way kissing session, caressing each other passionately. Maria looked deep into my eyes and kissed me for one last time before she departed.

She spoke in broken English. "I loved the way you-a were with me last-a-night. Jasmine has my informatioone. I want you again." With that, she kissed me, descended to the lower floor to dress, and went on her way.

Jasmine and I sat at the kitchen table sipping coffee and engaging in a deep intimate discussion. I found out that Maria was a very wealthy woman. Money was never a matter of concern for her. She even wanted to bring me to Bari again and stay with her.

Jasmine then confided in me that a private group of rich women had encounters in the secret room regularly. It was usually drinking at the bar first until the secret book case entrance opened for playtime. Avriel was part of the wealthy elite that enjoyed satisfying women of class and distinction. Jasmine would join in as requested by others. After we ate, we picked up Anna at the dorms and life moved on as if nothing happened.

As the week progressed, Anna and I went on many site seeing tours that included the caves, cruises, and wine tasting. Our love making continued but to a lower intensity than before. At night, we seemed to sleep further apart. I would rise very early in the morning as Anna was sleeping to enjoy a cup with Jasmine. Jasmine and I would make love quickly in the hidden room before Anna arose. Anna often wondered why Jasmine and I were bare chested in the kitchen but never realized what had transpired.

The plane ride was silent between Anna and me as we made it back to Carcene. After the trip, I saw little of Anna except when we waved at school from a distance. I had plenty of invitations to dine but declined many offers. However, erotic thoughts of Maria and Jasmine plagued my mind. So, I kept in contact with them through emails while planning my next trip to Italy.

Before starting my last year of college, I experienced many bike rides along the rue de pasture during the summer months. However, I rarely returned to paradise creek to seek its private moments. Most times, I preferred spending time on the beach to connect with females while I sunbathed on the sand.

By September of my last year in college, cooler weather set upon us. Summer had ended as the feeling of desolation and longing swept through my heart. Then, I remembered the words of Mama.

"June will soon be here before you know it."

Chapter 39

Conclusion

After uploading the required paper into the school's portal, I electronically signed and submitted my completed application. The paper had set my thoughts back ruminating, recapturing, and reliving my most impassioned memories since childhood. Now, fully divulged to the review committee, my erotic experiences were no longer hidden secrets from the world.

Alexia had entered the room unnoticed. She came up behind me, putting her arm around my shoulder giving me a soft kiss on the cheek.

"All done.... so soon," she said.

"What do you mean?" I inquired.

"Just considering what experiences we had, plus your own adventures, I thought you would be enslaved on the keyboard all night long."

"It was an amorous ride. But we know it's far from over."

"We're going to miss you at home. Things will be quiet until the summer. But Papa promised we'll travel to Italy making a special trip to see you. Of course, it will have to include wine sales."

"Business and pleasure. That's Papa and now you. Well, I will see you at Christmas but next summer it's going to be Bari. I will always look forward to seeing my best sister. However, the way you keep busy at work, I don't think I'll ever see you."

"Now, that's not true."

"When money is to be made, guess what comes first?"

"You always come first, sis.... But do you really think they will accept you into the master's program at the University of Bari? You always seem very optimistic."

"Maria thinks so. She already prepared the room."

"I hope you will not feel disappointment if you're turned down."

"Alexia, how could you say that?"

"You still should reconsider and join the business. Valise and Jacque will miss you tremendously."

"Well, all I can tell you is that there is an elite society of woman in Bari's that awaits my coming. Besides, Maria has some close bookcase friends on the acceptance committee."

After Alexia left the room with a perplexed look on her face. I sat back in my chair, thinking about how much we enjoyed playing on the beach as though tomorrow was endless. We dipped naked into the warm bay water, feeling free of inhibitions. We basked in the natural beach scene and observed beach goers through the secret spyhole. The spirit of the bay always offered spontaneity among the crowds. Within its presence, we were content, instinctively unrestricted, and always welcomed. The beaches at Carcene were our childhood. Time could never lose those wonderful moments planted in the mysteries of the ocean. Merely a slight breeze, scent, or mist could easily trigger those cherished memories once more.

Ingram Content Group UK Ltd.
Milton Keynes UK
UKHW020631160323
418667UK00016B/1419